Tracy Farr is an Australian-born, New Zealand-based writer and former research scientist. *The Life and Loves of Lena Gaunt* is her first novel.

Visit the author at www.tracyfarrauthor.com

The Life and Loves of
Lena Gaunt

AARDVARK
BUREAU

The Life and Loves of Lena Gaunt

Tracy Farr

Aardvark Bureau
London

An Aardvark Bureau Book
An imprint of Gallic Books

First published by Fremantle Press, Australia in 2013
Copyright © Tracy Farr, 2013

First published in Great Britain in 2016 by
Aardvark Bureau, 59 Ebury Street, London, SW1W 0NZ

A CIP record for this book is available from the British Library
ISBN 978-1-910709-05-4

Typeset in Perpetua by Aardvark Bureau
Printed in the UK by CPI (CR0 4YY)
2 4 6 8 10 9 7 5 3 1

For my grandmothers.

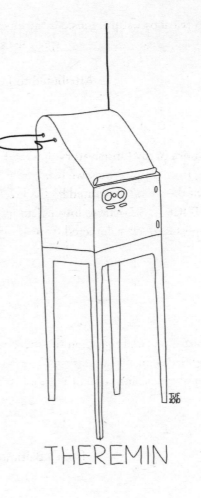

THEREMIN

I am electrical by nature, music is the electric soil in which the
spirit lives, thinks, and invents.

Attributed to Ludwig van Beethoven

NASA's Chandra X-ray Observatory detected sound waves, for the
first time, from a super-massive black hole ... In musical terms,
the pitch of the sound generated by the black hole translates into
the note of B flat ... 57 octaves lower than middle-C ... this is the
deepest note ever detected from an object in the universe.

NASA press release,
9th September, 2003

To see [her] play a piece of music on the theremin is to be reminded
of a boy doing tricks on a bicycle. For, like a boy who rides with 'no
hands', [she] plays this instrument without touching it – by merely
waving [her] hands over it.

Mary Day Winn
from a Baltimore newspaper, 1948

COTTESLOE
1991

Transformer

THEREMIN

All of us are old at this hour, on this beach; the heads in the water are all grey, including mine. Mostly we move gently, we older, early-rising swimmers, the water buoying us in our slow choreography. But if we're all old and stale, still the water smells fresh – somehow like watermelon, and salt. It's glorious, the water in the morning, when it's calm like this, when you can just bob on the surface, like a seal, watching. How *well* it makes me feel, how calm; how light and how heavy at the same time: like heroin – a little bit like heroin.

The waves this morning are gentle, lacking the roll and boom of the afternoon, when the breeze is up and the swell catches and the great mass of water feels deeply oceanic. Now it's silky, almost still. A little wave forms and moves towards me. I concentrate on watching its path, its sinusoidal shape. It breaks on me, gently, and I let it push me under the water, then I push back up and my head breaks the surface.

Looking down – through air, through water – I see myself distorted, my black swimsuit the negative of the pale thin legs extending long below it, and I feel disconnected from the body and legs I see under the water. From this perspective, I look the same as I've always looked; the water washes the years away, or at least hides them under its surface.

I move my arms in wide arcs in front of me, pushing water out to the sides and back again. I can feel the stretch in my shoulders, the tendons tense and twist. Bubbles form up my arms, trapped in the tiny pale hairs, tickling like the bead in champagne. Moving my fingers in the water effects tiny changes in the waves that effect bigger movements. Action at a distance; just like playing the theremin.

Muscle memory takes over from my conscious brain as my fingers and hands move under the water's cover. I know the movements, not just practised for tonight's performance, but from a lifetime of playing. Under the surface of the water my arms have dropped into the position they adopt to play – right hand raised around shoulder height; left hand dropped nearer to my waist. My hands too are in place – the left hand palm-down, flattened, to stroke volume from the theremin's metal loop; the right with fingers pinching lightly in towards thumb to form an eye, to pluck and twitch in the tiniest precise movements, like pulling the thinnest silk thread, a filament too fine to see.

I let myself sink under the water. Expelling air from my mouth and nose, I hear the waveforms and harmonic intervals of *Aetherwave Suite* rise to the surface in the bubbles, the sound waves mixing in the air and water, undulating, soothing, readying me for the performance tonight.

Music from a theremin can sound like a human voice, or

an electronic scream; like an alien spaceship imagined for a B-movie soundtrack, or like the low thrum and moan of a cello, warm with wood and resin and gut. The best players can tease all of these sounds – more – from the wood and wire and electricity that is a theremin, form a limitless range of notes and sounds. And I *am* the best player – after all these years, old woman that I am, not bettered. I, Lena Gaunt, am a legend.

The inaugural Transformer Festival has been keenly anticipated, written up in *The Wire* and other music magazines, discussed in earnest tones. A music festival offering the best electronica and eclectica that 1991 can deliver, I'm told. I understand I fall into both categories.

I first heard of Transformer nearly a year ago via an invitation from its organiser, Terence Meelinck, to play at his festival up in the Perth Hills. His pleading, his enthusiasm for the music and the instrument – and, yes, I admit it, his flattery – won me over. And so, here I am, committed – for better or worse – to play tonight at this festival of Terence's. There is my face staring at me from the programme. I look so old amongst the other faces, so old.

I close the programme and place it on the table in front of me, in the campervan that is my accommodation for the night. The van is tiny, but adequate for one. Thankfully I do not have to share it; fame and age guarantee certain comforts. It is parked in a group of vans, large and small, circled at the edge of the festival's compound, far enough for the music from the stage to reach only as a slightly dulled thudding, distorted through the evening air.

I have already dressed for the stage: silken grey trousers, voluminous and flowing, each leg so wide it could double as a skirt. A simple black tunic, sleeveless, leaves my arms free; its shape reminds me of a mediaeval knight's dress, appropriate for battle. I take a mirror and lipstick from the make-up case next to me on the divan, apply dark red to cover my old lips. My hair is short, white-grey, platinum-grey; it catches the overhead light, like velvet. I stare at myself in the mirror: I will do.

I sit on the divan. There is nothing more I can do to prepare for my performance. I place my feet flat on the floor in their rubber soles, rest my hands on my knees, breathe deeply to still my body. I think of the beach this morning, the gentle waves, the watermelon scent, muscle memory; my fingers twitch lightly on my knees.

There is a knock at the door of the van and I open it to see a young man, the minder Terence has assigned to me. I lock the van on the way out and hand him the key as we slide into the car to slowly drive the short distance to the stage.

Steroidalab have finished their set and are backstage when we arrive. They're in a post-performance huddle, a closed unit as I walk past them at the top of the scaffolding steps that lead up to the stage from ground level. The crew are on stage, busy, packing away synthesisers, computers, microphones, until the stage is almost cleared. I stand where the stage manager tells me to, out of the way, but ready.

I hear Terence on stage. He starts speaking and, even though I am waiting in the wings, even though I know I am about to walk on to the stage and perform, it takes a beat before I realise: he is talking about me.

> *She has been an extraordinary part of the electronic music scene since before most of us were born. She was at the birth of electronic music sixty years ago. She's travelled the world performing on the instrument that started it all, the theremin. She reminds us that nothing we do is new. She's playing for us tonight on irreplaceable vintage electronic equipment. We're truly blessed to have had her back in this country for two decades, and we're honoured to have her here to play for us. Join with me in welcoming to the stage the remarkable, the beautiful, our very own, Dame (beat) Lena (beat) Gaaaaauuunt.*

And so I breathe in deeply and step onto the stage to deafening, thunderous applause.

I walk from the wings, legs pushing my trousers to swirl and billow and sweep the floor. When I reach the spotlight, I bow from the waist, my black tunic swaying, the heavy pendant around my neck hanging to almost touch the surface of the stage in front of me.

I raise my head, square my shoulders. The audience is invisible behind the bright spot that shines, reaching in behind my eyes, almost blinding, almost hurting. The spotlight widens around me, my cue to raise my arm to gesture, as if to welcome another performer onto the stage. A second spot appears at stage left and, as the light reveals it, I raise my arm towards my theremin as if in a distant embrace. The audience roars; they stamp, they hoot, they call like cats, like cattle, like owls, like mad things. This is what they've come to hear, to see: this instrument, this tangle of wire I have played for so long, made for me all those years ago, not a museum piece but a working musical instrument, that has seen more and lived longer than any of them; nearly as old as me, it is my darling, and I play it like a lover I cannot touch.

I raise my hand, palm flat towards the audience, and slowly, reluctantly, they quieten. I start to move across the stage to the theremin, my arm outstretched towards it. A layer of air exists between my skin and its wire, wood and glass. A low hum issues from it, the sum of the capacitance of my body, its effect on the electric currents.

I steady myself behind the theremin, and the spotlight tightens its focus, excludes all else into darkness. I raise my hands again – one to the loop, one to the wire – and hear the deep low that is almost the sound of a cello and yet is its own thing, its own sound; this deep lowing issues from the theremin, is amplified and channelled to the speakers behind me, swells to fill the night air and I once again wring magic from the wires by simply plucking and stroking my fingers in the aether.

The echoes of the last notes of the final movement of *Aetherwave Suite* hang above the crowd for only a moment;

that quiet, magic moment when the sound is ringing in their ears and they are stretching to hear the low notes rise and fall in the still, dark air. Then the applause, jolting and unmusical, starts and builds in wave upon wave of sound, directed back towards the stage, to me.

I bow low, my arms hanging loose, my hands almost touching the floor, then I rise, straighten. I lift my arms to the side, to the front, as if to acknowledge the audience, but really I want to acknowledge it all – the night, the audience, the music, the air that carries the sound and hums it back in endless loops of wave upon wave of glorious, vibrating music. The audience's applause and shouting form a thunder that hurts my ears. I raise my arms, my hands drawing through the night air, raise my hands up and bring my palms together, draw them to my face so that the fingertips touch at my lips. I hold the pose – *namaste* – for a beat, *two, three, four*, nod my head, drop my hands to my sides, and walk from the stage.

Satisfied after hearing the much awaited *Aetherwave Suite*, the audience lets me retire – without an encore – with grace, with dignity, from the night's performance; how could they in good conscience call an eighty-year-old woman back onto the stage at this hour of the night? They've watched me standing, arms raised, energised, my whole body channelling the music. They know not to expect me back on stage; I know they know. I can hear the crowd, can imagine them start to turn away from the stage, to fragment into smaller groups, to turn from being a mob, a hive, to individuals humming with the energy of what they've just heard and seen, ready to reform into a single mass of audience as soon as the Gristmonger boys step onto the stage.

Backstage my minder meets me, ushers me past the members of Gristmonger bouncing in the wings, leads me away through snaking leads and amps, down the scaffolding steps. People mill, congratulate me; I beg off, *so very tired, please forgive me. Of course, of course; goodnight. Thank you, Dame Lena! Thank you so much!* I am led to a car, handed into the rear seat. The minder drives me back; it is not far, maybe half a mile, but he drives at no more than a brisk walking speed to pass slowly through the crowds, between the tents and vehicles, back to my campervan for the night. I step up to the door and unlock it with the key the minder hands me.

From the top of the step, framed in the doorway, I thank him, remembering that his name is a pretty name, Jasper. *Yes, I am fine. No, I don't need food – it is late, I have tea, I will sleep; thank you, Jasper, thank you. Goodnight.* We nod at each other, smiling, backgrounded by the sound of the audience roaring, music swelling in the distance. As Jasper turns to leave, I close the door, lock it, and the noise of the crowd, of Gristmonger's music, fades to a hum.

At the tiny bench that passes for a kitchen I fill an electric jug with water from a plastic bottle, flick the switch on the jug and, as it clicks and mutters, I take a teabag – Russian Caravan, appropriately – from the box on the bench and drop it into a mug. The jug boils within a minute; I pour water over the teabag, and the smoky steam rises, whetting my appetite. I transfer the mug of tea to the table, then settle myself, move a cushion behind my back for comfort, for support, for balance. I breathe in then out with a heavy expiration of breath, my palms resting on my knees, feet flat on the floor, back straight against the cushions on the divan.

From the hard-shelled make-up case next to me I take a small metal vessel shaped like a squat teapot, and place it on the low table in front of me. I take a silver tin, prise the lid off, and place lid and tin next to the pot. There are a dozen capsules in the tin, arrayed as if in some form of code, or like a photograph I recall seeing in an encyclopaedia, of bacteria under a microscope. I withdraw one capsule, twist it in a quick, familiar movement and pour the pale powder into the pot, place the lid back on the tin, the lid on the pot. There: ready.

I have only to turn slightly to my left to light the small gas burner on the kitchen bench; I can reach it without moving from my seat on the divan. I place the pot on the burner, over the hissing blue flame, and wait, not long, anticipating. I know just how long it will take to heat; can hear, almost feel, the changes occur within the vessel. And when the heat is at that point, just at that particular point, I flick off the gas, lift the pot down to rest on the trivet in front of me and, blocking my left nostril with my fingers, I inhale with my right nostril over the spout – close to the spout, but not touching it – with the smoke from the heroin spiralling up, filling the gap between my nose and the vessel. I inhale lightly at first, then deep, deep, filling myself.

And as I inhale hard, the opiates rush my blood and my brain, making familiar connections. My mouth dries; I feel my skin flare red and hot; and then the wave rushes over me, the pull of it, the surge of it, buoying my heavy arms, making my mind dance. I settle against the cushion, my eyes close; I hear the music, the crowd, their voices becoming distant, buzzing and humming as the drug changes the shape of the waves of electricity forming and reforming, fluid, in my brain. My breath is shallow and on it drifts the scent memory of ocean waves: salt, and watermelon. I am on the divan. My feet are no longer flat on the floor, but curl at my side. My fingers – heavy, slow – twitch on my knees, patterning music.

PISS-TAKE

Although it is so long since I have played such a festival, I recall the feeling still; the day after a concert is always a comedown.

I wake early, musty with sleep, with the aftermath of adrenalin from the performance tempered with residual opiates. Noises from outside the van wake me: birdsong, peoplesong, the humming and coughing, laughter and shuffling of the people collected there, the bands, the roadies, the audience, the organisers, the makers of food and the emptiers of porta-toilets. Generators, still humming from the night before, throttle up to a whine as the power load on them increases; breakfasts are cooked; I smell the salt fat smell of frying food. I make tea in a mug, and sit on the flimsy bed to drink it, my knees pulled up to form a tent under the covers. I get up, dress in the light cotton trousers and loose shirt I wore to travel to the festival site. I fold my stage outfit carefully into my overnight bag, and wait for my lift back to town.

Terence is arranging to have my gear – he calls it this, *your gear*, my musical equipment, the theremin, its speaker – packed securely and returned to me, so I do not have that to deal with. I wonder distractedly if it will be secure, but the thought is fleeting; what will be, will be. It is tough old *gear*; it will survive, as it has done all these years.

The boy Jasper, my minder from last night, knocks on the door of the van. He's looking the worse for wear: hair all over the place, up on one side, and he smells of something distasteful; he wears a t-shirt with a single word, *Crass*, written across it. His eyes are red and staring. Nonetheless he smiles at me as I open the door, and asks if I'm ready to go. I hand my bag down to him, step down onto the ground, and ease into the car's passenger seat, relaxing into its shape. As we pass through the gate of the fence that surrounds the Transformer site, he pushes a cassette into the machine in the dashboard; Steroidalab, turned to a pleasant volume, dulls the burr and whine of the car's engine. Jasper needs all his remaining faculties to concentrate on driving, so conversation isn't required. Through the window of the car I watch trees give way to buildings, as we circle the outskirts of the city and motor down the hill to the ocean, to home.

I direct him to my street, point to the path that leads to my cottage; politely refuse his offer to carry my bag; thank him for the lift, for his help, and wave him goodbye as he takes off towards the ocean at the end of the street. As the car accelerates away from me, the sound of Steroidalab gives way to Gristmonger, played loud.

I walk down the path from the street, unlock the door of my cottage, and walk into darkness. I leave my overnight bag in the hallway, hang my keys on the hook behind the door, and go to the kitchen. The red eye of the machine under the telephone blinks at me. I push the button to play the message.

'Dame Lena. Good morning. My name is Mo Patterson. I'm sorry to call you so early, but I was at Transformer last night and I saw your performance – can I thank you for it? Congratulate you on it? You were exceptional.' The voice clears its throat, resumes. 'Ah, I was wondering if I could come and meet with you about a proposal I have, for a film I'd like to make.'

The voice rattles off a number. I let it run, neither saving the message nor deleting it, nor writing the number down. I wonder what her agenda is. I wonder where I have got the term 'agenda' from. I wonder if it is too early in the day for a gin. The sun is over the yardarm, I decide; I pour myself a short measure over ice, slice a lemon and drop two juicy slices onto the surface of the oily liquor. *Salut*, I say to myself. You weren't bad, for an old girl. The gin is clean in my mouth, the lemon tart, awakening.

I take my gin outside, sit in the sun filtering through the vines into the courtyard outside my kitchen door, and listen to the surf crash, a block away; to seagulls wheeling; to the cars luggering down the road, looking for somewhere to park to disgorge their occupants who tomorrow will be at school or university or work but today are heading for the cool and salt of the sea.

I sit in the noisy, humming sunlight, sipping my gin and thinking about last night. It has been so long since I've played at a festival, at anything of that size. It felt – extraordinary. Wonderful. I realise I have missed it, and this surprises me. There was a heat that I felt from playing; I'd almost forgotten that rush. I surfed on its wave, last night, and it felt good, very good. Still feels good; it is lingering, in my extremities and in my core.

The phone rings. I hear the same woman's voice faintly across the room as she leaves another message. I hear its timbre, recognise it, but cannot hear the detail of what she says. Her name seems familiar, as if I have heard it or read it before. But not familiar enough to make me go to the phone. For now, I will enjoy the sun, the lemony oil of the gin, and the memory of last night, the residue of the rush of performance, the tingling in my fingers and my ears and my heart.

On Monday morning I wake to the sound of houses emptying into cars, cars escaping to their weekday destinations. Only the old and the aimless, and mothers and their young, are left behind to populate the suburbs. And builders; the men working on the house next door arrive early to recommence their banging, smoking, and tuneless singing to the radio. I raise my hand at them as I pass them on my way to the shop on the corner to buy the newspaper, and milk for my coffee. They wave back, nod, mutter assorted 'morning's and 'gidday's at me; *It's gunna be a hot one.*

At home, I don't get to the newspaper until I've made coffee, savouring the burbling burnt smell of it. Hissing on the stove, it's almost musical in counterpoint, in syncopation with the tang of the builders next door, their percussive metal on metal, the whump of nailguns. I

26

settle at the table, my hands warming around the coffee in its glass, stare out the window through the foliage that surrounds me and listen to their noise, try writing it in my head on a musical staff, annotate it *pianissimo, forte, da capo al fine*. But the builders' noise reveals itself as what it is: noise, not music; the common variety of noise, mundane, unplanned.

I drain my coffee and unfold the paper, spread it on the table in front of me. I love reading this parochial tabloid, full of blustering politicians, vain, potatoey men with too much money and expensive suits, huge ads for cheap furniture, chicken drumsticks, and bulk packages of toilet paper. I love the lists of drunk drivers and loan defaulters, bankrupts and divorcees, school children raising funds and painting murals, ads for cheap rental cars and skimpy bars. But today, it is me. I am there, large as life, in black and white, all the clichés in the world; I am in the news as I once was so often and have not been for so long.

There is a photograph, which is what I see first. It is of a thin figure on a stage, dwarfed by the girders and scaffolding that form the stage's shape and hold the lights that shine upon it. I realise that the thin figure is me.

THE RETURN OF THE
THIN WHITE DAME

The Transformer Festival was, as promised by organiser Terry Meelinck, a celebration of the best and the most eclectic electronica this country has yet seen. The sold-out show held in the Hills this weekend saw local and international acts come together to entertain the more than four thousand-strong crowd that camped overnight at the site.

Though much anticipated, Dame Lena Gaunt's performance — her first in nearly twenty years — is hard to characterise and harder to review. The audience applauded earnestly after each shrill piece, but this reviewer found it laboured, dated, irrelevant. Like The KLF's recent offering with Tammy Wynette and the Justified Ancients, there was a definite whiff of novelty act in the air. Ancient, yes. Justified: not really. Her famous Aetherwave Suite sounded all of its fifty-plus years of age.

So it was none too soon when Gristmonger hit the stage. The crowd resurrected itself to mosh and grind to favourites like 'Monkey Tiger Christ', 'Wedding Schmedding', and the evergreen classic 'Crass (As You Like It)'. The Gristers never sound better than when they perform live. The bpms were solid, frontperson Delly Watts was in fine voice, with an edge that's not always immediately apparent on their recordings.

I can't read any more. Good Lord, they think it was a piss-take. They think *I* was a piss-take.

The phone rings. I pick it up without thinking; it's the voice, the woman who called before.

'Dame Lena? My name's Mo Patterson, I'm a filmmaker.'

'Yes. You've left messages for me.' I am curt, though not, I hope, impolite.

'I was at Transformer on the weekend, I saw you perform.'

'I see.'

'You were extraordinary. I can't tell you how much I enjoyed your performance.'

I say nothing. She talks on into the silence.

'I'm calling really to introduce myself, because I'm in the early stages of making a film about electronic music, and women musicians. I'd love to talk to you about it, because I want you to be involved in the film.'

I can almost hear her holding her breath. I give my response quickly, cleanly.

'I'm afraid not. I'm a musician. I'm not interested in making films.'

'But I think you could—'

'No, I'm sorry, Miss – Patterson, is it? I'm quite certain. Make your film about other people. I wish you luck. Goodbye.' I hang up before she can say any more.

Why would I want to tell my story now? Why open up my quiet life by the sea to scrutiny, to piss-takers and filmmakers?

THE PATTERSON WOMAN

Norfolk Island pines line the streets where I live. They cast tall conical shadows on the houses, making them dark. They're far enough from my little cottage not to cast their shadows on me. My shadows are cast by the jacaranda tree that drops its purple carpet to drift onto my verandah all the late spring. A path leads from the street down between the high wall of the front house and the fence that separates this block from that of the house next door, then down past the jacaranda, up a step and onto my verandah. The path is almost always dark, except when the sun is directly overhead, like the slit in an ancient tomb designed to catch the sun at midsummer and point to treasure.

A lemon tree blocks in my garden at the back, glossy green and yellow. Productive. I like that in a tree. The garden's other end is enclosed by a grapevine that climbs and gnarls up and around and over, clutching at the back wall of my cottage. When I sit in that courtyard I can smell the sea, salting the air.

The cottage was built as servants' quarters, as the gardener's house, perhaps as stables – no one remains to remember any more. It is my house now. I've lived here for twenty years, and I will die here, if I'm lucky.

My theremin usually stands in the dark of the front room, with the speaker behind it. The diamond-shaped speaker cabinet – a metre across at its widest, and nearly three metres high – only just fits into the room; thank God for high ceilings. The theremin and speaker have not yet been returned from Transformer. The room misses them. There are marks on the floor, on the carpet, where they normally sit.

My feet nestle into the indentations on the faded silk. Father bought this rug, long ago, from the *pasar*. It covered the floor in Mother's bedroom in Singapore. There are shapes within shapes, where sunlight has fallen or been forever excluded. The shapes overlap, touch at corners. They have formed over months or years, but sometimes generations apart. The faintest outlines still exist of Mother's bed and her dressing table. The outline of my theremin just touches the edge of the ghost note of Mother's dressing table; just lightly kisses its edge.

*

Dear Dame Lena,

I hope you'll forgive me writing to you, when you were so clear about your decision not to be involved in my film when we spoke on the phone today. I couldn't let go without making a final attempt to entice or persuade you; to convince you of my excitement about the project, and my respect for your work, your music, and above all, your right to privacy.

I suspect the latter is at the heart of your reluctance to be involved. I'd like to assure you that it would be paramount for me, in working with you, to ensure that your privacy is maintained, and that the material that forms and informs the film is sensitive to that.

If you would agree to meet with me, just briefly, I'd be so very grateful for the opportunity to speak with you directly, openly, and honestly about my ideas and aesthetic for the film I'm planning. If you are interested, I could also show you the footage I shot at Transformer — with the permission and assistance of Terry Meelinck — as well as a short film I made some years ago which has as its subject the artist Beatrix Carmichael, to whom I know you were very close.

I enclose some information as a background to my work: a brief biography and list of my films, and the transcript of a talk I gave at the Film and Television Institute in Fremantle late last year, where I mentioned the music project I was then just beginning to formulate.

Respectfully and hopefully yours,
Maureen (Mo) Patterson
Enc.

I shuffle through the pages she has sent me. My own name leaps from the page. *Carmichael's portrait of Gaunt, Electrical by Nature, was the first I knew of Lena Gaunt. That painting inspired me to make my short film,* Beatrix. Words, then phrases and whole sentences come into focus. She talks about art, and art school — *I didn't finish my diploma, but my training as a painter has influenced my approach to composition, to lighting* – and about film as painting, as representation – *Making a documentary is like painting a portrait and, for me, the best portrait tells you as much about the artist as it does about the subject.* Holding her pages in my hands, I'm struck by memories – the smells of paint and canvas, cigarettes and oranges, smoky tea and long, late nights – as vivid as if I've only just lived them.

There is paper in the drawer of my desk. I take a blank page, a pen, and place them in front of me, set the filmmaker's papers aside. I turn my head, just slightly, and glance at the two paintings over my mantelpiece: Beatrix's self-portrait, and the other, her portrait of me. I keep the paintings shaded, in the dark of my bedroom, keep them out of the sunshine, out of the light. I pick up the pen. It feels heavy in my hand. I roll it back and forth between my hands, my palms, until it's taken up all of my warmth, and matches me; now, I can barely feel it. I hold it against my face, rest it horizontally in the hollow below my mouth, my lips, and press it there, roll it to my chin, then into my hand. *Dear Ms Patterson,* I write. *Your letter and other material received, and read with*— Read with what? Sadness? Nostalgia, tinged – perhaps – with a little fear? She doesn't need to know that.

I turn and look again at the paintings that I see every night, every day, that keep me company, and that I keep in the dark. I wonder if what she's written – *the best portrait tells you as much about the artist as it does about the subject* – is true. I wonder what portrait she could make of me now.

*

Dear Ms Patterson,

Your letter and other material received, and read with interest.

Would you come for coffee on Tuesday next, at 10 am? You have my address.

Cordially,

Lena Gaunt

*

It's a warm morning on what will be a hot day. I wake early, in a tangle of sweated bedsheets. The thought of the beach is soothing. I've not swum since the morning before I played Transformer, and I have missed it. The Patterson woman is due at ten o'clock, so I have time. I unpeg my beach towel from the clothes line outside my kitchen door. It is stiff with salt, bone dry. I crack it to fold it, fit it into my straw bag, take my hat and keys from their hooks and, locking the door behind me, walk to the footpath that heads straight to the ocean.

The light's only just showing in the sky over the rooftops and spikes of pine trees behind me. The houses I walk past are still dark. There are straw-coloured whips on the footpath, dropped from the Norfolk pines. I stop to pick one up and run its overlapping scales through my fingers, scales that are dry but silken smooth, as I imagine the skin of a snake to be.

At the bottom of the street, a path descends from the roadway to the beach, between limestone walls that contain the sand dunes, retain the water, let grass grow for picnickers and sunbathers and cricket players. As I

34

pass under the arch that forms the base of the old bathing pavilion, I touch the pale stone lightly, as a million other fingers have, feel its cool roughness, its runnels and imperfections.

I kick off my sandals. My feet sink into the sand, squeaking fine and sharp with a clear tone and high pitch. I drop my bag, my sandals and hat; strip off my long cotton shirt and let it fall; and I walk towards the water, feeling the sun higher, warmer on my back now even than it was when I left the cottage. *It's gunna be a hot one.*

It's an easy walk up the slight incline from the beach towards home. The sun is up now, though low, and my eyes squint against it. The street is busier; cars move in the low light, windows and curtains are flung open to admit the morning's cool air.

I shower, dress in light, loose cotton trousers and shirt. I leave my feet bare. I'm filling the pot with coffee grounds when the telephone rings.

'Dame Lena!' Terence's voice is as animated as ever; I can hear the exclamation marks in his speech. 'I'm so sorry I haven't managed to catch you before now. It's been crazy, this past week!'

I hear him draw breath, perhaps inhale on a cigarette, before he goes on.

'Anyway, I'm just calling to thank you, congratulate you, for the festival. You were wonderful! As I knew you would be. Absolutely wonderful! I hope you enjoyed yourself as much as we enjoyed your performance.'

I wipe each hand in turn on the tea towel hanging from

the hook by the stove, then sit down on a kitchen chair. I don't know how I want to answer Terence. I hear in his voice the enthusiasm that I've always heard from him, the lack of a piss-take. But after the newspaper review, I'm no longer sure.

'I enjoyed myself immensely. And from your point of view: was it successful? I mean, of course, did you make money?'

He makes a noise like a cough, a half laugh tacked onto the end of it. 'If I was in it for the money I'd be a constant disappointment to myself. We covered our expenses though, and that's saying something.' He pauses. 'I've personally supervised the packing up of your gear – I can assure you it's in good hands, safe and secure. I'm having trouble getting hold of a truck before the weekend, though. Could we deliver it to you next week? Say Tuesday? Will you be at home?'

He credits me with a fuller social calendar than I have. 'Next Tuesday will be fine. Thank you. I'll feel – happier – to have it at home with me. Let's say middle of the morning – would that suit?'

'Sure, sure, no problem.'

He keeps talking, piling words at me. We dance around the perimeter of the review without acknowledging it, speak glowingly of the other bands and acts, and of little things. He promises to send me a cassette tape he is compiling from the festival. In the midst of the wash and flow of his words, I catch the sound of a name.

'Patterson, did you say?'

'Yeah, that's right. Mo Patterson,' he says. 'She makes

movies. You've probably heard of her. She's dead keen on music, and she's even more keen on you. She was filming at the festival – it was in the release you signed, you might have noticed as you read the fine print! Anyway, I've given her your number. I hope that's okay. She's good. A Kiwi. Lives here these days.'

There is a gap, a silence. I realise he is seeking reassurance.

'That's fine, Terence. I've spoken to her already in fact.'

'Oh.'

'No, it's fine. Really. She's due here, actually, any moment. So I won't keep you.'

I hear him exhale smoke with a sigh, as if through tight, pursed lips.

'Well, I guess that's it. It's been a pleasure working with you.'

'And you, Terence. Thank you for the opportunity to play. It felt…good.'

Good Lord, I can think of nothing more erudite to say to the man, and wish he would go away. At which, mercifully, there is a knock on my front door. I excuse myself, hang up, and breathe deeply. The breathing clears the slightly unpleasant taste of the phone conversation from my mouth. I smooth my hands down the front of my trousers, and go to answer the door.

MAKING FRAMES

The woman pushes sunglasses back onto the top of her head, her pupils contracting in the light that filters on to my front verandah. She holds out her hand towards me.

'Dame Lena. I'm Maureen Patterson. Thanks for agreeing to see me.'

Her hand is cool, dry; her fingers long, neat and fine. She is tall, nearly my height. She smiles as we shake hands. She has strange eyes, pale grey-green. She wears no make-up that I can see, but for dark red lipstick defining her smile. I find myself aware of my own older, meagre, pale mouth.

'Ms Patterson, good to meet you.'

'Oh please, please call me Mo.'

'Mo, then. Come in.'

She steps over the threshold. She carries a large bag looped over her left shoulder. It looks heavy. I reach past her to close the front door and smell perfume, citrus and clean. She seems half my age, perhaps forty. So young.

'Please, come through to the kitchen.'

She's wearing black, so that she almost disappears into the shadows of the hallway, but is framed in silhouette by the doorway into the kitchen. She's a tall pear on long legs; narrow shoulders and waist, plump arse. She wears trousers wide and a little too short, a black shirt loose over them. There are heavy boots on her feet, long laces tied around the tops.

In the kitchen I motion to the chairs, the table. My beach towel is draped over the back of one of the chairs, already almost dry; I fold it, excusing myself, and ferry it through to the bathroom.

'You've been swimming already,' she says, as she takes a seat at the table. 'So early?'

'It's ten o'clock, Ms Patterson. Most people wouldn't call that early. However, I do try to go most days, the earlier the better. And you? Are you not a swimmer?'

'Mmm, I never really got into it, to tell you the truth. Back at home – I'm from New Zealand, originally – it's just like here, most people like to think they're born on the beach, live all their summers barefoot and sunburnt but, well, I just never really liked it. I'm a terrible swimmer, too, so that doesn't help. And I'm not very good at mornings.' She smiles, looks apologetic.

'Ah well.'

I busy myself with coffee, the ritual of it, while she ferrets in her bag, brings out a spiral-bound notebook and a pen, and places them on the table. The notebook remains closed, though; she is prepared, but not overeager. She removes her sunglasses from their position on top of her head, places them on the table above the notebook – centred, straight, aligned. Her hair, released, is smooth, long, and as red as her lipstick, but for a long streak of theatrically white-blonde hair hanging from her right brow, across her forehead like a draped curtain, and down the left side of her face, framing it.

Neither of us has said very much. We have busied ourselves with *business*, as they say in the theatre, with props; with notebooks and sunglasses and coffeepots and chairs. Coffee on the stove, I sit at the table opposite her.

'Well,' I say. 'Why exactly are you here?'

'I make films, Dame Lena—'

'Please, just Lena.'

'Lena.' She nods her head. 'I make films. That is, I've made several films – documentaries, some feature films as well. I sent you some biographical material, I hope that was useful for you.'

'Yes. It was certainly interesting.' The coffee bubbles and gurgles on the stove. I excuse myself to bustle with coffee and cups and milk and sugar, which I bring to the table. She realigns her pen and sunglasses in parallel with the spine of her notebook. She sighs lightly and starts again as I sit down.

'Thanks.' She touches the coffee cup. 'I was so inspired by your performance at Transformer. Terry Meelinck would have told you I was filming there, and in fact I was planning on making a documentary that focussed on the festival. But, after watching you play, I find that I'm more interested in making a documentary about *your* life, your ideas, your work, your music.'

I feel the bitterness of the coffee on the back of my tongue.

'Your life's been so, well, interesting.'

'Has it?' I look up at her. Another piss-take?

'You've had a long, successful and, let's face it, fascinating life.' She's animated now, her hands in arcs across the table. 'You were like, I dunno, Madonna before she was even born. You've been through waves of fame and relative anonymity, but it seems to me – from the research I've done since Transformer – that you've always been represented as a caricature. I hope you don't find this offensive...'

'Go on.'

'It seems to me that what most people associate with you is weird music, a bizarre instrument that they don't understand, and a vague whiff of scandal. It's a kind of early version of the sex, drugs, and rock'n'roll stereotype, and – again, I hope you don't find this offensive – I think, if anything, it shows you as a victim. I want to focus on you as a survivor – which you clearly are – not a victim. But I also want to show you as an innovator, and as a champion of your art, and your lifestyle.'

She sits back, takes a breath, after what sounds like a prepared speech, a pitch.

'I'm not sure...' I start to speak but, in truth, I'm not sure what it is that I'm not sure about. She seems sincere, this young woman, with her soft, soothing vowels. She talks on, low and constant, about the film she has in her mind, about angles, about themes and stories. About women, and feminism. About music. She has done her research – she speaks of things I have done, things I had almost forgotten I had done, the things that are in the history books, that made the gossip pages of long-ago times. She talks about my music. She talks about my Beatrix. She talks about her

41

vision; her hands move constantly together and apart as she speaks, making frames, containing and releasing images. My hands rest on the table in front of me, one crossed over the other.

She stays for an hour. At eleven o'clock, she looks at her watch, gathers her notebook, pen and sunglasses from the table in front of her, thanks me for my time, and says she mustn't take up any more of it, not today anyway.

As she pushes her notebook into her bag, she brings out a video cassette tape. She holds it in front of her in both hands, looks at it almost shyly, then holds it out to me.

'This is the film I made, a long time ago now. I don't know if you saw it, I don't suppose you did. It's called *Beatrix*.' She looks at me as if waiting for some acknowledgement. 'Well, anyway, I've brought this for you. I thought you might be interested. I know she was important to you.' She holds it out to me and I take it, hold it tentatively, feel its lightness.

'I don't have anything to play it on.' I don't meet her eyes.

'Well, I could bring you a VCR, you know, a video tape player. Or you'd be very welcome to watch it at my house, any time, just say so.'

'Oh, no, I wouldn't want to——'

'No, no, I understand. Well, maybe somewhere like the local library?'

I hold onto the video, squint at the label on it. 'I *would* like to keep it, if I may. Borrow it. There is a machine at the university, the School of Music. Perhaps I can play it there. I still go in, on occasion.'

'Of course,' she says. 'And please keep it, if you like. It's just a copy. I don't need it back.'

I place the tape on the kitchen table. I see her smile as she watches me.

I walk behind her towards the front door, open it to let her out. She turns to me – she outside on the verandah, lit by dappled sunlight, facing me inside, shaded – and holds out her hand as if to shake it. I take her hand, and she places her left hand over mine, so that my right hand is cupped, contained within her hands. We do not shake hands; we still them.

'Don't decide now', she says, 'about making the film. Think on it, and we'll talk next week.'

She releases my hand, hoists her bag onto her shoulder, and starts up the garden path. She turns and waves to me, then disappears into the dark up the side of the house.

BEATRIX

Iturn the video tape over. Block letters on the paper label
spell out *BEATRIX*. I trace it with my finger. Underneath,
in smaller letters, is written © *1975 M. Patterson.*

I did not tell M. Patterson the truth. I'm not sure why.
I do have a video cassette recorder. It is in a corner of my
bedroom, underneath a small television, the two of them
perched on a small, old wooden table, designed perhaps as
a plant stand, or an occasional table. I rarely use either of
the machines, but they are there, in that private room, just
for me.

She doesn't need to know everything.

I play the film on the machine in my bedroom. It is not a
documentary, it's – how best to describe it? – a portrait,
or an improvisation; Beatrix jazz. It's very beautiful. I see
myself in it. Literally: there are images, parts of paintings,
some of them paintings of me. It is full of colour and
movement. Like Beatrix. There's a bit I love, particularly,
where the camera pans across a black-and-white photograph
of her. The photograph has colours and lines washing across
it; it's alive with patterns drawn or painted or scratched

onto the film – that must be how it's done; shapes jump and judder across her face, across the screen. I press the button on the remote control unit to pause the video as it pans across the photograph. Her face – partly obscured by the colours, and by cigarette smoke as it often was in life – is just as I remember her, from our time in Sydney, that glorious time. Perhaps I took this photograph, with Beatrix's camera? I peer in closer at it, trying to recall, until I am so close to the screen that I can't see it at all.

I move back, sit on my bed, staring at the stilled image on the screen. The remote control is in my hand; I hold it at arms-length, and press the button with the symbol most likely to mean *eject*. The tape slides out of the machine, spine towards me. I see the words I read on the side of the tape repeated on the spine label: *BEATRIX © 1975 M. Patterson*.

M. Patterson: sly bitch with a muckraking agenda, or genuinely interested? Either way, with this film she may have bewitched me. If I'm not careful I'll find myself telling her the story of my life.

SINGAPORE, PERTH
1910–1927

The symphony of her dressing table

THE SOUND THAT BEES MAKE

If I were to write the story of my life it would begin, in a nutshell, like this: I am Helena Margaret Gaunt; I call myself Lena. I was born, the only child of Australian parents, in Singapore, where my father chased the riches of the booming rubber and export businesses after escaping the humdrum of work as a clerk in the bank in Tambellup, two hundred-odd miles – two days by train – south and east of Perth.

I was a solitary child, lacking companions my own age, but I was not lonely. I was happy in my own company, dancing to my own drum. My earliest memories are of making music, patterning music. They linger, these memories, watery, hazy, in the back of my mind.

I remember opening the door into Mother's bedroom, the dark back bedroom in the little brick bungalow in Singapore. I pulled the rattan stool from the corner, dragged it across the floor until it was next to Mother's dressing table. I clambered up onto the stool and reached across, past the dressing table set, the crystal tray, the dish with Mother's rings, the perfume bottle with its bulbous ting-ting lid. I reached across, and took the tortoiseshell comb.

Someone must have taught me this: I took a piece of thin tissue paper, wrapped it around Mother's comb. I held the papered comb to my lips and hummed. The paper vibrated; the air formed bubbles that moved as waves between the tissue of paper and the teeth of the comb.

I hummed quietly at first. The comb made the humming strange, changed it. I hummed into the comb; then I pulled it away and repeated the refrain – the sound was softer, quieter.

I could not have been more than four years old. But I remember the feeling of my lips, buzzing against the paper and the comb.

One time in my life – only one time, long ago and far away – I had a pet. Father bought him from the *pasar* in Singapore, a sweet little monkey, chattery, who when he found he liked you would settle and nestle into you, snuggling in under your arm. I called him Little Clive.

When Father brought him home and handed him to me that first day, I squealed and let go, and he was up the tree in a flash. There he stayed, peering down at us while sucking on his thumb just as a human baby would. He sat up there for three hours until Father ordered Cook's boy to shin up the tree and get him down.

Father said that Little Clive must be tied up after that. So Cook's boy, Malik, found a long piece of hemp rope, and plaited it to form a neat collar at one end, to slip firmly over Little Clive's neck. Little Clive couldn't undo it, even though his nimble fingers worried at the rope much of the day. Malik tied the other end to the verandah post. The rope was long enough that Little Clive could run, and even climb the trees closest to the house, but he could only climb so far – not far enough to get himself tangled, nor far enough to climb onto the roof.

He would sit on the long rail at the front of the verandah and chatter at anyone who passed, like one of the old Chinamen at the *pasar*. Malik brought bruised fruit from the kitchen. Little Clive would sit and carefully peel the fruit, turning it over and over in his hands then stuffing it piece by piece into his mouth until his cheeks bulged and his eyes almost goggled from his head. At night he would wrap himself in an old sarong – against the mosquitoes, we always thought, but perhaps from watching me swaddle my doll in her blanket and hold her to me like a baby.

Our garden was full of insects, and among them were bees, swarming and buzzing on their quest for pollen, staying only for an afternoon, a day, then passing on, leaving silence where their humming had been. They could engulf a hibiscus in minutes; the dizzy big plates of scarlet and orange circled our house, each flower with its nodding sticky pistil a syrupy flag of welcome to the bees.

And poor Little Clive, perched there in the hibiscus with his hands and face and belly all sticky with the juice of mango and pineapple and rambutan and papaya, poor Little Clive was there one day when the bees passed through. And he was on his hemp rope and couldn't get away when the bees swarmed him. He tried to fight them off, poor thing, he squawked and screamed, he fought with his sharp little fingernails, but the humming buzzing mass of them settled on him like a cloud.

Father wouldn't let me outside, though I screamed for poor Little Clive, but the truth is, I didn't want to go, not with those buzzing, stinging bees there. We stood inside, safe behind wooden shutters, and watched.

'They will leave,' Father said. 'They always do.'

And Father was right, as Father always was. The bees passed on and left Little Clive as suddenly as they had swarmed him. One moment he was writhing, black and thick with bees; the next, just his thin bee-less self remained, drooping, barely holding on to his perch in the hibiscus, fruit dropped to the ground below him.

Father opened the front door and we went towards Little Clive. When Father stretched his arms towards him Little Clive screamed. I could see hard, round lumps already forming on the soft skin of his belly, the size and shape of the jade beads Mother wore around her neck. The little monkey scrambled to try to climb higher, away from Father, but the rope tightened around his neck and would let him go no further.

Father got a mango – a good one, not a bruise on it – and tried to tempt him, but Little Clive just shuddered and shivered at the end of his rope, just barely keeping his balance in the V of the hibiscus branches. Even when night fell, he would not come to us. His little eyes stayed bright and watchful, not letting us close.

Before I went to bed, I watched Malik put an enamel dish of water and a banana on the ledge of the verandah, close to Little Clive – like putting a glass of sherry and a slice of Christmas cake out on Christmas Eve. I went to my bed but I could not sleep. I could hear Father and Mother in the dining room, clattering cutlery, tinkling glasses. I crept quietly down the hallway and managed to open the front door without making a sound. On the verandah, my eyes adjusting to the moonlight, I could make out the shape of Little Clive in the hibiscus, where we had left him. His outline was smooth, draped, and as my pupils widened I could see that he had wrapped himself in his old batik sarong. He held the sarong over his head, like the little old Madonna at the Catholic church, and he picked the lumps on his belly with careful fingernails, picking the beestings out of the centres of the hard lumps. He looked at me and squinted his eyes, as if to let me know it hurt, so much.

'I'm sorry about the bees, Little Clive,' I whispered. 'Goodnight. Get well.'

I believe he nodded at me.

In the morning he was dead, wrapped tight in his sarong, hooked like a hammock on a branch at the base of the hibiscus. Cook's boy buried him that morning, buried Little Clive in his old sarong under the hibiscus, and I picked a bunch of flowers – orange and scarlet, magenta – and placed them on the small mound above him. I played him a tune on Mother's comb. I played him a tune like the buzzing of bees, a requiem that made my lips puff and sting.

NOT DROWNING, WAVING

I thought of my life as lived in a fairy tale. *Once there was a little girl named Helena Margaret Gaunt, who called herself Lena.* Sometimes it seemed almost as if I observed myself from a distance. Without other children to play with, I played all of the parts in my own little life story.

Lena sat on the path by the verandah at the front of her house, pouring water from pot to cup to make tea for her dolly, whose name was Enid. The girl and her doll sat in the cool of the garden, flowers around them, hibiscus big and bright and open, frangipani fragrant, moon-coloured, milk-coloured. She picked frangipani blossoms and put them on hibiscus leaves, and served them, *one for Enid, one for me.* She pretended to bite them, but didn't quite touch them to her mouth, mindful of her mother's warnings not to eat anything straight from the garden. As she pretended to eat, she nodded her head towards Enid, pursing her lips, as her mother and her mother's friends did when they took their afternoon tea. Her mother and her mother's friends all sat on the verandah that afternoon, in the deep cool of the shade, around a low table of tea things: pretty china from Home, daintics on plates, milk in a jug. Lena could hear them, just yards away from her, tinkling china and low chattering and the whoosh and rustle and delicious slip of dress hems against ankles.

As she and Enid sat on the path in the shade by the house, enjoying their frangipani dainties and water-for-tea, a butterfly appeared and hovered above them, just out of reach, as big as one of Mother's best dinner plates, but more brightly coloured. Suspended above her, it seemed to block out the sun, the whole sky. The butterfly's wings were every colour the little girl loved: mango, hibiscus, blood red; purple of the sky at night; silver of fish gleaming on Cook's plate; blue of Mother's eyes. The butterfly was so big, so very big, that its wings made a sound as they compressed the air underneath and above them with each beat. The girl stood, lifting Enid in her arms, smoothing Enid's soft mango-yellow hair.

'Look Enid, butterfly. *Rama-rama.*'

She held Enid aloft, and as she did so the butterfly moved ahead of them, just a little. She took a step closer, so that Enid could see. With each step the little girl took with Enid, the butterfly moved just out of reach, just away but staying close, as if they were attached by a fine filament that the girl couldn't see, as if the butterfly was pulling her and Enid along behind it. It stayed close enough that she could hear the sound of its wings, the waves through the air. The butterfly stayed above her head, so she was looking up, but she got tired of holding Enid up to see. So she tucked Enid under her arm as she continued to follow the butterfly, quite quickly moving far from the tinkling teatime ladies on the verandah, towards the dark jungle at the bottom of the garden. Magicked by the butterfly, she ignored the warnings drummed into her: stay close to the house; stay away from the old well; don't go near the dark trees at the bottom of the garden.

The butterfly came to rest on a twig at her eye height. She stopped, held her breath so the butterfly wouldn't be scared. She reached out her arm, her finger outstretched, then took a step forward – just a tiny step – towards it.

And then her world dropped from beneath her, the butterfly flew up as if the filament was jerked by an angel in the sky, and the girl felt a rush and a drop and all the air above and below her pushed her down and she disappeared below water, the air replaced by water all around her and above her and below her, and she didn't know how deep it was, or how wide. She felt herself fall through the water, felt her body move through the water and make it eddy and roil, felt bubbles rise in her wake and turbulence all around. Enid was there, above her, her mango-yellow hair around her head like a halo, like a dinner plate, like a sea anemone's tentacles, like a star. Enid held her arms out towards the girl, then rolled in the water above her and faced away, her hair tentacling around her, blocking out the sun, the sky, the world, the air above. The little girl waved her hand at Enid, waved at her to turn back, to not go away, but Enid did not respond. The little girl stopped waving. The water was warm. It pushed against her ears, a pressure she heard inside her head as a single note, humming, musical, low. It sounded like the black strip near the bottom of the piano. But it wasn't played on the piano, it was a different sound, not a hammer on a wire; it was a humming, inside her head, like the sound bees make.

As the sound in her head changed, the little girl felt a clasping pressure on her chest, then a rush and then the water moved past her and she was pulled, blinking, spluttering, abruptly back into the air.

The panicking eyes of Cook's boy were above her, close to her eyes, as big as plates, wide in his face. She breathed in deep, and smiled.

'*Selamat pagi*, Malik,' she said.

'Miss, you were in the water!'

'Where's Enid?'

'Enid, Miss?'

'Enid went with me. We were having a tea party. Enid was in the water. I saw her. We followed the *rama-rama*.'

The boy's eyes panicked again, and he looked to the well, freezing for a moment before leaping up, imagining another pale girl, this one floating on the surface of the water, eyes open, not seeing.

He leant over the well, peering into blackness. But he turned back smiling, showing her Enid, bedraggled, hair like yellow seaweed over her beautiful face and dress.

'Enid!' the girl squealed, and then she coughed, and then she was sick, more water than sick, water flowing in waves from her mouth, more water than a little girl could hold coming out and coming and coming as if it would never stop.

THE MEMORY OF WATER

Mother came to us trailing a wake of afternoon tea friends, oohing and aahing, each with her hands to her mouth as if to stop anything coming out. They stood around us, our little tableau in the jungle at the bottom of the garden: me lying on the ground by the well, Malik crouched over me, holding Enid out to me like a prize, all of us covered in watery sick. Mother scooped me up in her arms, the sick and the water and Enid's hair all dripping down her dress, making it stick to her, making a sound of scraping and sucking against her legs as she walked, carrying me – me carrying Enid – the ladies all trailing behind.

Mother strode up the steps to the verandah and gently lowered me onto the thin mattress on the rattan lounge. The ladies gathered around me, muttering, their concern a lower register than their earlier tinkling clinking teatime sound. Mother's hand plucked at my clothes, and the ladies' muttering faded to a low hum. And then, from that moment on, my memory fades, fades on the face of Enid as I held her close to me.

*

After the water, I lapsed into a fever. The doctor was called, and Father came early from work. Although I do not remember it, I imagine the doctor, Father and Mother all huddled around me. I must have been taken to Mother's room, had my wet clothes stripped from me, been towelled dry and tucked into the big bed in her dark room at the back of the house, the window shaded by large trees, the whole room smelling of powder and coconut oil, of lavender and Mother and mothballs.

I stayed cossetted in that soft, dark room for days and days as the fever ebbed and flowed, dimmed and raged, and then finally left me for good: weak, pale, but well. The cause of the fever was never determined. Its source was *something in the water*, Father would always say. The water had been inside me and outside me and all around me. And then the fever took its place: inside me, outside me, all around me. The water had been warm. The fever was hot, my brain turbulent with imagined things, terrible things, burning hot things. I remember them as a hot dark cloud, buzzing in a minor key, indistinct, swirling.

My mother stayed close to me for that long season after the water, after the fever, sleeping on a low rattan lounge by the side of her bed, where I slept. I recall looking down at her hair spread on the pillow. She made a soft breathing sound, and her hands were tucked up, one under her pillow, the other under her cheek, resting lightly on the fine cotton.

I recall the symphony of the dressing table. It is what I heard as I came out of the fever from the water. I have held this with me, and can hum it still. It is the sound of my mother at her toilette, and it played for me each morning, the bristle and rustle as her hairbrush ran electric through her hair before it was trussed and tamed into its daily knot, its bun at the nape of her neck. The hairbrush creaked and crackled, released tiny purple-white sparks, like stars, in the dark dry air of the bedroom, tapped percussion as she placed it on the dressing table. Crystal rang like tiny chimes, and her rings sang gold and silver against the china tray she dropped them onto.

I became attuned to all the sounds I heard. I would sing them under my breath when she had gone, sing them in the dark before the shutters were opened, before breakfast was brought to me.

But when I sang them to myself, I corrected them, wrote the music properly in my head first, then in my throat and my ears. Because Mother didn't make those sounds in the right order, the right rhythm. She didn't make the notes last for as long as they should. It was as if she didn't hear the music properly, as if she didn't hear how it should be.

Mother made the dressing table sing. But I perfected it, made it right.

I am unsure how long I slept in Mother's bedroom after the fever from the water. Enid slept with me, by my side in the big bed, her hard little body a companion, a comfort. I grew stronger as the fever left me, fed up on mango and papaya and good white rice, and a sherry glass each day filled with the dark, strong Guinness stout that the Chinese drank as a tonic. Soon I was able to swing my own legs over the edge of the bed and hop down without assistance. Finally I was moved back into my own, smaller room at the side of the house. It smelled musty, from me not being in it. Enid still slept next to me. Her hair did not recover from its dunking, and its straggling thinness never failed to remind me of the water.

I was left with another reminder of the water, even after the fever had left me. The doctors told Mother and Father that my heart had a leaky valve, and advised them that I would do better living in the southern Australian climate. The humidity of the tropics would only worsen my condition, they said. And although it was never made clear, I associated that leakiness, that fault, with my time in the water. That leaky heart of mine was what made them send me away from them. For my health, they said, but I always felt that somehow it was my failure to stop the water leaking in, or leaking out, that caused it.

UNCLE VALENTINE

So it was that my parents sent me away – *back Home*, they called it – aboard the mail steamer *Arcadia* in the care of the ship's stewards. I was four years old; it was 1914. I can barely remember that trip, arriving in Fremantle Harbour to be met by my mother's brother, my uncle Valentine, in his fresh new uniform. I did not know what a war was, nor what it meant. Uncle Valentine deposited me at the private boarding school Father had booked me into, the school run by the Misses Murray in Lesmurdie, in the Hills above Perth, where the air was too cold in winter and too hot in the summer. I can recall my arrival there as if observed, not experienced: the little tiny child in a dress sewn for the tropics, shivering in the foyer of that winter-dark school building. My uncle patted me on the head, waved me goodbye, and left. So deposited, I settled into my life with the Misses Murray well enough, their solid teaching of all things musical the distraction I needed to replace the gentle first music – of dressing tables and bees – that my family could no longer provide. I would not see my uncle again for five years, and it would be twelve years before I returned to Singapore.

*

Of my twelve long years boarding with the Misses Murray, the less said the better. They taught us and disciplined us in the manner of the day, their aim to turn us all into little ladies, the sensible, well-spoken wives of cockies and bookkeepers, of doctors and clergymen. We learned to write letters for all occasions, to sew a trousseau, to mend a sock or a bedsheet, to launder each Monday, to iron each Tuesday, roast a joint of meat to its grey melting point, to bake scones and sponges and fruit cake for a shearing gang or a church fête. Miss Murray the elder taught art, leaning too close behind each of us in turn as she peered at our watercolours and pastel sketches, her breath sour and slightly wheezy, eager and hopeless all at once.

Miss Murray the younger, though: Miss Murray the younger taught music and it was she who uncovered and nurtured my musical abilities, starting me at the piano when I was so young that I learned the musical notes before I learned my alphabet. The symphony of Mother's dressing table faded, replaced by the cleaner notes from the keys of the piano, notes that I could control and order. As it became apparent that I had both perfect pitch and perfect recall, Miss Murray the younger gave me my head, letting me roam through pieces considered too difficult for a child. The word *prodigy* was murmured – with a mixture of wonderment and distaste – but never knowingly in my presence; vanity was almost as dangerous as talent.

My days shaped themselves around the piano in the music room, around the locked case with its treasured music manuscripts behind glass. Music released me from the humdrum of so much at the Misses Murray's. My leaky heart did the rest: my parents had entrusted me to the Misses Murray with instructions that I was not to join the other girls in swimming, nor in any strenuous endeavours. And so I was left to my devices in the music room, my weak heart beating time with the piano's hammers, hammers on wires.

Although we knew that the Great War was raging – for the Misses told us so – it seemed a far away thing, cloistered as we were, we girls, in the little school in the Hills. It came closer when the Misses took us to Guildford to see the men march down the main street and onto the train, with all the population of the Hills down to send them off. We waved at them and their fine uniforms, and we draped the classrooms with paper chains to celebrate our soldiers.

As time went by though, more and more girls returned to the Misses at the end of each holiday break ashen-faced, quiet, sombre with stories of fathers or brothers lost or wounded. I learned the word *elegy* then, learned the feeling of *lentissimo* and *larghissimo*, from the music Miss Murray the younger played us.

By the time the war ended, I had almost forgotten that my uncle Valentine existed, or at least thought of him only in the abstract.

His voice came as a shock when it rang from the foyer of the school, rang through the closed doors and into the music room. I heard the Misses Murray muttering, their footsteps tinkering beside his boots until he burst through the door in a fresh grey suit that even I could tell was cut from expensive cloth. He stopped a good step away, and frowned at me.

'Helena Margaret, it is you, is it not? Good God, look at you, the spit of your mother, and almost as tall. Welcome your uncle home from the war, there's a darling,' and he held out his arms towards me, as no one had done since my arrival at the Misses Murray's. I stepped eagerly towards him. He smelled of soap and tobacco, and held me tight against him, patting my back, *there, there*, almost humming the words.

My uncle had me play for him. He laughed and clapped as I finished each piece, shouted *encore!* and *brava!* and stamped his feet on the polished wood floor. Miss Murray the younger brought him tea on a tray, and a dish for his cigarette ash, and stood behind Uncle Valentine's chair, her hands clasped in front of her, listening.

'Such playing deserves a treat,' he said, rubbing his hands together. 'An outing, my girl, you should have an outing!' He stood and gathered me up from the bench at the piano. 'Miss Murray, I'm taking Helena out for the day. We may'— he paused for effect, wiggling his eyebrows at me – 'be a tad late home. Don't keep her tea warm tonight, Miss Murray, she won't be needing it!'

Uncle Valentine's car, black and shining, was parked right by the door at the front of the school. I had not been in a motor car since Uncle Valentine had deposited me at the school five years earlier, but I remembered the smell of the red leather seat, remembered it pressing my skirt to the backs of my legs. As we wheeled down the hill towards town, I watched through the window as the bush slid by. We followed the river past the tall buildings of the city, past the stinking brewery and on to the edge of the land, to the sea.

I had not seen the sea since I'd stepped off the *Arcadia* five years before. How had I forgotten its smell, the sticky salt everywhereness of it, its thunder? Uncle Valentine parked his car on a headland high above the waves, the car with its nose pointed out above the ocean like the prow of a ship. Even on a calm day, as it was then, the power of the ocean was evident. The water thundered within itself, even as it whispered at the sand in foaming curves on the beach below us. I could hear the roar, *basso profondo*, underneath.

Uncle Valentine and his bottomless pockets bought me a swimsuit that day. We paid our halfpennies to use the changing tents, met up again dressed in our woollen togs and walked down to the water's edge together.

'Can you swim as well as you can play the piano?'

I shook my head.

'But you *can* swim?'

I shook my head again. 'I'm not supposed to. My heart…' I put my hands to my chest.

'Oh good God, well forget that nonsense, we must get you into the water, there is nothing as bracing as a dip in the Indian Ocean! Come with me. No harm will befall you if you stick with your Uncle Valentine, I am unsinkable.'

He took my hand and we walked to the water. It tickled at my feet, effervescing. Again I heard the bass notes underneath. I shuddered.

'It's the salt that keeps you afloat. Old Briny. Taste it. Go on!' He bent down, scooped his hand through the water and up to his mouth, rubbing it over his face. I did the same. It was cold and salty, but clean, crisp, metallic. It was different from the buzzing water that once was inside me and around me and all about, all those years ago.

'Ready? Easy at first.' Uncle Valentine was by my side. He took my hand in his. We both faced out to sea.

'Ready,' I told him.

My confidence in the water grew. At first I happily paddled in the shallows, bobbing in the clear green sea, until I became brave enough to swim out, just a little, just far enough to catch a wave into shore. I did not venture deep. I preferred to stay in close, where the water was pale. Uncle swam out to the dark water, the deep water. It made me anxious to watch him get smaller and smaller then disappear in the chop. But I learned that he would always come back, huffing and blowing from the exercise.

RESONANCE

On that first day, as on many later outings, we retired to Uncle Valentine's big house by the sea, after we had swum. Afternoon tea was served in his front room, where the piano sat waiting for me. I was allowed to play whatever I wanted to play on his piano, and Uncle Valentine encouraged me, clapped and stamped as he had on my first day at school. During the week I would learn new pieces to please him, complicated pieces to show off.

Then, after I had played, it would be Uncle Valentine's turn to show off. He would play me gramophone records on the His Master's Voice player that stood against the wall, the latest recordings ordered in for him by the music shop in the city. We did not have a gramophone at the Misses Murray's up in the Hills, and I had only the very slightest recollection of the cylinder phonograph Father had so rarely played in my earliest days, in Singapore. I had never before seen – let alone held, or examined – a gramophone record. Uncle Valentine, himself enthralled as much by the technology as by the modern sounds it let him hear, was keen that I should share his delight. He explained to me in detail each part of the machine, how it moved, how it worked with the next part, and the next, all of them working in concert. He would let me wind the gramophone, gently move the arm to place the needle in its groove, and then I would sink into the soft chair by Uncle's side, in time to hear the hiss before the music, the hiss and pop that was the lead-in, the signal for what would come after.

In this way, I came to hear the pieces I had learned to play on the piano in the solitary music room up in the Hills; but now I heard them with their full orchestration. I heard sounds I realised I'd been straining to hear, the gaps between the notes I'd played, timbres unreachable by the piano, heard resonance above and below and through and around.

And one day I heard it: the low sound, like a human voice, low and warm, deep blue like the dark deep water. It hummed then sang out from underneath the piano, rising from the amplifying horn above the rotating recorded disc.

'That sound,' I said. I rested my hand on my uncle's arm, and he covered my hand with his.

'Casals. Playing the cello, darling. Beautiful instrument. Bigger than you, probably.'

'Can I play it?'

He looked at me. 'I suspect you can play anything you put your mind to, Helena. Would you like to try?'

I pulled my hand out from underneath his, grabbed his big hand in both of mine. 'Can I? Oh please, please, can I?'

On the way back to the Misses Murray's, Uncle Valentine drove slowly past Spanney's, on Hay Street. We stopped the car, and Uncle tried the shop's locked door. We peered in through the windows, leaving wet smudges, leaving empty-handed, unable to see what the shop's dark interior held. But three days later, the Spanney's van pulled up outside the Misses Murray's school and delivered me a half-size cello, packed in a hard black case lined with red velvet. In the music room I lifted it out – even this fractional size was as big as I was – and fitted myself against its back, its body, smelled rosewood and spruce, touched horsehair on the bow. I shaped the curve of my arm to its body, ran my fingers down the thick strings and heard them hiss and screech – just lightly – under their breath. With my right arm, I reached the strings and plucked the thickest, heard its resonance, its low growl. I turned my back on the piano, picked up the bow and measured its weight and heft in my hand, and started the long process of learning to play my first true love, the cello.

I became completely absorbed in learning the cello, then and in the years that followed, throughout the remainder of my schooling with the Misses Murray, to their horror and despite their protestations to my uncle that the violoncello was not appropriate for a young lady, that its tone was too deep, too manly, that the posture one had to adopt to play it was – well, unladylike. But Uncle Valentine's winning ways overcame their protestations. The not inconsiderable matter of providing me with a teacher was also dealt with by my uncle, who engaged a music tutor, Mr Coulson from the boys school in the city, to travel up to the Hills to give me a weekly lesson. Mr Coulson taught me the rudiments I needed to play; showed me how to hold the cello as if, he said, it was a standing child leaning backwards, trusting, into my lap; taught me how to bow, taught me *pizzicato*, *vibrato*. While Miss Murray the younger had guided me ably in my early years learning the piano, her greatest contribution to my cello-playing was to leave me alone. As soon as I completed my schoolwork for the day, I sought out the music room, frowning and growling at anyone else who thought they might colonise my space. Beyond my weekly lessons, I developed my technique by listening, with my ears and my whole body, to the sounds I made, by changing and reflecting and responding to the music I played.

I remained a solitary child, happiest in my own company. I did my work well enough in the classroom, but I didn't care for the games and silliness of the other girls, who teased me, for my way of speaking – formal, grown-up, foreign-sounding – as much as for my obsession with music. It was Uncle Valentine, not the girls my own age, whose company I cherished. He continued his visits, and we continued our outings. There would be gaps and unexplained absences when I would not see him for months at a time – *fingers in pies, and so on, my dear*, he would tell me on his return – but then, unannounced, there he'd be, swooping up the hill in his big black motor car, sweeping into the music room, to drive me away for the day, to the beach or, increasingly, straight to his house by the sea, to settle in the big soft chairs in the front room and to listen to recordings on his gramophone. We would only leave the Misses Murray's after I had performed for him though, something I loved, a piece I had kept safe in the forefront of my brain knowing it was a piece for Uncle Valentine, that he would love its intricacy, its gaiety, its depth or its modernity.

As well as music, my uncle's house was filled with the many modern conveniences that his comfortable income allowed. In contrast to the ancient, dark austerity of the Misses Murray's, all blacked wood stoves, Coolgardie safes and draughty fireplaces, Uncle Valentine's kitchen gleamed with the newest electric appliances, the stove and refrigerator kept humming and full by his housekeeper, Mrs Anderson. Well-thumbed issues of the magazines he loved – *The Wireless World*, *The Electrical Experimenter*, joined later by *Science and Invention* – fed his enthusiasm and curiosity for all things new, and prompted many of his purchases. He was an amateur, a buyer of others' inventions, neither a tinkerer nor an inventor of his own.

'I leave the inventing to the geniuses, and the building to those that are good with their hands,' he told me. 'But you and I, my dear Helena, we get to enjoy them; we get to play with them all, all of these wonderful new toys! How very lucky we are to live in this fabulous century.'

Infected by his vigorous enthusiasm, I too flicked hungrily through the pages of *The Wireless World* and *Science and Invention*, intrigued by the poetry if not the detail of anodes and ohms, connections and resistance. In those magazines of my uncle's, and in the slim literary volumes on his shelves, I found pages alive with the buzz of the next new thing. Like me, they were of this century, not the last; they looked forward, not to the past. If these are possible, I thought – this machine, or this poem – if these are possible, then anything, *anything* might be possible.

STUDY HARD, BEHAVE YOURSELF

During my many years with the Misses Murray, once I had learned my letters and words, I wrote to my parents every Sunday, a single page of onionskin paper, topped *Dear Mother and Father* and tailed *Your daughter Helena*. And Mother wrote to me each week, a letter to match, a page. Mother's letters were as invariable as the tropical climate she and Father lived in: *I am well; your father is busy; we had the Atkinsons for tea; it is so warm.* My letters to them matched hers: *I am well; Uncle Valentine is busy; it is warm*, or *it is hot*, or *the rain has come*, or *the wildflowers are out*. I live for my music, I wanted to tell them, but somehow did not. Father would sometimes write a line on the bottom of Mother's letter, almost always a variation on *Study hard and behave yourself*. They were so far away. I can't say with certainty that I missed them.

It was towards the end of my school days that I received a letter addressed in Father's handwriting. My first thought was of illness or disaster. I left the letter resting for an hour on the closed lid of the piano, behind me, out of sight, as I played my cello.

When I finally opened the letter, it was businesslike,

as Father always was. I was to finish school this calendar year. I should reside with my uncle until passage early in the new year could be arranged for the two of us to Singapore, where Father would meet us for the trip home to Malacca. *Home*, he called it. My parents had moved there, from Singapore, ten years before, but I had never lived in Malacca. *Employment will be arranged for you here*, he wrote. *There is an excellent school for the English community, they will take you on to teach. Your mother is delighted at your imminent return*, he finished. *Study hard and behave yourself.*

And so, that December I said goodbye to the Misses Murray, shook their hands firmly in mine and climbed into Uncle Valentine's car with my trunk, my cello and my leather valise of sheet music piled in the back. We drove down the hill for the last time, to the big house by the beach, where we sprawled all summer, my cello and I. Uncle Valentine would go to his office each morning, wearing his too-hot business suit, his forehead already sleek with sweat before he left the house. But in the evenings we would sit together in the cool of the breeze blowing from the ocean, sipping whisky while we listened to gramophone records, or I played my cello. Uncle taught me to smoke, those hot summer nights – said it was good for my health, and just the most modern thing. I studied the photographs and advertisements in magazines, and copied the poses they showed, draping myself languidly on Uncle's lounge, crystal tumbler of whisky in one hand, cigarette in the other. Uncle's gift for me that Christmas was a fine silver case, which I kept well-stocked with cigarettes from the carved wooden box on his desk.

I spent that summer in luxury, glorious luxury, back and forth between Uncle Valentine's house and the beach as the summer became hotter and hotter. My cello's tuning suffered more each day.

One morning at the height of summer, after a week of temperatures well over a century and my cello almost melting, I saw the music store truck pull up at the front of Uncle's house, and watched as two men delivered a familiar-shaped case to the door.

The cello inside the case was gleaming aluminium, all metal except for its wooden fingerboard. I had never seen anything so beautiful, so modern. It was like a machine, polished to a mirror finish; I saw myself reflected, wide-eyed. Uncle Valentine watched me, smiling.

'Worth every penny to see your face, Helena. And for you to stop your whining about the weather. It's the latest thing from America. The advertisements say that it won't crack or warp, that it'll last forever. Might just survive the trip to Malacca, eh?'

Full-size to my smaller wooden cello, this beauty had a different voice, at once deeper and brighter. Despite the heat around us, the cello was all cold beauty against my skin. When I pressed it against my legs and plucked the strings, it felt electric, new.

That same day a telegram came from Father, addressed to me. I held it with fingers callused from playing my new cello, perspiring from the day and the playing. The message was short; my skin felt cold on reading it. Its words ran together, not making sense at first, but finally the sense they made was unavoidable. *Mother contracted fever buried today suffering brief. Maintain planned passage north. Father.*

In the days that followed, as Uncle Valentine and I stepped quietly and carefully around each other with the strange formality that death seemed to require, I realised that although my mother's death saddened me, I could not say that my sadness was deep. Twelve years of polite but repetitive letters had distanced me from her. I remembered her for her music of the dressing table, from long ago, remembered her sleeping next to me, as I came through my leaky fever. I did not miss her, it occurred to me, quite as a girl should miss her mother. If anything, it was observing my uncle's grief for his sister that saddened me most.

Still, I played the music I remembered from the end of the war, *larghissimo, lentissimo*, the annotations like a string of saints' names muttered over a nun's beads. Ringing from the clear, bright cello, music cut the hot air, elegiac.

COTTESLOE
1991

Mythologies

SWEET SPOT

My theremin has been returned to me this morning, unscathed. They've taken care of it, at least. It was returned to me packed in cardboard, held rigid and protected within a wooden frame – like a large tea-chest – constructed around it. The two young men who delivered it set themselves to unpacking it on the footpath when they realised the crate would not fit down the path between the front house and the side fence.

I found one of them attacking the wooden framing with a crowbar while the other watched and scratched his head. I suggested – sternly – that they take care with the crowbar, and told them I would wait for them in the cottage. It took them nearly an hour to unpack the instrument, carry it to the cottage, and install it in the front room; to unpack and install the speaker to which it attaches; and then, bless their mothers for teaching nice manners, to clean away their mess, and make their polite farewells.

The boys have placed the theremin approximately in its accustomed position, marked on the floor by a dark, flattened patch on the rug. I tense my body against one side of the machine, feel it hard against my body. I waltz it gently across the rug until the position is perfect, just so.

I connect leads, plug the instrument into a transformer, the transformer into the electrical socket, and flick the switch on the outlet. A light hum starts, almost inaudible at first, but increasing in volume as the machine warms and glows into life. I wonder, not for the first time, if I can really smell ozone as electricity arcs and sparks. Can I smell it? Or do I just imagine it, the lightning and rain smell of it, impossibly damp and dry at once.

I adopt a playing stance: address the machine, face it, raise my hands, take a breath and bring my hands in to draw a note. Yes; *there*. I play a note, a trill, a run. I play a scale, C major, *legato*, then D major, *pizzicato*, pinching each note off from its predecessor and its successor. The sound is fine, good; no damage has been done in the shipping to and from Transformer, and I feel my shoulders relax with the knowledge. I should have known that it would take more than a ninety-minute journey by truck and two silly boys with a crowbar to cause damage. It's lived a long time, this machine, travelled well in its long life; followed me in mine.

I test the instrument and my fingers, my memory: I play Shostakovich, the first concerto for cello, the *allegretto* movement. I feel my head nod and drop away.

Over my soaring playing I just barely hear a banging, a knock, and realise it is sounding from my front door. I drop my hands mid-bar, the resultant discord hanging in the air as I turn away from the machine.

Through the screen door I see the filmmaker is holding the same shoulder bag, wearing the same sunglasses as last week when we first met. I open the door. She smells of the same cool citrus perfume.

'I'm so sorry. I've interrupted you, haven't I? I heard you playing,' she says. 'As I came down the path, it got louder, and I realised what it was. I couldn't tell whether it was a recording though, or if it was you playing. Actually playing.'

'It was me. It's just been delivered home from the festival. I wanted to test it, make sure it hadn't been damaged in transit.' I wave her in, usher her with my hands into the dark hallway.

'And?'

'Oh'—I make a dismissive noise with my lips, a dismissive wave with my hands—'it's fine. I suspect it's indestructible.'

'Do you have someone who can, I dunno, repair it for you? Is it like a car; does it need regular servicing to keep it running?'

'The man who made it for me—it would have been, I think, 1930 this one—always said I didn't need to know how it worked, but I should be able to maintain it. There are things I do, to keep it running. Routines. Yes, I suppose, a little like oiling and fuelling a car, like replacing spark plugs.'

'Could I see it, do you think?'

'Of course.'

In the room, she stands slightly to the side of the instrument, and too far away to touch it. The ozone smell and the warm, dry hum of the instrument fill the room.

She moves closer, takes a step, puts her hand out, but not in any systematic way, not as a thereminist would approach the instrument. As her hand nears the pitch aerial, I reach past her and, as my own hand trills up the straight metal rod, a series of notes sound, wobbly and incomplete, poorly formed from my awkward position.

'God, it's – strange. Strangely beautiful. The sound; it's warm, isn't it?'

'It's the valves. Old-fashioned glass and solidity. Here, let me.'

I move in front of the machine, into the playing position. She moves away to the side, far enough that she won't affect the sound. I reprise the Shostakovich she heard me play as she arrived.

The filmmaker watches me, prowling the room as I play. I notice her looking at her hands, looking down. I hear a heavy click and mechanical wind; she is looking down into the viewing lens of an old-fashioned camera, held low at her belly.

I finish playing, trail off just shy of the lead-up to the movement's ending. I turn to face her. She stands, leaning against the wall in what I know to be the room's sweet spot, where the sound from the speaker is pure and as perfect as it gets in this little wooden shack. If she has found that spot from five minutes listening, then she has a fine ear, a very fine ear. If she is there by chance, well, she is there by chance. These things happen.

I reach out and touch the camera.

'Your camera is almost as old as my theremin.'

'That was beautiful,' she says.

'Thank you.'

'Was it the Shostakovich? The one you played at Transformer?'

I nod.

'It didn't sound quite finished. Sorry, maybe that sounds rude, or just ignorant. That wasn't the end, was it? It sounded as if – well, I wanted more, wanted you to keep on playing.'

'No, you're right. There is more, but I didn't play it. It seemed a little too – perhaps too showy for before we've even had coffee.' We smile at each other.

As I turn to leave the room she places her hand on my arm, just above my wrist, stopping me. 'Thank you for playing for me. Thank you so much.'

'It's nothing.'

'No, it's not nothing. I'm sorry, but I just can't get over how beautiful it sounds. Your playing. You draw out the most astonishing sounds. It's what struck me the other week at Transformer. I've heard it played by other people – it can sound so tinny, so gimmicky. You make it sound beautiful.' She shakes her head, slowly, drops her hand from my arm. 'Magic. Just magic. No one plays like you.'

'You're very kind.'

She follows me out of the front room and into the hallway. I find myself saying to her, not looking at her as we walk, 'I would like to help you make your film.' It's her finding the room's sweet spot that has done it for me. That she should be there, just there; that she can hear that. That talks to me in a way I can trust. I know – without knowing, without reason – that this is the right decision.

THE VIEWING LENS

We sit again in the kitchen, coffee hot on the table in front of us, weather hot outside. She has asked if she can set up an audio tape, to record our conversation. The tape spools turn in the machine, a lead snaking to a microphone on a short stand on the table between us. She pushes her hair behind her ear, and picks up the pen from next to her notebook.

'So,' I say, 'how does this work? Do you have a list of questions to ask me? Will you start filming first?'

'No, I like to start with this' – she touches the tape recorder – 'some audio, and the images from my still camera.' She has placed on the table the Rolleiflex she used to capture me in the front room. The heavy black camera sits on soft black fabric, with velcro tabs that close it snugly around the camera like a swaddling cloth.

Why do you really want to film me? I want to ask her. Why do you care? But instead, I gesture towards the camera.

'A fine machine. I had one – well, used one – you know. Long ago.'

She hands the Rolleiflex to me. I look down into the

viewing lens, see her framed in the window, the stove behind her.

'I'll take some stills,' she says, targeted in the crosshairs as I watch her through the lens, 'some ideas for shots perhaps, but often more a reference for me as I go. And I'd like us to talk a little before we start filming, just find our feet I guess, get comfortable with each other. It'll be good to record that on audio tape, those preliminary talks, like today, get some ideas for the filmed interviews. Sound okay?'

I raise my eye away from the viewfinder, and hand her back her camera. 'It does.'

We talk, for an hour or more, about music, about the garden, about swimming, about time. It is comfortable; I do not feel as if I am being interviewed. When I close the door behind her departing back, I lean against it, kick my shoes off, walk to the bedroom and draw the curtain across the window, leaving cool darkness.

I sit on the bed, my feet flat on the the floor. Opposite me, perched on the table, is my small television, the spine of the video cassette filling the mouth of the VCR machine below it. I have only to lean forward and press my finger against the spine, against *BEATRIX*, to launch the tape into the machine again, to watch her contained on the little screen.

Now the filmmaker wants to film *me*, to make a film about *my* life, *my* art. Movies were made before, long ago. Newsreels, once upon a time. Then later, in New York, the people around me made movies all the time, used cameras that were supposed to be mounted on tripods, carried them in their hands, made films that wobbled and swerved, focussed in and out and all over the place so you almost suffered seasickness as you watched them played back. Black-and-white films, or saturated colour, people sitting on beds and smoking, or at festivals, or talking about sex, or music, or art, or nothing. Lots of films about nothing. Faces staring into the camera. The soundtracks of these movies, more often than not, were found sounds, looping swirls of rhythm.

You see fragments of these films, occasionally, as part of earnest compilations at film festivals. You read about them, more often, or about the mythology around them. This film of hers, it will be different, from what she tells me. I wonder how much of those old mythologies she has absorbed; how much do they stick to me, these different mythologies from the past?

MALACCA
1927

A low hum

A VOYAGE BY SEA

My cello, my uncle, and I left Fremantle just a few weeks after my mother's death, boarding the MS *Kangaroo* on a hot summer day in 1927 to sail for Singapore. My memories of the voyage are vivid and detailed. Perhaps grief's legacy was to render my mind receptive, perceptive, for surely I did not grieve deeply otherwise. My uncle put a brave face on his sadness at our loss and, I am sure, was relieved at my own stolidity. Grief had also, somehow, made me aware of the limitations of the books and recordings and reproductions I had held so dear. I was ready for life, for *experience*, ready to hold every sound and sight and smell in my mind and retain them, keep them airtight, watertight, forever.

I sat on my trunk in the stinking February heat, my shoes flat on the grubby wharf below me, my fingers tapping time with the clanking of the chains against the side of the ship and the wharf. Uncle Valentine returned from the booking office with our tickets stamped.

'Rustle yourself,' he told me, 'we've a boat to board.'

My passport, newly obtained for my voyage, spelled my name at its top: Helena Margaret Gaunt. My place and date of birth were recorded below my name: Singapore, May 31st, 1910. The captain held the piece of thick paper, with its government stamp, its copperplate writing, at arms-length, peering at it; he recorded my name in a small book he held. He leered at me, nudged the man next to him who leaned on the railing of the *Kangaroo* counting boxes on the wharf still to be packed aboard.

'Going home, are you, my darling? Don't look like a Straits coolie to me, eh, does she, Georgie?'

'Yes, Captain,' I replied, ignoring his rudeness, and muster-ing all the hauteur my sixteen-year-old self possessed. 'I am going home.'

The MS *Kangaroo* was old, stuffy and poorly designed – a little like the elder Miss Murray, left far behind me in Lesmurdie. She had black sides, a clipper bow, and she rolled abominably – I will say it again, the resemblance to Miss Murray was remarkable. The *Kangaroo* was crowded, with more passengers than sleeping quarters. Uncle Valentine, though he need not have, chose to camp on deck with the younger men.

'To take the air, my dear! There's nothing like sleeping in the open to give a man an appetite.'

The crew were mostly Chinese with some Malay deckhands. The passengers were squatters and pearlers returning north after holidays in the city; there were few women among the passengers, and fewer children.

We left Fremantle late in the morning and by night we were well out past Rottnest Island. We sailed for two days in calm seas to Geraldton, then on with a heavy roll developing until we berthed at Carnarvon jetty. From there we sailed not on sea but on land, over the Carnarvon salt flats to the township. Our transport was a truck on a rail line, driven by a sail. Passengers piled onto the back of the truck, many standing, some of us seated on rough wooden planks. I clung to my cello in its case, clamped tight between my legs, pushed against my skirt by the mass of baggage piled on the truck. Uncle Valentine stood towards the front, leaning back jauntily while his arm gripped tight to the railing. The captain climbed into the front with the driver, and two men raised the sail up a sturdy wooden mast clamped to the truck. Unfurled, the canvas hung loose, empty for a moment and then, with a whoomp, the wind caught it, filled it to a billowing belly-fullness, and with a jerk the truck was underway.

I looked up through the sail's swell to the endless sky above it as we sailed into the railway station of Carnarvon town in a cloud of canvas and dust. How wonderful we must have appeared! But the people of the small town barely raised their eyes to us, so mundane to them was this marvellous apparition.

The railway station was a tin shed on the port side of the town, close to the best hotel, the Gascoyne, itself made of concrete, corrugate and pressed iron. The Gascoyne had ample rooms, and Uncle and I took a single room each. I went to sleep that night with the wind buffeting the window, the tin roof creaking and crackling as it cooled, and dreamed of sailing over the land, a full sail above me, powered by the wind, powerless to change course.

We were to wait two nights in Carnarvon for the arrival of the bright new motor ship *Koolinda* to continue on the next leg of our journey. I passed the time playing my cello, tuning and retuning it as the heat of the day flattened the pitch even of my gleaming aluminium machine. My sheet music was packed in my leather valise; I would prop it on the dressing table in front of me, pull the dressing table's chair in and perch between the bed and the table, straddling my cello, play to resonate the room, to make the whole creaking building, the whole dusty windy township, reverberate with Haydn, Brahms, and the Bach I loved best.

We left Carnarvon on the *Koolinda* and steamed steady up the coast past Onslow, berthing at Hedland and Broome. We carried on to Derby where we took on a great stinking, lowing herd of cattle in addition to the cargo of sheep already destined for Singapore. We reeled out of King Sound on the swirl of a rip past Sunday Island, the ocean surging under us with the power of the sound's tides. The animals muttered, as if under their breath, and only occasionally bellowed and roared with discomfort or displacement or fear.

We were in open seas, the land hazy, far-off. Flying fish leapt and soared, glistening blue-green, reflecting the sun; we saw whales like dark islands spouting, and sea snakes curved like bass clefs on the glassy roll of the ocean.

Despite the gentleness of the seas, and the claims of the Aluminum Company of America for the indestructibility of their instrument, I found myself unprepared to expose my cello to the extreme elements on board the vessel – so it stayed in its case, away from the salt and moisture. Still, I found myself itching to play. I would take out my sheet music and read through it all, fingering the pieces in the air, wielding my bow across the space where my cello should be. I hummed the music as I played it in the air, taking my beat from the engines of the *Koolinda* as she moved, *lentissimo*, on the swell of the ocean.

The heat was oppressive, the air heavy with all the smells of sheep and cattle, of oil, of garbage from the galley. The saloon boys and Chinese stewards stretched out on the decks and hatches on their backs as we forged ahead over a leaden sea with an oily roll. I felt peevish and quarrelsome, and snapped at the stewards when they brought me tea.

But the tension broke when it rained, as only the tropics can rain. Decks flooded from hatch to scupper, the bows of the ship were hidden from the bridge, cascades of water ran from the boat deck and down to the saloon deck below. The rain thundered, the noise of it drowning the grind of the *Koolinda*'s engines. Half speed and siren hooting, we steamed through the pouring, pelting rain. Then, just as suddenly as the rain had started, we steamed out into the bright daylight again, everything dripping wet and glistening with water for as long as it took the sun to raise the steam. Steam rose from the deckhouse, from the lifeboats, decks and winches; even the passengers steamed happily in the sun. Everything in sight was washed clean; even the surface of the sea seemed brighter.

I stood with Uncle Valentine on the deck. And as we stood there, out of the cloud appeared mountain peaks to starboard. Bali lay ahead of us, high and magical, like a fat woman squatting on the sea, her buttocks and hips obscured in cloud, her head rising high, held proud in the dazzling blue sky. All on board stopped to stare at her, transfixed; Uncle Valentine and I stayed and stared as the afternoon lingered then left. As night fell we saw lights on the shoreline ahead, then here and there twinkling lights higher up the slopes. Strange metallic music drifted across the water, bell-like over the sounds of voices, of shouting and calling and selling, from the night market.

'That's gamelan, that strange music,' Uncle Valentine told me.

Such words! Gamelan, junks, sampans, flying fish; and Bali. I felt as far from dry old Lesmurdie and the Misses Murray as it was possible to get.

Night fell while we made for port. Uncle Valentine and I persuaded the steward to bring us our evening meal on the deck, and so we sat, we two, eating our meal and watching the land grow nearer. The sound and smell of the land seemed to come to us over the sea. We stayed on deck, smoking and watching the lights, until the captain called the watch.

I awoke early. I could see the cone of the island's peak, a faint breath of steaming, lazy smoke curling up from the crater. Boats came out to meet the *Koolinda*, poled out from the shore at first, then a hoisted sail caught the breeze and they scraped alongside our ship. They were laden with pretty, small Balinese cattle, the colour of strong milky tea, destined for the Singapore market, so the steward told us. We gulped our breakfast in a flash, eager to get ashore.

We were paddled towards a white beach, long and

smooth as the eye could see, with small boats just above the high-water mark and coconut palms leaning their heads down towards the sea, listening to it as a mother leans forward to catch her baby's whisper. The sea beneath the *prahu* that carried us to shore was a clear, transparent jade green. We touched a small jetty and scrambled ashore.

Up the gently rising slope of the road from the jetty of the little town we walked. Gaudy fabrics were everywhere, scarlet jackets, bright batik, and brown women in semi-nudity, for they wore only a sarong from waist to calf. The *Koolinda*'s stewardess and I were the only women among our small party, and she slipped her arm through mine and walked with me, said I might feel more comfortable in the company of a married woman and mother such as herself in the presence of the naked native bodies all around us. But I was too thrilled to feel a blush even had I been guilty of one, and the beauty and naturalness of the Balinese women made their state seem not bold nor brazen, but perfect, natural. I heated and sweated under my heavy Australian clothing, yearning to shed my blouse and feel the cooling breeze against my own white skin.

As we came upon the marketplace, the *pasar*, I put my hand to the notebook in my skirt pocket. On the way north from Fremantle to Broome, Uncle Valentine had written in the small notebook phrases of Malay vocabulary, that I might gain some familiarity with the language, and quite a deal of my time on the *Koolinda* between Broome and Bali had been spent poring over the words which, written, were so strange to me. As the sounds of the market reached my ears though, and I matched them to the words in my little notebook, whispered them back to the hot air as I heard them, so I remembered the language in some fundamental way, matched it with sounds murmured above and around me in the Singapore of my earliest years.

The roadside stalls were piled with strange fruits: mangosteen, green oranges, rambutan, durian, bananas, coconuts and piles of glossy scarlet chillies. Over each small stall presided a brown woman, beautiful, smiling, and naked as far as the eye could see as the stall hid the lower part of her, clothed in her batik sarong. The women wore their jet-black hair drawn back severely from generous foreheads, as the Misses Murray had taught us to do for dancing. I wished the Misses Murray could be there to see the lines of women with their ballerina hair and their bosoms on display; how their faces would burn, their eyes pop!

The *pasar* was crowded with buyers and gossipers, young mothers with naked brown babies slung in sarongs astride their hips; vendors of sweet drinks, Chinese coolies drawing heavy handcarts loaded with coconuts and bamboo. The Chinese laboured hard and breathed heavily; the Balinese chattered and giggled; an occasional Arab swept by in a long cloak – and ourselves, white skin red with sweating, buttoned up and staring – all of us in the early morning sunlight in the lee of the towering peak. We bought fruit, we became confused with the unfamiliar coins; I tried my notebook Malay on the stall keepers, who laughed and seemed not to understood a word of it. We loaded up with rambutan, bananas and heaven knows what, after the inevitable haggling which, so Uncle Valentine told me, all Orientals love. A fleet of pony carts carried us back to the jetty with our treasures, then on to a sampan and back aboard the *Koolinda*, sweaty and hot in our heavy clothes in the heat of the day, ready for the cook to ply us with lunch, and to steam ahead to Singapore.

FATHER

We pulled slowly into the thick heat of the port at Singapore, the *Koolinda*'s crew milling and busy. Uncle and I leaned against the guardrail, shading our eyes, watching the strange place approach. Uncle Valentine grabbed my arm.

'There he is! Look!' He shouted, waved both arms in the air. 'Hi! Charles, hi there! Hi!'

A tall man, strange to me, looked up at the sound of my loud uncle. He peered through narrow eyes, raised his hand briefly in salute. We watched each other without further signal – my uncle and I from the ship, the thin man from the shore – while the *Koolinda* was made secure. When, some ten minutes later, we were allowed to disembark and make our way down the gangway, he appeared from the busy crowd, and stood waiting to meet us where we stepped onto land. He shook my uncle's hand, then turned and clasped me briefly to him, announcing himself as my father.

He stood back to assess me, as I assessed him. He was immaculate in white ducks, white socks and shoes, and white topee, smoking a fragrant cigar. He did not look like a man who had just two months before buried his wife, but then, what did I know of how such a man should look? He did not speak to me of my mother, so I in turn kept my silence.

My father waved down two rickshaws to take us from the port. I rode ahead with him; I looked back at Uncle Valentine perched on the seat of his rickshaw, his arm around the waist of my cello case next to him, leaning into her shoulder like a lover. As our rickshaw toiled up a steep hill, Father gave the boy loud directions that sounded to my ears as *Go to Tangling Kechil*. It was, he told me, the house of an old friend from his Singapore days.

The McKenzies' house was a brick bungalow three steps off the ground, its verandah rich with glazed pots planted with masses of maidenhair ferns and other tropical plants I could not name. The glossy leaves and strange flowers seemed faintly familiar, perhaps recalled from early childhood, from faded memories of the garden I had played in.

The front door opened as we stepped onto the verandah, and a thin, ginger-haired man appeared. He led us into a room filled with bowls of tiny white flowers, exactly like tiny birds hanging onto a spire of woody stem by their beaks. Their fragrance filled the air, made it heavy.

'Pigeon orchid day today,' Mr McKenzie told us, by way of welcome. 'These wee white flowers. According to native tradition, anything that happens on pigeon orchid day is blessed. I'd say that augurs well for your journey.'

The McKenzies made us comfortable. Mrs McKenzie fussed over us and brought us tea and cakes and fruit on lovely china. She sat down next to me, pressed her hand onto mine and whispered to me, 'Your mother was a very fine woman,' then patted my hand twice before withdrawing it to pour the tea. She asked me about school, and fashions at home, and I answered her nicely but I barely knew what to say, and sat in silence, speaking only when I was spoken to, smiling and sipping my tea. I caught my uncle's eye over the teapot, and he smiled at me, wiggled his eyebrows in his silly way. I wished we were back at his house by the beach. Father turned his chair towards Mr McKenzie and spoke of rubber prices and officialdom and of people I did not know. He spoke with a voice like a whip, cracking but turning back on itself, swallowed into the back of his throat. He clipped his words tight from his tongue, and he did not smile, unless the straightening of his lips into a thin line when Mrs McKenzie offered him cake could be termed a smile.

The next morning, we departed once again – this time by land – for Malacca. Father had booked us first-class passage on the train from Singapore, across the bridge that connected the island to the mainland of Malaya. In contrast to my voyage by sea, I would retain in my mind little of that unpleasantly hot and sweaty journey up the coast, by train and by truck. I clutched my cello to me the whole way, staring from the windows at the hot green land we passed, a tangle of jungle too solid for sound.

Our house, Lanadron, was much like the houses of other Europeans in Malacca: built of wood, high off the ground for the cooling effect as much as to avoid the occasional flooding that accompanied the monsoonal rain. The house had two storeys above the ground. The living rooms, the kitchen and scullery, the dining room and the big verandah were downstairs, and our bedrooms upstairs, up the wide dark staircase that bisected the house. My bedroom overlooked the verandah at the front of the house, facing onto Jalan Kuching. It was my vantage point on the world of Malacca as it passed by our front gate on its way to Town, to the wider world.

After only two months in Malacca – hot, quiet months – I had come to know and hate the house, the unchangingness of life within it. I understood Mother's letters, their constancy. I was, it seemed, expected to be the woman of the house in Mother's place, to manage Cook and the boy who brought the water and the man who did the garden, while Father did his work, talked to men at the Bank and at the rubber sales. Uncle Valentine disappeared when he could, to tend his business interests, he said, but in truth I wondered if it was the dullness of the house he was escaping. I understood that Father's intention must have been that my education and care in the hands of the Misses Murray would prepare me for the role as his helpmeet and house manager. All prospect of my taking work, of teaching, was seemingly dismissed since Mother's death.

It was stultifying. My mind was dulled by the boring routine of the very air around me. I could not match this boredom with the excitement I had felt on the journey here, up the coast, the glorious fervour of Bali. I could barely even rouse myself to play my cello. The languor upon me was heavy, enervating. No wonder Mother had died.

In the two months I had lived in Malacca with my father, doing the job my mother had done not so very long before, he had not mentioned her. He was distant, my father, hard. I did not think that my mother had been the same; but I could not clearly recall. There was just one connection – one moment, one gesture joining Mother, through Father, to me. On the morning after our arrival at the house in Malacca, when I appeared for breakfast, a royal blue shantung-covered box rested on my plate. Father, at the head of the table, sipping his tea, nodded at me without his eyes meeting mine.

'Those are yours now. Take care of them.'

I opened the box. Within it rested a circle of jade beads, each the size of a pea, the whole string joined with a silver clasp. Drop earrings, looped with silver, nested in the centre of the circle of beads; my mother's jewellery, just barely remembered, milky green against fine skin at her throat, the sound of marble-hard beads against china on her dressing table.

Lying stretched to my fullest length on the polished wooden floor next to my bed, relaxing my back into the cool dark, I could feel the sound from the party below me – voices, music, the clat of fans, the tink of glasses – vibrating the wood and transmitting itself up through my skin to my breastbone, feel it echo in my skull. It wasn't possible to pick out detail, to distinguish one sound from another. Rather, sounds merged in an undulating wave, low, oscillating to match the pattern of my heart. I rolled on to my side, pressed my ear to the floor in an effort to get better definition to the sound, but it remained a hum, a long, low hum, undefined, blurred at the margins.

I rolled onto my back, drew my knees to my chest, and swung myself to my feet. My dress felt hot, heavy in the humid night; I lifted its light cotton skirt in my hands, as if to make a dainty curtsey as the Misses Murray had taught me, but instead I wiggled the cotton fabric in my hands, wafting it to make a breeze to cool my legs, my bare underneath. The air licked light and luscious up my thighs. I let the dress's fabric drop. I sat on the chair at my dressing table by the open window. From the drawer of the table I took a blue enamelled dish, paper, tobacco in a tin, and matches, and rolled myself a cigarette. I lit it, drew in deep to fill my lungs with the sweet smoke, then hoisted myself up onto the table, the closer to send the smoke outside. I picked a shred of tobacco from my lip, flicked it from my fingers out through the window into the night, into the garden, drew in hard again on the cigarette, and ashed it into the little blue dish perched in my hand.

The men's voices lifted up to me from the verandah, hummed and ebbed, clear in the warm night air. They were all Europeans, of course – they were always all Europeans when there was a do at Lanadron. I could hear Mr Holland, my father's business partner, among them, and Mr Williams from the Bank, and Uncle Valentine; thank God for Uncle Valentine. Their voices were fragments, deep and low, carried on waves of whisky fumes volatilising from their wide crystal tumblers, peaty on the hot air. Smoke from their cigars mixed with the thinner smoke of my own cigarette.

'Well.' Uncle Valentine's voice drifted on fragrant smoke, up and through my open window. 'Music time, Charles, eh. Rally the troops.'

The men shuffled; there was a sound that was surely a hand slapping a back, matey. The door squeaked, as it always did, then closed with a click as the men moved inside the house.

It was time for me to join the party downstairs, where Father expected me to play. He was proud of his cellist daughter, of what I had learned while I had been away from him. My skill, my talent – and my perfect, contained demeanour – reflected well on him.

I took up my cello to tune it before going downstairs. In the heat and moisture of the tropics, even my aluminium cello slipped and slid out of tune with each passing moment, with each note played. I turned the pegs, stretched and tightened the strings, the cello's endpin firmly on the floor, wedged in the gap between floorboards. Happy with the tuning I'd restored, I took a cloth from the case and wiped fingermarks and rosin specks from the metal, polished it to gleam and shine.

With both hands I drew my hair back from my face, twisted it into a tight knot at the nape of my neck and secured it with two tortoiseshell slides. I clasped Mother's jade beads around my neck, slipped the silver hooks of her earrings through new, raw holes in my earlobes, dusted my face with powder from a silver case on my dressing table. I picked a pinch of coloured cachous and fragrant fennel seeds from the dish on my dressing table and popped them into my mouth to freshen my smoky breath. Then I took up my cello and bow, ready to join the party.

I played in the dining room. The table had been moved to one side, the chairs rearranged for the older ladies, the younger ones standing behind them. The men stood towards the back of the room, spilling out into the hallway.

I seated myself, settled my cello in front of me, wiped my hands back over my forehead as if to sweep back hair that had escaped from its clip, but none had; all was in place. I took up my bow, and looked at the audience. Their murmurings had settled to quiet, and they all faced front and centre, towards me.

And so I played, and they held their breath, as they heard the beauty of the music, so like a human voice, yet so beyond it. I drew the bow across the strings. The first notes of the Bach Sarabande sounded in the room and I felt the sound waves travel through me, through the body and guts of my cello, through the endpin and into the wood of the floorboards and through the feet of the audience and up through their skeletons to their hearts and into their brains and the music reached their brains and their hearts at the same time – each of them, it hit their heart and their brain at exactly the same time, for sound travels according to the laws of physics, and I saw the light behind their eyes catch fire and heard them intake breath as they felt the rush of the music take over their bodies, aethereal and corporeal combined.

Even Father, at the back of the room, even Father's eyes lit up in response to the music. I felt his eyes upon me, as all the eyes in the room were upon me, as the cello leant warm against me.

THE PYTHON IN THE FOWL HOUSE

As the months passed, I felt chained to the house on Jalan Kuching, unable to leave. My days in Malacca developed a pattern. As soon as I heard the front door slam behind Father in the morning, I would lock myself in my bedroom and play, cramming the precious hours with music, not so much stretching my skills as maintaining them; the heat seemed to drain me of the very will to do anything more than that. I would become lost in the music, locked in my room, sound reverberating. When I heard the footsteps, the creak of the front door, that signalled Father's return from the office for lunch or at the end of the day, I would lay down my bow and retire my cello to her case. A quiet, biddable companion was what my father wanted, and each day, when he returned to the house, I put my true self aside – returned like my cello to her case – and played the role required of me, reporting quietly, demurely on the running of the house, speaking when spoken to.

I ingratiated myself with Cook, offered to run little errands for her, to go to the market, to do anything to break the pattern of my days. She wouldn't trust me at the market, but she let me collect the eggs for her from the fowl house by the kitchen door.

The hens were tiny colourful things, not like the sturdy, bosomy hens at the Misses Murray's. They scratched in the garden during the day, and would roost in the fowl house at night. I liked the Malacca hens as little as I had liked the bigger hens in Lesmurdie, with their flustered ways and their pecking and scratching. As I unlatched the half door that led to their roost I would coo to the hens, as I had learned to at the Misses Murray's, coo under my breath, *chook-chook-chook-chook*, and they would chortle back at me, flustered at the interruption. I would collect the heavy, chalky eggs into a tin bowl, then sit on the back step and clean away the hen dirt using an old cloth before handing the bowl to Cook.

One day though, when I chook-chook-chooked and unlatched the door that would let me reach in to collect the dappled eggs, there was silence, a sour silence, a dry rustling. As my eyes adjusted to the lack of light, I saw the piled sinuous muscle of a python coiled in a great fat pyramid in the centre of the fowl house. Its triangular head lifted, slowly, directly, its tongue slipped from it to taste me in the air, then its head dipped back slowly, slowly, slowly, coiled in on itself as I had seen a kitten tuck its head under its tail to sleep.

I stared for some time, perhaps a minute, perhaps longer. I realised that I had not breathed. I closed the door, latched the latch. I sat on the back step to the kitchen door, with the empty bowl on my lap, the old cloth in it, nothing to polish; I sat there, and I smiled. Finally, something interesting, *dangerous*, had happened.

I didn't tell anyone I'd seen the python in the fowl house. Later that day, the boy who tended the gardens came shouting to Cook that half the chickens were gone. The cause was never determined; Father said we would simply make do with fewer birds. I never saw the python again. I imagined it sliding down to the bank of the canal that ran behind our house, sleeping there in a damp hollow while it digested our runty chickens and their soft, unlaid eggs.

It was soon after I saw the python that I took to wandering the streets and bridges of Malacca at night, to escape from the feeling of the house, its dry rustling, the heat trapped inside it, the slow, squeezing death it seemed to offer. As Father slept – as the whole household slept – I'd slip my cigarettes and matches into my pocket, and step out through the kitchen door, past the downy scratching of the chickens settling, and out onto the street, seeking cool air, seeking music, seeking escape.

I'd walk past the night market, the *pasar malam*, past silk merchants cheek by jowl with dried fish shops with bags of rice on the footway, rice from Siam, rice from Patam and Saigon, shark fins and dried fish livers, leopard skins, bags of dried chillies, shallow boxes of eggs encased in lampblack, kettles, pots and pans from Germany; past tinsmiths, and herbalists, and shops with wall scrolls of paper depicting devils, josses and other characters in

Chinese lore; past shoe shops and boot shops and shops selling nothing but wooden clogs, green clogs, yellow clogs, clogs by the thousand.

The Chinese merchants, the men, wore a *towchang*, a queue, a pigtail, and these were as varied as the wearer, some plaited with black thread, some with blue thread, some red; men in mourning plaited theirs with white. Even little toddlers had their few inches of pink woollen yarn plaited through tender hair standing up off the back of their heads, the hair too short and soft to hang down. The Chinese women kept their hair long, its glossy black glistening with coconut oil, pulled back tightly from their foreheads and secured in a bun at the nape of their neck, held in place by big pins of silver or ebony or jade or wood.

I too would sweep my black hair back tight from my forehead, copying the Chinese women's style, feeling the pull on my eyes and my cheeks. In the cool of the night, in the busy *pasar malam*, I felt indestructible, invisible, although I was not. Eyes watched me constantly, but Father's friends would never walk here, would never see me where I should not be, sitting at the Chinese stalls and drinking cold beer, rolling my cigarettes, blowing smoke into the night.

I'd cross the bridges that joined the western bank of the river to the eastern, follow the tide of people across the Old Market Bridge to Kampung Hulu, follow the river for part of its course, past houses leading down to it, houses packed together; and then back over the Chan Boon Cheng Bridge, its steel ringing under the clogs and bicycles that crossed it. I'd turn near the point where Christ Church rose up, the building's glorious red showing dark in the night, the solid squat Stadthuys my signal to retrace my steps and return home, shuffling past the chooks in their house, in through the back door to the kitchen, then up the stairs, quietly, and into my bed, to sleep, to dream.

One night, drawn to the scent of the sea, I did not turn back at the Stadthuys. I turned instead down a narrow road, then followed the path along the bank of the river to the docks, where the river widened towards the sea. I heard the clanking syncopy of metal on metal, the ting of brass fittings, the slap of water. In the dark, I could just read the names of ships, and their home ports, painted on their sides in straight or curving scripts. I imagined myself in these elsewhere places – Hong Kong, Peking, Roma, Sydney – anywhere that was not Malacca.

Turning back, I seemed to lose my way to Christ Church. I walked down side streets, past the doorways of establishments where I imagined men went to gamble and smoke, to whore. From the street, the rooms looked long, narrow, and deep, their darkened interiors smoky, velvet-dark. Men pushed into them, and spilled out of them, Chinese and white men and Malays and all, but I saw no women. Three men – white men – stopped in front of me in the narrow street. I was not sure whether to be afraid.

'Ya lost?' one of them said to me, and the others nudged him and pushed him and jeered, and before I could speak, they moved on, stumbling into the night.

An old Chinese man sat smoking a cigarette on a rattan chair at the door the men had spilled from. He looked up at me, staying seated, as I approached him.

'Excuse me,' I started to say, 'I need to get back to Christ Church.'

He nodded his head at me, singsonging words I could not understand, and waved his hand towards the door.

'Come in, Missus. Come in.'

Smoke spilled from the doorway. I moved forward. He laughed the laugh of a little child, giggling, musical.

'Come in. Come in, Missus.'

There was even less light inside than the moon and stars had provided outside. The darkness, through the door, was soft, velvet, smelled of grog and men and spices and smoke with, underneath those rich smells, something sharp, ammoniac. Voices were muffled, low. As my eyes adjusted to the dim light, I saw bodies reclining on divans and benches, on cushions, against walls, pipes to their lips. Metal tinkered against metal, ceramic clinked, as lids were lifted and replaced. I watched a man roll his palms together, like a child rolling balls of salt dough, slow and careful. Everything happened slowly, as in a dream. I smelled resin, sweet smoke.

A curtain hung at the end of the long, narrow room, heavy and concealing. An arm looped it, swept it aside and up, and figures tumbled from behind it into the velvet dark of the room. They were four men: a large man, a thin man, each of them molten against the side of a smaller, slighter partner, two small coffee-skinned men, smooth-faced and young. The large man – Uncle Valentine – saw me first, as the two small darker-skinned men melted back behind the heavy curtain, melted back so quickly, so smoothly, that I wondered if I had imagined them there between my Uncle and Mr Holland; if I had imagined the money slipping from Uncle Valentine's hand to that of the young man close by his side, his fingers lingering on the thin brown arm.

'Good God, Helena, what the hell are you doing here?'

I embraced my uncle, hid my face in his shirtfront. He smelled of musk and curious smoke, and a combination of other smells I had not before encountered.

It was Uncle Valentine's companion – Father's business partner, Mr Holland – who told Father where they'd found me. Father was roused from sleep that night as the three of us arrived by rickshaw back at the big house in Jalan Kuching. An explanation was not required from me – there could be none, in Father's eyes. I had brought inescapable shame upon his house, his name. I could damage his name in business, he roared. I was sent to my room, while the men talked, and Father raged. Again, I did not care. There was nothing to hold me to this house in Malacca. I opened my cello case and brought my cello into my arms, between my skirts, and played a loud lament into the night air, drowning the sounds of Father hammering on my locked door.

HOME AND AWAY

I tapped ash from my cigarette out of the upstairs window of my bedroom. The squeak of the gate signalled Father's return. I pressed my cigarette against the enamel dish to extinguish it, popped a cachou into my mouth. Running my tongue around my teeth, I tasted tobacco smoke.

The dining-room door slammed below me; the crystal lid of the decanter clinked. I imagined Father standing by the cabinet, drinking whisky from the cold crystal, feeling its smoky burn in his throat, its comforting warmth hit his belly. I heard Uncle Valentine's voice, heard its register but could not make out distinct words as he spoke to Father in a low and urgent tone. Father's voice, in response, rose in pitch and volume, punctuated by a sharp noise – a door crashing, perhaps a book being slammed with force onto a table. There was silence then; and then again, their two voices, each in counterpoint with the other.

I tucked an enamel pin into my hair, smoothed my hands down the front of my dress and, as the clock in the hall below me struck the hour, I left my room and walked downstairs.

I pushed open the door to the dining room. Uncle

Valentine looked up at me and almost smiled as I stood just inside the door. Father stood at the long window at the back of the house. He clutched a tumbler, his hands together holding the glass under his chin, his head slightly bowed, as if in prayer.

'Good evening, Father. Uncle.'

Father nodded his head in reply, but did not speak. I stood as I was – my hands by my sides, my body tense, on tiptoes. I realised that I was holding my breath and, as I realised, I willed myself to exhale. Father turned from the window, draining his glass. He moved towards the cabinet, addressing me without facing me.

'Helena. Join your uncle and me in a glass of whisky.'

Father had never offered me anything stronger than sherry. I didn't hesitate to accept.

'Thank you.'

As he filled the glass his hand was steady as a rock, as it always was. He handed the glass to me. We stood, the three of us, what passed for family. We had formed a circle without meaning to, facing inwards. Father raised his glass, not quite looking either of us directly in the eye.

'Good health.'

'Health,' Uncle Valentine echoed.

'And happiness,' I added.

I felt the welcome fire down my throat. But Father's words, wafting with his whisky breath as he spoke them into the quiet of the room, hit me in the belly before the whisky could.

'Helena, as I have just told your uncle, you will leave Malacca. You will travel south as soon as passage can be arranged. Your uncle is leaving too; he will return home with you; his business interests require his attention.'

Uncle Valentine had moved a step backwards, broken the circle we had formed. He leant against the back of a chair. His eyes pointed downwards, did not meet my eyes. There was a look of distaste on his face that I imagined matched mine.

Father continued to speak; Uncle Valentine and I continued in our silence, receiving his words, passive. *You will leave; there is no need for discussion; there is nothing to keep you here.* He stopped speaking. His final offering, something about a small allowance to be paid to me, I failed to take in properly, although I registered his final words, the first time he had mentioned her.

'It is money from your mother.'

It had taken little for me to disappoint my father, but in truth, he too had disappointed me. *Father, home, family;* empty words, without meaning for me. I was sick of these places my father called home: of his home in Malacca; even Uncle's home by the sea could not draw me back. The faint taste of dishonour in my throat made my lip curl. I would go south, as Father dictated, but I would not go home. I would find a new way in the world – my own way.

I left Malacca with the promise of a quarterly allowance from Father, and with an adequate but not generous bank note that I could cash on my arrival in Australia. Uncle Valentine and I arrived in Singapore glad to leave the sticky boredom of Malacca behind us, Uncle ready to sink back into the comfort of his house by the sea, far to the south of us. But I had heard stories on the journey south from Malacca, stories of a city that called my name, a bigger city, modern and vibrant.

And so, Uncle Valentine and I parted company on the docks in Singapore. He kissed me, hugged me tightly, then boarded a ship headed south to Fremantle. I took the *Houtman*, bound for Sydney.

COTTESLOE
1991

Like jamming, like jazz

HIGH EIGHT

The filmmaker continues to visit. She comes with a camera now. A video camera, she is quick to tell me, *high eight*, she calls it. A lesser type of camera; tape, not film.

She films me in the front room, the music room. It is just her and her video camera; to get the feel of things, she says, to run through some setups. I sit in my accustomed chair, settle back into the worn leather. She brings one of the hard wooden chairs from the kitchen. She sets up the camera, a light, a microphone on the table, talks to me as she puts each piece in place, adjusts their positions.

'When someone makes a film,' she says, 'or writes a novel, or creates a painting, they choose what to leave in, what to leave out. That's storytelling. You know, that's the craft. Even when you're making a documentary, or writing a newspaper article – they're supposed to be factual, yeah, accurate, historically correct?'

'Of course.'

'Well, maybe. But I think often they're not. There are a million and one choices the artist makes about the story they're telling. And that's not even factoring in the veracity of the information they have to hand – whether they've done enough homework, enough research.'

'And have you done your homework? For this film?'

'I've done some. But that's why I want to just talk with you now, and probably for a few weeks, before we start filming properly. I want to hear your version. Your story. You know, collect it, capture it. Now, how's that light? Are you getting used to it?'

The light is not bright; the camera is small, quiet. I'd forgotten the process of being in front of the camera. At first it's all you think about; head up to avoid a double chin; good side to the camera, watch your words, watch your expressions, keep it clean. But a good interviewer has that magical ability to make you forget about the camera, distract you.

'Oh, I've brought these. From my first – maybe second – visit; remember? What do you think?'

She hands me a manila folder. In it are photographs, eight-by-ten prints, black-and-white. I flip through the photographs. In each of them, the light is dim, the exposure long. The photographs appear pitted and bitty, the print all contrast and darkness and light. You can feel the movement in them.

'I used fast film. It gets that grainy, gorgeous look.'

'I look as if I'm moving. Yes; what you really see is motion. Very good.'

'I love this one. Your hands. I want to make sure we film this.'

It's a close-up. They almost don't look like an old woman's hands; the fingers are long, sleek, busy. The fingernails are neat. The loop of the theremin looks cold and hard behind my skin.

'Your hands are so busy. Even when you're not playing. The rest of you – your body – stays very still. That's the kind of detail I want to capture. That's part of your playing.'

I hand her back the folder of photographs. I rest my hands in my lap, consciously keeping them still. She laughs.

As we work, I find myself opening to her in a way I had not expected. I feel my shoulders relax. I feel my torso relax, my gut. We talk, as the camera hums, until her talk becomes questions, and my talk answers.

TAPE RECORDER MEMORY

She is here today with the video camera, and with another woman. They talk of lights and camera angles. They are filming me again, in the front room. The new woman, who she introduces as Caroline, operates the camera, takes control of the lights, shoots photographs with a Polaroid camera. The filmmaker concentrates on me; am I comfortable? Is there anything in particular that I'd like to talk about to start with? The women work well together. Watching them, I start to see how the process itself will work.

They stay for longer today, but it is not tiring. The pace of their work is measured, careful; they are quiet. When they confer, their heads close together as they stare into the camera's eyepiece, or figure notes in a notebook, they murmur *sotto voce*. I listen to the soft rise and fall of their voices, catch the hiss of sibilants, but miss the meaning.

The filmmaker tells me she's reasonably happy with the footage she's getting so far. It's starting to be a story, she says, starting to flow.

'But we need to watch the tape recorder memory thing,' she tells me.

'I beg your pardon?'

'You know, when it feels as if you've told it before, as if what you're saying is rehearsed, or learned. Like lines in a play. Or like a recorded version, played back. I've come across it before. I call it tape recorder memory.'

'Well, it is what it is. I remember it, and I tell you what I remember.'

She screws her mouth up, waves her head back and forth, clearly not agreeing. 'I think – well, I think it might be particularly common among performers. Like learning to play a piece of music; you've learned to perform a version of your life, and it comes to seem real to you. And maybe it is. But maybe it isn't, too.'

'Are you suggesting that there's a lack of truth in what I say?'

'No, no – look, I'm sorry, I don't mean to suggest that at all. Tape recorder memory; it's not pure memory, it's retelling the story the way it's always been told. There's remembering what happened, then there's remembering how to tell the story, and that's like remembering the way the music is written down, and remembering how you've always played it.'

'Hmmm. Perhaps.'

'So, maybe what I'm asking you to do is to improvise. Like jamming, like jazz. Maybe that's a way of getting your story to flow in new ways, true ways. Making it fresh.'

I roll the idea around in my mind. Improvising makes

a sort of sense. I risk alerting her to the appeal that it has for me. 'But doesn't improvisation move even further from the score – the text, the truth – than any practised performance? Surely that moves away from the truth, not towards it?'

'Maybe. But remember that I'm not looking for strict documentary, a strict retelling of history, of reality. I want to acknowledge that there's memory involved in all of this, and I need to find a filmic way of showing that. I want to make the camera move the focus, mirror it in and out of sharpness, like memory moves the focus in your head. Someone said once that a documentary is in between inventing and capturing reality. I want our documentary, this project, to sort of acknowledge both things, both invention and reality. I guess I need to know what the reality is, though, if I want to show it. At this stage, I feel as if I'm still missing pieces. These interviews – this is supposed to be the reality, not the invention. I dunno. Maybe it's just something we need to keep in mind as we move through the process.'

She sighs, gathers up her notebook and pen from the table. 'Look, it doesn't really matter. I'm sorry if you thought I was suggesting that you haven't been up-front with me.'

'Not at all.'

'I was thinking out loud. I do that.'

'It's fine. I understand.'

'Well – do you have energy for one more session? Or would you like to stop for the day?'

'No, no, let's keep going. I'll try improvising. Extemporising. See what bubbles up, shall we?'

I follow her down the hallway to the front room, where Caroline has busied herself with cameras and lights while we've been in the kitchen. I sit down in the chair. Caroline flips a switch, and the light flares. I close my eyes, blocking it for the moment, until I need to face it. I have never enjoyed improvising. I prefer a fixed score.

When they have finished, while the camera woman is in the front room packing the lights and camera, the filmmaker goes to the kitchen, where she has left her bag. I retrieve the video tape from my bedroom. In the kitchen I hand it to her, thank her.

'Oh,' she says, 'are you sure you don't want to keep it?'

'Thank you, but no. I have watched it. I don't need to watch it again. It's a fine film. You must be pleased with it. You were young when you made it, I think.'

'Yeah, twenty-four, twenty-five. I discovered Beatrix Carmichael's work a few years before, when I was at art school. She really stuck in my head – her work did. Actually, I have a confession...'

She fishes in her bag and brings out a postcard, a reproduction of the blue painting, the portrait that Beatrix painted of me, the painting that everyone knows.

'It was this painting that I was really taken with. You know that experience when you have a postcard, or a photo from a magazine, and you stick it on the wall by your desk, or above your bed, almost as a talisman? Like a fan, like a schoolgirl crush? Well, I'm afraid that was me, with the Carmichael portrait of you.' She holds the postcard out to me, in both hands, like an offering. '*Electrical by Nature*. I loved it. It gave me goosebumps. Still does.'

I reach out and take the postcard from her. 'How fascinating.'

'Oh, it gets worse! I can't believe I'm telling you this. I really identified with the image in the painting. I used to wear my hair in a bun, you know, I dyed a dress the same colour silver – or I tried to, but it came out a kind of dull murky grey. In the end, though, it helped inspire me to make the film. So I've always felt a very strong relationship with Carmichael. I'm sorry, that feels really presumptuous to say to you.'

'Oh, don't apologise. It's – flattering, if anything. It explains the film, perhaps. It seems that it's somehow about you, as well as Beatrix.'

'I think that too, yes. She was the inspiration for the film, of course, and so was the painting of you. But I think it's exactly that – when you watch one of my documentaries, you're seeing as much of my story as you are of anything else, no matter who or what the film's about.' She rolls her eyes. 'Well, anyway, I wanted to confess to you how much I've always loved this painting.'

I hold the tiny reproduction away at a distance I can focus on. I cannot speak. I don't know what to tell her. *The painting is in my bedroom.* No; I think not.

'It's a shame. In this, the colours aren't true at all. As I remember it.'

'It's very faded. I had it on my wall for years. Look,

pin marks in the corners. You can see the colour's brighter where the pins covered it.'

'I was very young, you know, when it was painted. It was so long ago.'

I am young, in the painting, and – I can say it now, when I am no longer – strikingly beautiful. My hair is drawn back to the nape, a polished black bun of hair, shiny, so black it's almost blue. I wear my silver dress, all sharp lines and curved folds intersecting, as if I'm wrapped in tin foil shot with blue light, gaping at the neck, at the breast, skin showing pale, almost luminous. The portrait is dominated by my hands. Beatrix captured the movement in my hands, even in repose, as if there's light and sound held within them. In the background of the painting is the edge – just the very edge – of my theremin, its dark lacquered brown struck with electric colour, duck egg blue, orange.

'Do you have any of her work?' she asks me.

I keep my focus on the postcard. I put it down on the table, tap it with my finger. I draw a box around it, like a frame, with my fingertip.

'Beatrix Carmichael?'

'Mmm, yes, Beatrix Carmichael.' She seems understandably exasperated at my response. 'She was very prolific. I just wondered if you had any of her paintings.'

I trace the postcard again with my finger.

'I moved a lot. It was difficult – sometimes difficult to keep track of things, to know quite where things were, or are. I lost my mother's wedding ring, you know, some other jewellery. Perhaps I'm not very good at keeping track of things.'

I pick up the postcard and hold it out to her. She takes it, biting her bottom lip with a rueful smile as she places the postcard back in her bag. She turns away and finishes putting her things together, packing her bags, coiling a microphone lead; tying up loose ends. The other woman, the camera woman, comes in from the front room and says she is finished. They both heave bags to their shoulders. I walk them to the door; they take their leave. They have film from me today, but nothing else.

SYDNEY
1927–1932

Without touching

MADAME PETROVA

On a cool day in the winter of 1927 the *Houtman* delivered me into the Port of the City of Sydney, marking the end of the journey that took me from Malacca – which I put far away, at the very back of my mind – by way of Singapore and Brisbane. I had packed my trunk and left it by my cabin door for the porters. I lowered my cello carefully down the steep stairway that led to the main deck. Sailors milled, busy in anticipation of our approach to the port, but few passengers were yet on deck. It was cold, the wind from the south biting across the ocean and across the bow of the *Houtman*. I pulled my light Malacca-weight coat tight around me, tucked my head down into its insubstantial collar, folded my arms across my breasts and pushed my hands deep into my armpits. I pressed my knees against the case of my cello, holding it hard under the overhang of the side of the ship, safe from water. The water, the wind, the salt, were cold but invigorating; glorious. I felt an energy that I had not felt during my time in Malacca. I was ready for Sydney.

We passed the Heads with their great swell of water, and steamed slowly into Sydney Harbour, rounding headlands dark with blue-green bush, sharp with the shine of iron roofing, the swell under us calming to the gentler rise and fall of the inner harbour waters. Buildings and roads became more numerous as we neared the city; houses dotted the land's edge and climbed up into the bush away from the water. But all thought of houses melted from my mind as we rounded a headland to my first sight of that most beautiful and most modern of constructions, the powerful iron curves of the new bridge. I could not have felt further from the low, exotic stink of Malacca if I had landed on the moon. The two arcs of the bridge approached each other across the water, but did not yet touch. We steamed closer on our route to the wharves at Pyrmont. Workmen swarmed like ants, like bees, across the bridge's curves, alive with construction, the noise audible and the movement visible the closer we drew to her flanks. The bridge seemed almost crystalline, its parts forming fragments that changed shape from each new angle of view. Stone pylons pushed her up from the earth at either end, raising her above the water, pushing the halves of the bridge towards each other. Girders, each alone straight and unbending, together formed curves and patterns as delicate as lace, as hard as steel. By now everyone, all the passengers, had come on deck to watch this marvel. We steamed under her, her shadow falling over us, our faces raised, like primitive man watching a solar eclipse. But we didn't run and hide. There was no fear among us. This was modernity in progress; we were part of the modern age.

Percussion sounded from the bridge as we passed under her, the pitch of the beaten, metallic notes changing as we moved in relation to the bridge. Sound bounced in every direction, both muffled and reflected, complicated by the water around us. The thrugging engines of the *Houtman* provided a steady background beat, and the sounds from the bridge sometimes fought and syncopated with the ship's rhythm, sometimes complemented it, ran with it, helped speed us along the water. We were part of the percussion, the music of metal and construction and water combined. I found my fingers tapping on the rails of the ship's deck, adding the rhythm of my body to the music I heard around me.

I was going to like this city, this place of modern song.

We steamed slowly through to Pyrmont, eased into place against the wharf. I watched from the deck as four strong men manoeuvred the gangway into position, secured it in place. Then I stood in line to step onto the gangway, to cross from the water to the land.

My first days in Sydney passed quickly, in the attaining of little miracles, a roof over my head being the most crucial of these. Within days I was resident in a room in a house on the genteel fringe where the rough-and-tumble of Darlinghurst sidled up alongside the opulence of Elizabeth Bay and Potts Point. The house was owned by Mrs Baxter, a stern widow of comfortable means. I paid her for two months on the spot, and settled myself into the small, shaded room that overlooked her front garden.

On the ship I had been taken under the wings of a wealthy Sydney couple, Mr and Mrs Britten, and it was Mrs Britten who had given me a letter of introduction to a cellist by the name of Vita Petrova. So I found myself, on the morning of only my fourth day in Sydney, lugging my cello in its case through cold unfamiliar streets from Darlinghurst to Paddington, to the terraced house in which Madame Petrova lived and kept her studio.

Petrova was a fat Russian who favoured shapeless floral frocks down to her ankles, and pinned her stringy blonde hair up on her head with a lacquered wooden spike to keep it out of the way of the cigarette that always hung from the corner of her mouth. As I would learn over the months to come, Petrova started each day with vodka added to her coffee, and fed for the rest of the day on sugary poppyseed pastries and potato pierogies from the Russian bakery on Oxford Street. And cigarettes, endless cigarettes, each one lit from the one before, her apartment a haze of smoke and vodka that would fade only briefly overnight before she started to replenish it again in the morning, her first black cigarette lit before she had swung her fat legs out of bed.

Petrova, though, to her credit and to my delight, could play the cello like a dream. But more than that, she had an ear almost as attuned as mine to the clarity and organisation of sound.

On the day I first rang her front doorbell, Madame Petrova appeared behind the opening door, cigarette in hand, ash trailing her down the dark hallway. I handed her the letter I had from Mrs Britten, and she kept me at the front door, her foot holding the door half open, half closed, as if I might be an unwanted evangelist to be kept from entering her house. Her mouth and nose wrinkled, moved, as she read.

'The Brittens, uh?' She sniffed loudly, drew on her cigarette, and coughed. 'You must come in, then,' she said as she finished reading the letter. Turning, she gestured at me with a wave of her hand to follow.

I padded after her down the dark smoky hallway, past closed doorways and into a heavily curtained room at the back of the house. Madame Petrova collapsed onto a chaise by the draped window and gestured again, flapping her hand languidly in the direction of a hard chair by a small table.

'Play for me, then,' she rasped, lifting her chin in my direction as she drew in hard on her cigarette, then ashed it in the saucer on the table at her side.

I opened the case, withdrew my cello. Madame Petrova blew breath from her mouth as she saw it, my aluminium beauty, made a noise of dismissal or of distaste, perhaps a laugh; I could not tell which. She shook her head – I watched her from lowered eyes as I checked my instrument's tuning, prepared to play – her eyes scornful, disdainful. I had ground to make up with her, it was clear.

'What shall I play?'

'For godsakes girl, play what you will, just play. Impress me, if you can, with your – tin cello.'

I played what came to me naturally, what I loved: Bach. I could play it without thinking, without needing to direct my fingers, my arms; my whole body knew how to play it. I heard it as if from across the room, as if sitting on Madame Petrova's ample knee and observing myself, heard and saw myself as she would: good posture, strength in the upper arms, yes, a good instrument despite its appearance, tuned well; interpretation very fine, nuanced; mellow, light and dark showing in the piece. I justified my tin cello to her.

As I finished playing, my consciousness pulled back where it belonged. I looked across the room at Petrova. Her fat feet shifted as I watched, uncrossing from right over left, recrossing left over right. Like a reef knot, I thought.

'Your name is Lena, you say.'

'Short for Helena. I prefer it.'

'Which? You prefer which? Say what you mean.'

'Lena. I prefer Lena.'

She had the curranty eyes that fat people have, disappearing into her face. She blinked them slowly.

'Lena. A name not uncommon in Russia, you know.'

She was silent then, drawing on the cigarette. I waited her out, silent too, just my right hand's fingers tapping time on the bow resting across my lap.

'Lena, Elena, same thing, they come from the Greek.' She sucked her top teeth, ran her tongue across them inside her lips. 'You know Greek, uh? Latin? Maybe even Russian? No. Yet you have some education, obviously.' A pout of breath, not a laugh, not a sigh, but something in between, escaped her mouth. 'Lena means *peculiar*, in Greek. Hmh!' She lit another cigarette from the stub in her mouth, drew in hard on it, then stubbed out the old one. She looked at me, expecting a reply.

'I'm sorry, I won't take up any more of your time,' I said, and started to stand.

'Sit, girl, sit!' she huffed at me, waving her hand in a flapping downwards motion, like a child waving goodbye. 'Peculiar but good. Peculiarly good. Yes, pec-u-li-ar-ly good. I thought you would be one of Delphine Britten's rich blonde dolls' – she sucked her top teeth again as she said this, raised her eyes in contempt – 'but no. Peculiarly good. You want work, I suppose? You don't want lessons, of course?'

'I would like…'

'Yes, yes, you would like what?'

'I would like lessons, I think, or – perhaps I should say – sessions. To play for you. For you to listen to me, to watch me. Help me get better.'

'You should go to the Conservatorium then. They would take you, I'm sure of it. I can give you an introduction; surely there is still someone there who knows my name.'

But the Conservatorium sounded old-fashioned to me, conserving, unchanging. Conserving was not what interested me. I thought of the bridge. I wanted its clanging modernity.

'No. I would prefer to work with you. I can pay.'

Petrova screwed up her nose, frowned, turned down her mouth at the sides. 'If you pay me, I will happily do that. Even I can tolerate this tin cello in my house.' But she smiled as she said this, with what I would come to realise was Madame's strange humour.

I came to Madame Petrova's house each Tuesday and Thursday morning from that week onwards, for what we called lessons. I had the money to pay her – thanks to Father's allowance – and she gave me a sounding board, a good ear against which to play. Sometimes she would play, on a large cello, well worn, with intricate flourishes of purfling and beading at its edges; she played carefully, and beautifully; but not often. In truth, I did learn from her, but by my own actions, by the bouncing of my sounds against her.

She also gave lessons to young women from the opulent neighbourhoods of the Bays, Mrs Britten's derided blonde dolls. She dragged them and their screechings towards genteel musicality, to please their rich or aspiring parents. These girls filled her afternoons, coming to her directly from school, smelling of paper and chalk and sweat and the tram. They would sit at the piano, or occasionally at the cello, backs straight in their school uniforms, strain or boredom on their faces. I knew this, because later I would help her to teach them.

But at first, my visits to Madame's place were limited to our twice-weekly morning sessions. Each session lasted for two hours and – after a few weeks in which we sized each other up and decided we rather liked each other, different as we were – would always finish in the same manner: with tea, with shots of vodka, and with smoking, with Madame telling me that Australians had tin ears, and me telling Madame that Russian composers wrote music only for battles, or for madmen.

TINY BAMBOO SLIVERS

My sessions at Madame Petrova's house filled only a small part of each week, but I managed easily to fill the remainder. When I was not playing the cello in my bedroom at Mrs Baxter's, I would walk the streets of Sydney, absorbing the city. The winter was exhilarating after the dank unrelenting heat of Malacca. I bought a thick wool coat, wrapped a scarf around my face and up over my head, and walked through the rain, or the cold sun-filled days of winter. I walked always towards the water – not a difficult thing in this city, built around the harbour – and I came to learn which streets sloped down to meet the water, and where the headlands afforded the best views of it.

I went often to places from where I could view the progress of the bridge. My favourite of these was the look-out known as Mrs Macquaries Chair. I'd catch the tram to Pitt Street, turn into Bridge Street and trudge up past the castellations of the Conservatorium, lingering to listen for music that might filter from its windows. Then I'd continue on through the Domain and the Botanic Gardens, down past the pond to skirt the edges of Farm Cove around to

Mrs Macquaries Chair. Just shy of the Chair, I'd sit on the point and watch the bridge.

As the weather warmed, from Mrs Macquaries Chair I'd follow the track around to the saltwater baths at Woolloomooloo, pay at the entrance to the timber and tin change shed, and swim and laze by the pool's edge in the weak late-winter sun. I learned to swim in the fashion of the time as I saw it practised there, Boy Charlton's famous crawl stroke, my arms first aching then strengthening with each lap of the pool. But I missed the open ocean, the thundering of the waves into the beach near Uncle Valentine's.

Walking through the city, I'd watch the women and men pacing its streets, observe their clothes, the docked, bobbed hair of the women, their lipstick red and bright, dresses sleek and modern, all straight up and down and beautiful. I bought myself such a dress, one day, from a flash shop on Pitt Street: a slim dress of silk, the colour of my cello; the colour of aluminium, which is really no colour at all. Shot through with metallic thread, it felt cool against my legs, slick. I did not bob my hair though. I kept it long enough to pull back tight from my forehead, like the Chinese women in Malacca, tight in a bun rolled to rest at the nape of my neck, pressing there, solid.

On the day I bought the dress, Mrs Baxter stood at the door to meet me on my return to the house in Darlinghurst. She held an envelope in her hand.

'A telegram. Not half an hour ago. I trust it's not bad news.'

She stood close to me as I opened the envelope. The terse

language of the telegram adviscd me once more of loss, leaving out more than it told. *Your father dead. Sudden. Buried today. Sympathies.* The sender was Mr Holland, my father's business partner. A picture of him flashed unbidden in my mind's eye, his moustaches and bald head like my father's, their suits and hats matching; and the longer I thought, the more I could not distinguish them, Father and Mr Holland, in my mind.

My uncle sent a telegram the next day: *Darling Helena poor Charles dead. So sudden no warning. Will write. Love always Val.* A letter arrived from him a fortnight hence, heavy with sympathy, bright with details. Holland had told of unrest – Uncle Valentine wrote – among the locals, and indeed there'd been attacks on Europeans throughout Malaya. It was rumoured – but not proven – that my father's death had been caused by the addition of tiny bamboo slivers slipped into his food, that had made their way through his body and perforated his innards.

He was buried next to your dear mother, my uncle wrote. *Holland sorted it all out, good man that he is. You're left well provided for. I remain your guardian in law, and your dear uncle, always, with love. Valentine.*

I tried to bring to mind a picture of my father, but I could not. All I could hear was his voice, his words bitten back into his throat as he spoke them; and all I could see were minute splinters of bamboo, surfing rivers of blood and salty fluids until they formed a microscopic log-jam. Such an effect – to make an orphan – from such a tiny thing.

ELECTRICAL BY NATURE

Winter had given way to sweet wet spring, then to the warmth of summer, but by February the heat had become humid and inescapable. Madame and I still met each Tuesday and Thursday in the smoky dark of her room, behind her heavy curtains pulled against the sun. It was on one of my Thursday visits to Madame Petrova that she first spoke of the Professor.

'A Russian, of course, as you would guess from his name.'

She blew smoke at me over her glass, then tossed the vodka down her throat in one movement. There was buffalo grass in the bottle on the low table between us, a thin discoloured stripe of grass bent by the low glassy meniscus where the vodka met the air. The vodka burned my throat; I had learned to toss it back in one hit, as Madame did, to let it rush through my blood and my limbs. I felt its warmth in my gut, and my groin.

'He is a little mad, I think. He says he has a machine, like a musical instrument, but electric – can you imagine!' She blew air through her lips and nose at the same time, somehow breathing in a circular way, unnatural.

'Interesting.'

'You should play for him, I think. He wants to find someone to play this machine for him, someone talented, he says. Perfect pitch is what he needs in this player.'

'I play the cello, you know that. Why would I learn a new instrument – not even an instrument, a machine!'

'But you have perfect pitch.'

'Yes, I have perfect pitch. Why does a machine need perfect pitch?'

'I don't know.' She blinked at me, shifted in her seat, waved her hand at her face and blew air from her mouth to emphasise the heat. 'But'– she shifted forward in her seat – 'are you not a tiny bit curious to know about this machine of his? He calls it'– she had saved this up for me, knowing my fascination – '*Music's Most Modern Instrument*.'

My curiosity was piqued, as she had known it would be. I thought of my uncle, far away across the country, at home with his magazines – *Science and Invention* – his gramophone, his poetry, all the products of this, his beloved fabulous century. How he, too, would itch to know more.

'On what does he base this – odd – claim?' I asked her.

She shifted again, sucked her teeth, dragged on the ubiquitous cigarette.

'Apparently'– she shifted further forward then, eager, the day's heat cast aside in the excitement of musical gossip –'this machine is played by the waving of hands, like conducting an orchestra. It is played without the player touching it, not with a bow, nor by blowing. It is neither wind nor string, brass nor percussion. It is a kind of – I think – electrical voice. This is how modern it is: the voice of electricity, and of the body, combined. Yes, electrical, somehow.'

She sat back in her seat then, settling herself back on the chaise. Her curranty eyes widened as much as they could in her fat face, in the sheen of sweat on pallid, indoor skin.

I could not imagine how what Petrova had said could be true. I could only wonder at how such a thing might be possible. And so I agreed; I would play for this Professor. I would play for the chance to see this magical machine of his. Such are the decisions we make in our lives, on a whim, at a word, on a feeling, and such are the decisions that change the courses of lives, not just our own. I could not know, that day, that this was such a decision.

Madame had arranged our meeting for a hot afternoon in February, and I recall dressing with care for the heat, recall dispensing with undergarments as I often did to allow the air to circulate freely, to cool me. The dress I wore that day – my favourite, worn often that summer – had vertical black lines like wires finely drawn over a white background.

I found myself face to face that day with the Professor in Madame's smoke-hazy back room – face to face for, like me, he was tall. He too was dressed in black and white that day – neat black trousers, a sharp line running down from belt to toe, defining the centre of each leg; a crisp white shirt and a rather pretentious cravat. His eyes were piercing green, and he blinked seldom; his hair and moustaches were tamed with Macassar oil and pomade, fragrant with perfume. He took my hand when we met, bent slightly over it, dipping his head in a nod. As he started to speak, his heavy accent overlaying grammatically perfect English, his eagerness and excitement over his invention were compelling. He seemed part salesman, part shaman. He described a wooden casing containing valves and wires and transformers that translated tiny movements of the hands to music, amplified not by the shaped body of the instrument – like the cello – but fed instead by wires to yet more electrical forms. I was intrigued; I wanted to see these things, to hear them. But first, Madame told me, I must play for him.

So I took up my cello and bow, seated myself, arranged my skirt – carefully, recalling the state of ventilation down below – over my legs straddling the instrument, and played for him, Bach, the Sarabande from the fourth suite. My eyes closed, my head lolling to the music, I lost sense of time passing until I reached the final bars; then I raised my head, and my eyes opened as I drew the bow across the string to sound the final note and let it sit in the air between us.

'Yes,' said the Professor. 'Yes, you must come and play my Aetherwave Instrument, this is clearly so. Come. I will show you.'

Madame nodded. I hastily replaced my cello into its case and snapped the case shut, eager to follow the Professor.

We walked side by side the two blocks to his building, not talking, stepping briskly despite the heat. He lived in a tall old house on Underwood Street, loaned its use by absent patrons, he told me as we walked. He stayed in a flat on the first floor, but used the large basement as his work room and studio. The cello case banging against my leg, I held the railing to steady myself as I descended into a small anteroom opening into a large, low-ceilinged space tangled with wires, tubes, conglomerations of leads and devices connected to other conglomerations, and then to others still. The Professor threaded a path through the midst of it all, beckoning me to follow him. I propped my cello in its case carefully against the door and followed the Professor, until we stood before a wooden box on a low tabletop. In the box, two tall tubes – like tin cans – were wound around with copper. The copper coils flanked glass bulbs, bulbs and wires within them, attached by black bakelite bases to a wooden platform. Ceramic cards, more coils, a large black box; all connected by wires, by clips, in seeming chaos. The box had a long metal rod, an antenna or aerial extending perhaps two feet into the air; and to the side there extended a teardrop-shaped loop of similar stiff metal. The Professor talked with enthusiasm of trimming condensers, of transformers and valves, of vacuum tubes and farads and induction, of capacitance and pitch, of limitless notes. I was lulled by the poetry the words made as the Professor spoke; but could he really, as he described it, create music out of the air with a wave of his hands?

He flicked an electric switch and the machine in front of us hummed to life. We waited while it warmed; a smell like lightning, like magic, like dry rain, rose from it, as bulbs glowed into life and heat radiated from the electrical components into the already stifling room. He warned me not to touch the machine's innards, warned me of the danger of shock from the electrical currents. I imagined I could feel its threat as I could feel the sweat trickling down my back and legs.

The Professor raised his right hand towards the upright aerial, while his left hand approached the loop. And as his hands neared the metal, there was a high wailing – a voice disembodied but somehow everywhere, aerial, electric. Magical. He moved his hands and fingers to change the pitch and volume, to swerve the voice high and low, soft and loud. He wobbled his right hand and a warm vibrato issued.

But the Professor's amateur noodlings quickly frustrated my perfect ear and twitching fingers – I ached to try to play the thing myself. He, frustrated by his inability to achieve the potential he saw from his machine, did not take much convincing. And so it was that on that hot February afternoon in 1928 I put aside my beloved cello and for the first time raised my sweating arms and drew my fingers through the air to cause music to issue from a tangle of wire, glass, bakelite and wood. I did not play perfectly that day – that would come after long practice, take some time to achieve – but that day, when I first raised my hands to the machine, that was when I first felt my hands disrupt the electromagnetic field, felt the waves swell through the blood and flesh of my body; felt electrical by nature.

In the many years since that hot day, this instrument has become known as the *theremin*. But the Professor and I, we called it by the names he coined: aetherphone, or Aetherwave Instrument. The first time I played the aetherphone, I felt the rush of the electrical field through my body. I felt like a god. I felt like a queen. I felt like a conqueror. And I wanted to play it forever. I can't describe the feeling accurately. It was part visceral sensation, part physics; the relation between body and air, electrons aligning. A crystalline cold swept through my body when first I played the theremin, swiftly replaced by a bone-warming heat, a calm like none I had known. I recall bowing my head in awe.

I hold one regret from that day: that I put my first love, my cello, aside. But it was to take up a bigger love, a greater thing; it was to step into the future. This was Music's Most Modern Instrument. And I was to become Music's Most Modern Musician.

BIRTHDAY

In the days and weeks and months that followed that first
meeting, I could not have been kept from my visits to
the Professor's studio by a team of horses. I'd go there each
morning; depending on my mood and the weather I'd walk
or catch the tram to Oxford Street, then from Oxford
Street I'd cut across and almost run the last three hundred
yards to the Professor's. Learning to play the theremin was
unlike learning to play the cello. There was no touching of
soft unaccustomed fingertips to thick strings taut across a
wooden neck, no blisters of skin to overcome, no calluses
to build. My arms were strong from swimming, so the
pain of muscles holding arms aloft was slight. My pains
came from the straining of fingers against nothing, against
the air, against the sound, against the letting go of my
preconceptions and the adoption of new ways of holding
my body. I became a novice once more; I had everything
to learn.

The Professor worked me hard each day; more to the
point, I worked myself hard. We worked closely together,
for long hours – physically close, as we experimented with
different ways that I could hold my body in relation to the

machine. But there was no hint of romance. The Professor was a man focussed on his machine, and his interest in me was purely as an extension of it, as the means of realising its potential. And my only care was to become as proficient a thereminist as I was a cellist, to prove myself a modern musician.

A week before my eighteenth birthday, I received an invitation on ivory linen stationery. It seemed that the Professor had been talking to Madame Petrova, Petrova talking to Mrs Britten, Mrs Britten to Mr Britten, and that it had been decided that I was to be introduced to society, to play the theremin at a party at the Brittens' house on the night of my birthday.

The Brittens were patrons of the arts. Musicians, painters, sculptors, writers; they gathered them all, opened their arms and their wallets to them, bought their first pieces, funded their concerts, even took them as lovers, if rumour could be believed. Mrs Britten had white blonde hair cut in a severe and fashionable bob, sharp tips curving in to emphasise her pointed chin. She was beautiful, despite – or perhaps because of – her severe look; her age was somewhere from forty to fifty-five. Her husband looked older, and had about him the stance, the demeanour, the very smell of a rich man. He was a lawyer with an eye for art and women, and the money to assure he had both.

On the night of my birthday, the Professor arrived in the Brittens' car to pick me up, although it was just a short distance, easily walked, from my house to their mansion in

Elizabeth Bay. But no, they had insisted, the Professor told me, and my silken shoes were thankful for it, designed as they were to swish and step the night away on a smooth, chalked dance floor, not to walk on Sydney roads. A man in a cap drove the car; the Professor handed me into the back seat and lowered himself in after me. We pulled into the short driveway that curved from the road, through gates, to the front of the big house in Elizabeth Bay, the night fiery with lights, murmuring with voices and soft music, scented with petrol and flashing with the headlights of cars sweeping around the drive.

The Professor stepped out of the car and onto crunching gravel. As I stepped from the car and straightened my back to stand next to him at the foot of the steps that led to the grand front door, he held out his hand to me, and I took it with mine. He was in evening dress. My dress was silk, cut on the bias, simple and clinging, fluid against my body. Its colour was oyster, or shell or ivory – the colour of something cut from an animal; an organic colour, a non-colour that both absorbed and reflected the colours around it. It had thin straps, slick and slippery. A short capelet capped my shoulders, the same fabric as the dress and tied at the front with thin ribbons of silk. I needed no coat or jacket to warm me; the night was mild, and I was young. The Professor faced me, took both my hands in his, and smiled.

'Enjoy this, my dear. It will be the first of many such nights.'

He patted my hand with his, turned to face the house and hooked his right arm towards me. I slotted my left arm through his, squared my shoulders, and we stepped up to the bright house in front of us.

The door was opened by a deferential man in evening dress, who bowed his head and ushered us towards the double doors that led from the entrance hall. The Professor opened the doors with a flourish, and led me through into a room of generous proportions. A semi-circle of people stood there, all dressed in their evening finery, black, white and silver dominating their dress as it did the room's furnishings. They turned to us as we entered. Mrs Britten stepped forward and introduced the Professor to the room. He bowed, low – a very Russian bow – and all in the room applauded gently, murmuring, heads nodding to each other. He raised his hands to the small crowd, smiling and accepting their applause as he took a step back, took my hand, and raised it in his.

'Mesdames et messieurs. Ladies and gentlemen. Thank you for your kind applause. But tonight is not for me. Tonight I give you a talented young woman who will soon be a famous young woman. You will not forget this night, my dear friends. This is the night I introduce to you, and to the world, Miss Lena Gaunt, and the shining star she will become.'

I bowed my head as he spoke, but was drawn to raise it as all in the room applauded. They applauded me. *Me.* I raised my eyes and looked around, saw the well-groomed faces, old and young, the fine clothes, the raised eyebrows, mouths moving with words or carved into smiles.

'Lena Gaunt – mesdames et messieurs'– the Professor pushed his hands through the air to call for their quiet – 'Lena

Gaunt will play for you tonight one of the most astonishing musical instruments you have ever seen or heard. Yes, Miss Gaunt has been working with me for some months now, perfecting the art and science of Music's Most Modern Instrument, and we can now reveal this to you, my dear friends. My most honoured patrons, Monsieur et Madame Britten – Edward and his lovely wife, Delphine – have bestowed their generosity upon Miss Gaunt and myself in inviting you all here. We will demonstrate for you – I give you – the aetherphone, this most magnificent instrument of my invention, played without touching, played by drawing the hands through the aether, by the modern science of physics and the human body combined.'

The Professor acknowledged the applause, waving his hands in the air. He stepped aside and turned, and so I too turned, to see the theremin set up in the centre of the room, the amplifying speaker looming behind it. A glossy black grand piano was set back behind them, Madame Petrova seated there, beaming at me, cigarette in her lipsticked mouth, nodding her head at me in encouragement, her hair piled more extravagantly than usual and looking in danger of flying off her head and into the piano's wires. The people still applauded; I turned at a touch at my elbow, to find Mr Britten had appeared. He led me to the theremin. It made a low hum as I approached. I touched a hand to it to silence it; not yet. Mr Britten stepped aside, raised his hands.

'My friends! Quiet if you will. Miss Gaunt will play for us on this amazing Aether Machine. Delphine and I've been looking forward to this evening very much. Miss Gaunt,' he addressed me, 'when you are ready, please.'

He stepped back into the crowd. They all faced me. The Professor was at the front, to the side, his hands held together under his chin. Delphine Britten stood next to him.

I lifted my dulling hand from the aerial, moved my hands and body to the starting position I had perfected, a neutral position: not touching the machine but positioned so that the tiniest movement would elicit the desired tone. I felt in control. I knew exactly the movements I needed to make with my fingers, my hands, my arms and my body to play for them.

The Professor nodded at me; I nodded in response, Petrova and I exchanged glances, and then I closed my eyes as I heard the first notes of Saint-Saëns' 'Le Cygne' from the piano. As the first note from the theremin issued from the speaker behind me, I heard a collective intake of breath. My eyes opened as I played, and I saw the response of the audience – some leaned away, almost fearful of the electrical machine; others leaned forwards, wanting to see, to know, to embrace this new thing.

I hit the high note at the end of the first phrase: perfect. My fingers' movement was all I could have wanted for this demonstration, this first outing of my technique, the notes crisp and sharp.

I finished the piece, lowered my hands to the resting position, the theremin quiet, just a low hum from the speaker behind me. I could hear Madame Petrova's breath heavy at the piano. From the silence, applause burst astonished from the audience, shouts of *brava* rang through the room.

As we had rehearsed, I played 'Vocalise' by Rachmaninoff, then Ravel's 'Habanera', the applause vibrant between each piece. The Professor stood to the side, nodding, his hands clasped to his face in a fist.

My final piece was Bach, of course. I played them the Prelude from the first cello suite, solo, without Madame on the piano. As I finished, I stepped aside from the theremin, and bowed low, the applause coursing through me, energising me. I smiled as faces started to distil into individuals from the blurred mass of audience. Delphine Britten smiled hard at me, raised her hands to me as she clapped them together. Mr Britten did the same, kissing his fingertips and throwing the kiss to me, his raised eyebrow lightly leering. Madame Petrova stayed at the piano, raised a glass of clear fluid, winked lustily, and downed the drink in a long single draught. The Professor moved towards me from the crowd, took my hand, raised it in his, and we bowed. Blood rushed to my head; this was extraordinary. I had received applause before, but polite, domestic. This felt different. Electric.

As I stared and smiled again into the crowd of faces, a critical eye creased – in laughter? In scrutiny? In approval? – and caught my own eye. Hair was slicked to one side across a face worn but warm, lightly lined but young underneath the lines. When I first saw Beatrix, for a moment I did not know whether she was a man or a woman. Beatrix seemed beyond gender; and so she was.

She was dressed as she sometimes dressed in those days, in a man's clothes – evening dress, sharp-creased black trousers, glossy black patent shoes, a white evening shirt. She wore a silk scarf tied in the fashion of a cravat, much like that the Professor had worn the first time I had met him. On Beatrix the scarf hung low, masked the rise of her breasts under her gathered shirt.

She caught my eye among the many present that night. She was part of the electricity, of the novelty of the night for me, the feeling running through my body that felt residual from the theremin, as if I had indeed been connected to it, been part of the electrical circuits the Professor had built, a connection as if made by wires touching wires, metal wound around metal. But Beatrix connected to me without touching, as soon as I saw her. She made me hum, even from across the room.

The Professor dropped my hand, and the crowd broke from its formation, its split between audience and performers – we all joined in a buzz of congratulations and conversation about the aetherphone, about electricity, about music. My connection with the world of music in Sydney had been limited, until this night, to Petrova and the Professor, and the Professor's connection with music was a product of his beloved machines, rather than love of the music itself. But, as much as I had craved this talk of music, as the crowd mingled, as groups formed and broke and reformed, I found myself searching for the figure I had noticed before, the eyes that had caught mine, the face of the woman I would come to know as Beatrix Carmichael.

Across the room, an arm described an arc through the

air, trailing cigarette smoke, standing with Delphine Britten by the fireplace. They stood before a painting hung on the wall above the mantelpiece. The painting was of a figure on an armchair, and I could see at once – despite the light and shapes and planes of the figure being sharp and unreal, unreadable, nonetheless I *could* read it – that the figure was Mrs Britten, Delphine. Clutching the chair's arm, she pushed herself upwards, bursting from the painting. The figure standing by the fireplace raised a hand to the painting once again, once again traced an arc through the air, close to the surface of the painting, tracing the arc of Mrs Britten's sharp jawline on the canvas. Then I watched as she raised her other hand, traced her finger along Delphine Britten's jawline, the real-life jawline in front of her. Mrs Britten raised her own hand to her face, pushed her hair back. I heard myself exhale hard, not noticing that I had been holding my breath.

Hands clapped sharply across the room, and all of us in the crowd turned to face the sound. Mr Britten, clapping as he walked across the room towards me, commanded our attention.

'Ladies and gentlemen, if I could ask you – if you could please give me your attention. Please.'

As he reached my side, all eyes were upon us. He slid his arm around my waist, kissed my cheek, held his other arm in the air as if conducting an orchestra, or hailing a tram.

'My friends, please. A moment more of your attention. Tonight, we have seen, and heard, history being made, I'm sure you will agree.'

Applause and shouts rang once more from the room. Mr

Britten waved his arms, pushed his hands down through the air and the noise lowered to silence.

'Well my friends, let's move from history to something more personal.' His hand, still at my waist, slid lower, to my hip. 'Today is Miss Gaunt's eighteenth birthday. Our clever Professor has prepared a surprise to help in its celebration. Professor, please.'

The Professor walked up to me and took my hand, leading me through the double doorway to the adjacent room, the crowd of people parting as we passed, all applauding politely. He led me to a small circular table, on which stood a cake large enough to perfectly fit the tabletop, white, decorated with flounces of sugar and small balls of silver in patterns of musical notations, treble and bass clefs, quavers and crotchets.

A candle stood in its centre with an electric light as a flame. A device was inside the cake, surely. As I approached, the candle lit, first flickering then glowing steadily. As I moved closer, the whole table started to rotate, going faster the closer I stood; then as I stepped backwards, the rotation slowed, the glowing candle faded to a flicker. I stepped forwards and backwards, my hands to my face in delight. I stepped away and raised my hands in front of me – almost in the position I would adopt to play the theremin – to see if the proximity of my hands was enough to rotate the cake, but it needed a greater body mass, a greater disruption of the electrical field than my hands could provide; it needed my whole body.

All the people of the crowd had moved around me, forming the shape of a crescent moon, oohing and aahing, clapping quietly. The Professor stood by my side, smiling at me, nodding as I understood what he had done, as I played his invention for him. The people in the crowd added their bodies and their arms to the influence of the cake and the table, and soon all were in a huddle, a scrum, hands and bodies moving together and apart in delight, in wonder. Mr Britten moved to my side and kissed my cheek once more, his hand straight to the small of my back and lower, caressing, and his breath in my ear was warm, wet, unpleasant as he hummed *Happy birthday, darling girl*, and I shrank into myself to avoid him, my eyes seeking the floor, seeking escape.

But then I saw the glossy patent of her shoes appear by the pale silk of mine, toe touching toe.

'Edward Britten, for godsakes leave the poor girl alone, won't you? You're dreadful, darling, honestly.' Her arm slipped around my waist, her lips brushed my cheek, close to my own lips; I caught her scent: the honey wax of lipstick, tobacco, turpentine faint in her hair. 'Happy birthday, darling Miss Gaunt. Your playing was wonderful. Don't mind Edward; he's a dreadful slut, and he always goes running back to Delphine, don't you, Edward?'

'Thank you, Miss...'

'Beatrix Carmichael, doll. Call me Trix. Run away and bring us drinks, Edward; you're not looking after your guests.' Her arm still around my waist, loose but warm, slipped lower – just slightly, just lightly – so her hand rested on my thin hip. She was shorter than me, the top of her head at the height of my eyes.

There was a shout from across the room as Madame

Petrova and the Professor clinked small glasses one against the other, and we turned, Trix and I, to watch them down the liquor in unison, shouting something guttural as they finished.

I turned back as Trix did, so that I turned my face into hers – we were facing one another, my face above hers, hers tilted up towards mine. I caught her breath under my tongue, smoke and whisky, as she said in a low voice, 'Come to the beach with me, doll. Let's go to Manly. Tomorrow.'

TRICK THE LIGHT

We met at Circular Quay. Beatrix was dressed in trousers, wide at the ankle. I saw her first from a distance; she faced away from me, yet I knew it was her. She turned, as if she felt my eyes on her, and as she turned, the legs of her trousers swished and moved like the sails of a ship, revealing ankle straps on her glossy shoes. Her face was lit with a smile. She wore a white fedora over bobbed hair, powdered face and the reddest of red lipstick on her wide lips. Yet while her clothes and appearance were a mixture of mannish and womanly, no one could see her at that moment and not know she was a woman.

Beatrix doffed her hat, winked at me, walked towards me, rested her hands on both my shoulders and kissed me on one cheek and then the next, in the European way I was used to from the Professor and Madame Petrova.

'Ready, darl?' she asked me, turning so that we faced in the same direction, towards the ferries, and taking my arm with hers. 'I took the liberty'– she squeezed my arm gently – 'of purchasing tickets for the two of us to travel. We're just in time. Hustle your bustle, doll.'

Whisked along as I would come to expect by Beatrix,

we joined the flow of people boarding the ferry berthed at Manly Wharf. The day was fine, and we secured a position on the deck, sitting close together on wooden slats that bounded the cabin. Beatrix took a packet of cigarettes from her pocket, and offered them to me. I took one, and Beatrix leaned in and lit it for me, her hand around mine around the match to shield the flame from the breeze.

We talked about everything and nothing on the trip to Manly; and we watched the bridge.

'Look at it,' Beatrix said, 'God, it's so beautiful. I love painting it. Not just the bridge. The water, the light. The shapes. The spaces between the shapes. The way they change as we move past them. I like to try to paint that.'

From the water, the view of the bridge was different than from anywhere on land – from that low angle, looking up, it seemed so much larger. Its overall shape had not changed since my view of it from the *Houtman* as I'd steamed into Sydney for the first time. The shape was the same, but denser, spaces filled, lines and curves connected. It looked stronger, more permanent, even though still the two arcs of the bridge did not meet. The air around and between the arcs hummed and rang with the sounds of construction from the bridge, of human voices drowned by metallic ringing.

The air had been still that morning, heavy with humidity and unseasonal warmth for autumn. On the water, air moved past us as the boat moved through it, creating a cooling breeze. It felt like an escape, to be surrounded by water, by its sound. The sweat on my back, under my arms, dried quickly in the breeze. I felt light again, released from the dragging effect of the city. I wore the dress I had worn for my first meeting with the Professor: black and white, elegant. I felt myself cool underneath the dress, felt the fabric move against me.

The ferry docked at Manly and the crowd of disembarking passengers streamed off onto land. Beatrix – she had said again, on the ferry, *call me Trix* – Trix took my arm. Her arm was cool; I could feel my sweat slicken the soft underside of my elbow against her dry skin.

Trix walked us to tearooms that overlooked the water. We took a table in the rotunda, outside but shaded from the sun. She ordered tea, sandwiches, and cakes. We talked as we ate. I learned that she was an artist, a painter, and that – born ten years from the close of the old century – she was more than twice my age. Having long ago escaped from the cold southern town of her birth across the water in New Zealand, more recently she'd returned to Australia from living in Europe, in places with romantic names, Paris, Vienna, Berlin. I spoke of my music, of my conversion from cello to theremin, of my interest and delight in the modern. We were loud, sometimes, over tea that day. We were looked at, by quieter patrons. I rested my hand on the table; Trix covered it with hers, cool and slight.

We walked down past the hotel and on to the beach, shoes off, sand crunching and squeaking between our toes. I could feel the stretch in my calves, felt myself push against the hard wet sand low on the beach. Trix linked her arm through mine. The waves were quiet that day, not booming, just a light, rounded swell. At the western end of the bay, where the beach curved around, long shadows from Norfolk pines fell on the beach, formed strips of shade on the white sand. We fell in and out of darkness as we walked.

We caught a late, crowded ferry back to Circular Quay. People smelled of beer and oil and sweat and fish. Trix and I resumed our places at the front of the boat, where the air moved the smells away, and the boat thrummed underneath us with its rhythmic tug. We were quieter now, all talked out. We listened instead to the talk around us, talk of football and fish and Missus this and Mister that. We smiled at each other, smiled at the same overheard fragments.

I looked at Trix. The light from the low sun glowed. She reached for my hand, resting in my lap. As she reached, tucking her little hand around my long fingers, her knuckles brushed against me, pressed the fabric of my dress to touch me lightly, underneath. I glowed with the sun, with the touch, with heat, a spark in me fired.

We arranged to meet again the next day. I waited for Trix at Circular Quay, watched her step from the ferry and stride towards me. She placed her hands on my shoulders, brushed her left cheek first against my right cheek, then her right cheek – slowly – against my left cheek. She breathed out hot breath against me, spiced with cigarette smoke.

'I've brought lunch.' She lifted a large, worn velvet bag. 'And a little drink.' She linked her arm through mine, and we walked together. I matched my long stride to her smaller step. We walked for hours in the autumn sun, through the Domain, the Botanic Gardens. At Mrs Macquaries Chair we sat and ate cheese sandwiches unwrapped from waxed paper, washed down with sherry from a tin bottle, all drawn from deep in her velvet bag. We sat close on the seat in the shade, so close I could smell the sherry on her breath. She lit a cigarette for me, and one for herself; she shifted closer to me, turned her body, just a little, so that she looked at me. We sat and smoked and watched the world, watched each other.

We walked back to Circular Quay late in the afternoon. Trix held her bag in front of her, low, almost dragging on the ground as she walked. As we approached the terminal, she turned to me, placed her hand on my arm.

'Come to my house. Come for tea. My paintings – I want to show you. Come on.'

We chattered up the hill from the ferry dock at Mosman to Trix's house in Royalist Road, leaning in on one another, giggling and scurrying like two schoolgirls. We climbed up the steps onto the verandah that wrapped around two sides of the house.

'Turn around, look!' Trix told me. 'This is where I paint, sometimes.'

From the verandah you could see the bridge. The shapes and curves of it, the two halves like the swell of full breasts, or pregnant bellies, reached towards each other, approaching completeness. You could imagine the arc the finished bridge would form; your eye drew it in, filled the space, completed it, connected the two pieces. We stood for a moment; I could think of no words to say. I could feel her next to me, and nothing else mattered.

The house was quiet, dark inside; no one answered Trix's *coo-ee!* as we slammed in through the front door from the verandah.

'Sherry? Mmmn, sherry, yes. Come on.' She took my hand and pulled me with her through to a lean-to kitchen where, on a shelf, bottles of liquid shone, next to glasses of every shape, none of them matching. They stood upon embroidered linen, next to candles in silver sticks, as if on an altar. Trix poured amber sherry into two glasses, one of panelled red glass, the other fine crystal. She handed me the red glass, clinked the crystal against it, and took my hand again.

'Come on. I want to show you.'

She led me down the hallway, through an open door. It smelled of paint, of turpentine, of smoke, of our sherry.

'Look,' she said, 'let me show you. The light. What we've been looking at. What I see. What I can make it do.'

She drew the curtain aside, let in the pale light of the dying day. The room was full of paintings. Canvas rested against canvas, some framed, most of them not. Paintings faced out into the room, or turned their backs to us, faced the wall. They were on the floor, on a bookcase, a desk. They hung on the wall, they sat on a well-stuffed chair by the window. She lifted one – small, barely bigger than the width of a dinner plate – and held it to me. I took it from her.

It was the bridge viewed from the verandah. Somehow, though, I could see it not just from the verandah, but from the ferry, from the other side of the harbour, from Mrs Macquaries Chair, all at once; all of those views and angles were combined. The painting was all about movement, and shape. It swam before my eyes.

'But how?' I said. 'How do you – how does it move like this?'

She took the painting from me, kissed my cheek – just shy of my mouth – and placed the painting on the chair by the window.

'Ah, see, that's why I wanted to show you. It's what I do. I trick the light.' She held her hands wide, inviting me, enticing me to move around the room. I looked at canvas after canvas of the bridge, the rooftops, the sky and the water. Still lives – the altar of wine and glasses – cigarettes and matchboxes. People I did not recognise, their faces and bodies formed in shapes and planes and colours.

'And this, look at this. Ah, it's old, but still…'

A cello was fractured into parts; not the parts of a cello, and yet somehow, combined, they made me know they formed a cello. The dun colour of the wood was enlivened, shot through with blue, light reflecting from glass under the instrument. It stood by a window; that was it, a window. Or was it water? I couldn't tell.

'I used to play – before the aetherphone – I played cello.'

'You told me.'

'It's beautiful. But I don't understand how you do it.'

'I interpret what I see. This is how I see the world. This is how I make it look.'

The cello in the painting was a cello, and yet not a cello.

'It makes me think – of the sound I make with the aetherphone. Not like a cello, but like it. Both more than it, and less than it, at the same time, and yet itself as well. I'm not making sense, I—'

'No, no, it makes sense. I think that's it exactly. Itself, and more than itself, and less. Everything connects.' She stubbed her cigarette out in a bowl on a table. 'Everything connects!'

She moved towards me, took the empty red glass from my hand, placed it on the table next to the ash-filled bowl. She reached up to place her arms around me; her hands hooked over my shoulders and her fingers reached under my chin, their touch gentle.

'Beautiful girl.'

I breathed in, almost could not breathe out. My face turned to the left and I kissed her finger.

'Oh.' She made a noise like *tsk*, with her mouth. 'Beautiful, beautiful girl.' And she raised up on her toes, and I leant – just slightly – downwards, and we kissed, our lips light at first, then heavy upon one another, smoky, sweet, intense.

We fell into one another. Beatrix took my body and fractured it into parts, so that I felt every part, every piece of my body with an intensity that was new to me, delicious. I felt the parts put together into a whole that was greater than it had been, before Trix. All of the planes and curves of my body were showing, all at once, inside me and outside me and all around me.

TOUCHING

Trix was unforeseen. My life became compartmentalised, split. I was working hard each day with the Professor, learning my craft – I had still so much to know. I wanted it all at once, to be better, more skilled with my instrument at the end of each day than at its beginning. Most of the time I was inventing the skills anew – there was no one who could teach me, who knew more about the aetherphone than I. I learned from my own body, from my muscles and from my ears and brain. The Professor made small changes to the configuration of the instrument, tweaking here and there, in response to the sounds and the music that I squeezed and teased from it – I would hit a limit, and he would manoeuvre wires and components until the limitation was overcome. In time, our machine became limitless. The Professor soared as I did, watching and listening beside me. This was the shape of my days.

But the evenings were for Trix, and a different kind of music.

Trix would arrive fresh off the ferry from Mosman at

the end of each day, come to get me when she'd finished painting. She'd ring the bell at the front of the house; Mrs Baxter would let her into the front room and knock on my door, *Your aunt, Miss Gaunt*. I'd introduced Trix as Mrs Carmichael, a widow, and had not corrected Mrs Baxter when she assumed – from our ease in each other's company – that Trix and I were family. On hot days, I would wait on the verandah, fanning myself with a sheet of paper or a leaf from the garden until Trix bounded onto the verandah two steps at a time and planted kisses on both my cheeks, squeezing my hands.

'Come on, doll. We are going to have a good time tonight.'

The Buzz Room was not the name over the door, but that's what everyone called it. It was easy to miss if you didn't know what you were looking for, down a laneway off the Cross, poorly lit, the kind of place to be warned about, to avoid. Through the door was a crowd, a push, a smoky haze of glory, of masculine women and feminine men, of all sorts and all kinds and nobody cared what. Trix would kiss my lips hard as we came through the door, our ritual; as we broke apart she would always say *There, because I can*, whisper it in my ear.

But almost best of all, there was music.

A raised stage filled one end of the L-shaped room, and the stage was always filled with musicians, a stream of them playing music to dance by, music to move to, music that wouldn't let you stay still. Bands would form and part several times a night; there was the same permissiveness to the musical groupings that pervaded the rest of the place. Women played; men played; jazz predominated, but dark, different; there was a wildness, a not needing to please, to conform. There was heat to the music, heat and fluidity.

Everyone danced with everyone, and no one – we just danced, with a freedom I'd never felt before. People would dance without touching, couples connecting with their eyes, or by mirroring or responding to the movements of their partners. They would connect by shouting out, calling, crying, *get hot, get hot*, mad cries would ring through the room, *yeah!* Coats and hats and bags piled in a corner, people piled straight onto the dance floor. We danced and danced until we dropped. And when we dropped, Trix showed me how to dance some more – from the Cross you could buy little glass vials filled with white grains. Trix tapped a small mound of powder onto her thumbnail, then onto my thumbnail; I mirrored her movements, hungry. You raised the thumbnail to each nostril in turn, as you held the other nostril closed and inhaled sharply, then flicked your tongue over the nail to lick the sparkling grains remaining there. A cold light would fire through you; first an ultraviolet black-and-whiteness followed by a suffusion of such brilliant energy and light. We would dance for hours more, topping up as we needed to with a thumbnail of snow, as I learned to call it. Trix took more than me, would top up more often. Her eyes shone with it.

With snow cooling our limbs and minds we could dance for hours, generating our own heat in response to the heat of the music. Heads bent for lips to kiss lips, arms were flung, bodies moved and touched and separated, came together, moved apart. The space was dark, the only lights shone on the players on the stage, and smoke hazed what little light there was. We didn't need light. We made our own light. The music soared above us; bass notes rumbled in our groins, tumbled from drums, from the double bass held wild like a woman between the legs and in the arms of the musician on the stage, sawing across her, growling bass. Saxophone pierced and lowed, animal and metallic all mixed together in an unnatural fusion, creating sounds unheard before, unheard again, riffed, jammed from the air. Sometimes the players on the stage would all seem to be playing a different music; there would be as many different songs coming from the stage as there were players on it. Then they would all fall into step and soar on a wave of sound, push it up to the ceiling and it'd rush down on us on the dance floor, hit us with a rush and a flow that was unbearable and glorious and gorgeous. A phrase I recognised – of Rachmaninoff, of Shostakovich, of Stravinsky – would flow into a new form, would bend and break under the weight of instrumentation and rhythm, take a new form that rose up from deep within the old, but liberated from it.

Faces and names, bodies and faces, limbs and necks and lips and hands. We were all doll and darl and honey and baby and skirt, daddy-o and baby again. There were more dark faces there than I would ever see in the streets of Sydney, crammed in, jammed in, dark face against white face, any colour melting into any other, skin on skin in the dark and the buzz of the place. Trix would tell me names – such-and-such an actress, so-and-so an artist – but they all swirled around me, nameless, beautiful, bright with sweat and snow, baby and honey and doll.

And sometimes, just sometimes, at the end of the night, we would go to the Chinese dens and, reclining, smoke sweet opium, concentrating the night, defusing the snow, smoke diffusing through our minds and flowing outside and up through the hot air, to the docks, to the hissing water in the harbour, out between the two halves of the bridge, across and over Mrs Macquaries Chair and out through the Heads to the ocean, deep, blue, unfathomable.

I moved into Trix's house in the late winter of 1930, August, when everything was green and luscious, the garden pushing dark and wet against the sides of the big Mosman house. I felt comfortable with the loose community of bohemians – writers, artists, intellectuals, no-hopers, musicians – who lived in the houses that crowded down to the water there, set into the bush. I had been spending more and more of my time at Trix's house, so it made sense for me to move my few things into the large room that became vacant when the painter who I knew only as Nora moved out, moved up to the Blue Mountains to join some community or other of painters and drinkers and opium-smokers.

Trix came with me to Mrs Baxter's to help me carry my few belongings. She arrived with a heavy old barrow with a wooden wheel; we loaded it with my clothes and books, the few things that hadn't yet made it to Trix's. Mrs Baxter waved us off from the verandah as we piled my neglected cello on top of the lot, then we wheeled it all the way to the ferry dock, onto the ferry, and off again at Mosman. It took the two of us and all our strength to wheel it up the steep street to the house in Royalist Road, where we collapsed in a heap on the verandah.

The spans of the bridge had been closing on each other, leaning closer and closer, filling the gap between them. Two days after I moved into the Mosman house, Trix and I prepared a picnic of bread and ham and wine and apples and cigarettes. Trix brought her new camera with her, the gleaming black and silver Rolleiflex she was still learning to use, her new modern tool to help capture subjects for her paintings. All of these we carried in a basket, down to the end of Milson Road and up the track to the end of the point, where Trix sometimes came to paint, and there we watched the gap close. We celebrated it, this joining of the city, the coming together, and yet Trix mourned it too. Since her return from Europe, since her arrival in Sydney, she'd been painting the growing bridge in parts, separate; in fragmented shapes formed of light and colour and sun and music.

'I'll miss it, you know.' Trix bit her lip in a habitual way I had come to know so well, peering down into the camera, adjusting it, framing the bridge. 'Somehow there's less of a thrill in breaking it into parts on the canvas when it's made whole in real life. Oh God, I don't know, maybe I'm

176

wrong, maybe it'll be better like this. But I've loved the idea of it being under construction, I suppose that's it, of it reaching across at itself.'

'Well, you can hardly ask them to keep it in pieces for you.'

'Ha! Don't you think I should? Mrs Carmichael the arteest requests the abandoning of the bridge project. Can't you see it, darl? I can.' She turned the camera on me, and I waved her away. 'Oh, let me!' I raised my teacup of wine towards her. 'Ah! Perfect!' She rested the camera in her lap, then picked up her teacup and clinked it at mine. She raised her other hand to my cheek, her finger lightly stroking.

'Oh well. To touching, then.'

'To touching.'

Trix and I maintained separate rooms in the house in Mosman, not for the sake of propriety – there was little enough of that at the house – but for the sake of sanity. We each needed our space to retreat to, to make or practise our art. And Trix remained a lark, while my owl tendencies firmed and extended. Trix would march into my room at noon to wake me, trailing her silk robe, vermilion and azure and scarlet, trailing lapsang souchong steam and Gitanes smoke. She would have been up for hours – she rose with the sun, whatever time of the year, whatever we'd been up to the night before – would have breakfasted, painted, cleaned, read the newspaper, had an argument, gone for a walk, written a letter. Trix was always active, always moving.

I settled quickly into my new room as the late winter lightened to spring and light filtered, warming, into the house. I set up the theremin and speaker the Professor had gifted to me, placed them in the centre of my room. I'd flick a switch and stand there, and play with the electricity in the air, fragment it, change it, affect it with my body's capacitance. My room smelled of ozone and wire, metal and hot ceramic. Trix, in her room, layered pigment and somehow captured air and light within the layers; colour shone from them. She painted the light on the water in Shell Cove, blue-green bush touching the edges of red-roofed houses, eggs glowing on a clementine-orange dish, the bridge cracked in two above the water of the harbour. Sometimes she even painted me – made light break and curve around me. Her studio smelled of cigarettes and turpentine, oranges and lapsang souchong tea; these were the smells of Trix.

FAME

Despite our differing internal clocks, Trix and I managed to spend nights together in gatherings in our big house, or in the houses of others we knew in Mosman, or down at the hotel by the ferry dock, afterwards to tumble and stumble and fumble our way up the hill to home. Or we'd go across on the ferry, go to the Cross, or to Balmain, to hear music, to dance, to talk, to argue, to come down after it all with a smoke in Chinatown.

In the meantime, music had – almost unnoticed – become my career, and I had attained a degree of fame through it. Through all the ructions and rumblings of the financial world tumbling to its feet, the Brittens seemed to retain their standing, even most of their fortune, and they continued as patrons to me, to the Professor, and to Trix, among the coterie of artists they still supported. After my first, not very public, performance on the aetherphone at the Brittens' house on my eighteenth birthday, I started to receive more and more invitations to play. I played small theatres and halls, at first, and initially accompanied only by Madame on the piano, with the Professor always in the audience, or in the wings, watching over us, watching and listening for ways to fine-tune his instrument. Soon my audience grew, and I was in demand, playing more and bigger shows. I was written about in magazines and newspapers and talked of on the radio. I was a product of the modern age, and the hunger of people for such a thing was great, even as money markets crashed and jobs became scarce. And so, through the early years of that new decade, I became, to my surprise, famous. I stuck paper bill notices for my performances into a bound book, cut reviews from newspapers, charting my rise in the public imagination: 'Creating Music from Aether with a Wave of the Hands'; 'Hands Create Radio Music'; 'Music like None Ever Played'; 'A Thoroughly Modern Woman'.

Trix made striking designs, cut into linoleum, from which to print the notices advertising my shows. They were variations on a theme: thin arms in black approaching a loop of metal, red rays emanating from them all. They were like nothing ever used before for the advertisement of music, and they caused as much comment as the music itself. There came to be built around me a notion – a mythology – of my fame and my music, a tying together of the music, the look of Trix's posters, the exotic otherness of the Professor, the magic modernity of the aetherphone. Somehow, I was expected to embody all of these things. I could feel the electric expectation of the audience each time I walked on to the stage. And I found that I could fulfil their expectation, and more than that, extend it. Reviews were enthusiastic. Invitations to play increased, and so did my repertoire and skills, and my fame.

As interest in the music I produced grew, so others started to learn to play the aetherphone. The Professor sold the license for production of the machine to a local radio firm, and they produced aetherphones for sale – by 1931 they were in the window of the biggest music shop in Sydney, with a photograph of me above them, my smiling endorsement an incentive to buy.

It was largely through Delphine Britten that I came to play my most famous shows. Delphine was a patron of the Symphony Orchestra, her father on the board of the State Theatre. My fame was such that by the summer of 1932, I suspect that the orchestra would have sought me out anyway, without the link that Delphine afforded. We played an unheard-of week of shows at the State Theatre. The tickets sold out quickly for all of the performances. The poster that Trix designed was as striking as always, yellow wave shapes forming a background under purple lettering, centred over the black arm, the loop, the red radiating lines, images that had become deeply associated with my music, and with me. I imagined the sound of my electric music filling the huge spaces of the new theatre as never before, soaring up to its famous chandelier, vibrating it, fracturing the sound as the crystals of the chandelier captured and fractured the light.

I worked with the orchestra on a programme that would fill the theatre and foreground the aetherphone, let it soar on the sound from the mass of instruments. The programme included what had become my signature pieces, and some that were new to me, that needed an orchestra to fill their spaces. We would play from Stravinsky's *Rite of Spring*; Rachmaninoff, Shostakovich, Dvořák would complete the bill. In rehearsals, I found that I required all of my concentration to work with the orchestra and the conductor; not to follow my own lead, but to play with others. We both, the conductor and I, made music by flinging our arms about in the air, flailing like mad things.

On the first night of performance, we achieved what I thought to be perfection. We exceeded it on the second night, and on each night that followed. And on the final night, a moving picture camera captured fragments of the performance that showed it for what it was: glorious, rapturously received. On this, as on each night of our performance, the audience on their feet called *encore* and, after the orchestra had taken their bows, the conductor and I ours, after flowers had been presented, after we had all walked off stage and Trix had held me tightly in the wings, as the applause continued and the stamping grew, I walked back onto the stage – just me – into a single light trained on the aetherphone. The stamping, the applause, rose to a crescendo as I stood, facing the glow of the audience. I raised my arms, and the audience became silent. I nodded, lowered my arms to my side.

I stepped behind the aetherphone, felt it attune to the presence of my body. I played the Prelude from Bach's first suite for cello, me alone, music filling all the spaces of the theatre, up to the red and golden height of it, to the honeycomb ceiling, through all the spaces, the arches and columns, into the arc of the back of every carved nymph on every fluted column, right on up to the gods.

*

Uncle Valentine sent me telegrams of congratulations, and bursts of flowers filled the house in Mosman. For a time, even in those early years of the financial depression, my fame grew; I drew increasingly bigger crowds, appreciative audiences. I rode on a wave of fame, in my adopted city of Sydney and beyond, travelled the eastern seaboard performing my music. I recorded my favourite pieces for gramophone, and these were popular throughout Australia and abroad; there was talk of touring to Europe, to America. While the Professor remained my mentor, continually improving his aetherphone design, replacing the instrument I played when his design improved enough to warrant it, he was soon drawn to chase bigger markets. Trix, Madame Petrova and I waved him off at the wharf on the day he left for America, to settle in New York City. His machines sold well overseas; the music gained in popularity. Madame Petrova's influence on me faded, as she no longer played to accompany me in concert; I would still visit her, perhaps once a month, but to sit in her dark studio and drink vodka with her, rather than to play.

But there came a limit to my fame. Or rather, it trickled away as quickly as it had flooded in. There was work, there were dates planned; and then, suddenly, nothing. I still played every day – played to the room, played to the light, played into the air – but not to an audience that paid. And so there came a day when we sat at the kitchen table in Royalist Road, facing each other, I with a telegram in my hand, Trix with a letter in hers. My telegram confirmed the cancellation of my American tour, on which I would have played at Carnegie Hall – *Financial crisis makes tour unfeasible. Cancel all dates.* The letter Trix held in her hand offered her a position teaching art in the city of Dunedin, in the south of New Zealand, where she had been born, and from where she had escaped twenty years before.

It took us little more than a week to pack our belongings into tea-chests and trunks in preparation for travel. We emptied our rooms in the Mosman house, jammed years of living into wooden crates, until all that was left was a mattress on the floor in Trix's room where we slept for the weeks remaining until our departure. Not that we slept much; we partied through those last weeks in Sydney with the musicians, the artists, the patrons, the writers of our circle; we played all night at the Buzz Room and the bars, until there was no one left to say goodbye to, no one left awake.

It was in those wild weeks before we left Sydney that they opened the bridge to traffic, and the two halves of the city were truly joined. We were two of those million people, Trix and I, who lined the shores and bays and headlands of the city that day. We stood on the northern lip of the bridge, pushed and jostled by the crowd, and pushing and jostling ourselves, although all was good-natured, in anticipation and delight. A man near us blew a trumpet; another answered, more distant, and another, and another, away across the span of the bridge, as if trumpets pinned it in place along its length. Flags waved, and hats; people held flowers, and bottles of beer. There was a sharp report as of gunshot, then we all joined in the cheer that surged at us across the bridge, across the harbour, folding in wave upon wave of sound. Beatrix held my hand, kissed my cheek, and we stumbled then regained our footing as we walked, in the crowd, across the bridge to the golden city on the southern shore.

COTTESLOE
1991

Mo, and Caro and Jonno, tra-la

PLAYED BACK

A small padded envelope has arrived in the mail. I open it, and a cassette in a case slides out onto the table. I peer into the envelope, looking for a note, but there is only a small card tucked inside the cover of the cassette; one of Terence's business cards with a note scribbled on the back which may or may not read: *Enjoy! T*. The cassette is labelled, again in Terence's scratchy hand, an only slightly more legible *Transformer – Sampler*.

I've been staring at this tape for half the day. It's on the kitchen table, on top of its padded envelope, Terence's card with its jaunty note next to it. I've *worked around it*, you might say, all day. I'm nervous about listening to the tape, hearing myself played back, juxtaposed between the youngsters, hearing the crowd's response. Will it match my memory of it? Did I dream the whole damned thing?

It's dark now. I've eaten a light meal, drunk a glass of wine, eaten cheese with a crisp green pear; washed my meagre dishes.

I sit at the table, contemplate the damned tape.

'Well,' I say aloud. 'Well, then.'

I pick up the tape from the table, walk to the front room,

slot it into the empty tape deck and press play, turning my back on the machine and moving to sit in my lounge chair, my listening chair.

The clean hiss of the leader tape gives way to the roars and shouts and percussions of the crowd, sounding as big and loud as I remember – bigger and louder, if anything. There is the sound of instruments tuning, just briefly – distonic, discordant – then an electronic whine over and above it all kicks in, cranks up and overcomes all sound, screeching, reaching high and ramping to a bright white heavenly, unearthly, hellish scream of beauty. As it reaches its peak – the peak that I can hear with these old ears – the crowd noise is mixed down and I hear Terence's voice-over.

You are about to be a part of the experience that is Transformer. People – Prepare. To Be. Trans. Formed!

Beats fade up over the crowd noise, rise and peak. I crank the volume knob on my stereo so that the house shakes and shudders with the noise of it. This is glorious, glorious. I nestle into my chair, my feet on the ottoman, my knees curled slightly to the side. Terence – I presume it is Terence who has mixed this – has done an extraordinary job; piece flows into piece, song into song, the crowd noise is up in the mix just enough, just often enough, to catch the feeling of the live performance, of the size of the crowd. There's even somehow the essence in there of an outside performance; not that I can quite hear cicadas, nothing as obvious as that. But the sonic feel of it is there, remarkably, and listening to it I can tell that this is not a recording that could have been made inside a building; it is not limited by walls.

Side one finishes, and the tape clicks off. I sit for a minute or two, smiling, absorbing what I've heard, before I get out of my chair, turn the tape over, press play again. I will be on this side. Steroidalab, Lena Gaunt, then Gristmonger will play out the tape, as we played out the festival that night. I return to my chair. I listen, waiting to hear myself, not afraid any more, not caring; not when the rest of the music is this good, when the sound is this good, when the mix makes it this good.

I hear Terence's voice announce me, say my name, say words about me; I hear the crowd. I can feel the feel of the trousers I wore, the swish and glide of them as I walked on stage, like walking on air, carried on stage by the sound of the crowd.

I listen to myself play. The sound of me playing fills the room, as I sit, listening, playing nothing. How remarkable it is to listen to oneself; what a privilege. I look down at my hands on my lap; the fingers are flexing and twitching, moving to play the notes I hear. My shoulders are taut, not tense, but taut, ready, in the playing position. God, it felt good to play that show. And, in this recording that the angel Terence has sent unto me, I have the evidence that it *was* good; I sounded good. Piss-take be damned; there was no piss taken, no mistake made.

*

I celebrate my self-discovery in the usual way, even though it is, as they say, a school night. Nothing much for this old dog to learn though, tomorrow or any day. I revel in the familiarity of the preparation, the anticipation, the regimen; I toke in hard, then lean back in my chair and wallow in well-earned self-congratulation, my body flooding with warmth and light and well-being.

LENA (UNDERSTOOD)

The filmmaker will bring her camera crew again tomorrow. I say crew, but really it's just Mo, the woman called Caroline who operates the camera and tweaks the lights, and a very beautiful young man named Jonathan who operates the sound-recording gear. They call each other Caro, and Jonno, and Mo. My own given name is so long unused that I almost forget it; everyone who used it is long dead now. I hear it – Helena, Helena, Helena. An aspiration fronting the name I use, Lena – an aspiration, the sound of a breath fogging glasses to clean them; of a laugh contained in the throat.

The name I use – I choose – is missing that breath. Or it is understood, parenthesised like the subject in a parsed sentence: You (understood). Lena is Helena (understood).

But I am distracted; it must be the junk.

Mo (and Caro and Jonno, tra-la) will film me tomorrow. She brought them both to meet me yesterday – just briefly, to chat over coffee. They were all on their best behaviour, as if meeting the Queen. Caroline has been here before, with Mo, but tomorrow will be the first time the three of them – the four of us – will work together. It will be a sounding out, a metaphorical walking around each other, a sniffing of bottoms. Yes, were we dogs we would sniff each other's arse. Perhaps one of us would attempt to hump the other, establish herself as dominant. Perhaps one of us would roll over, submissive, on our back, pale belly exposed, paws pathetic.

But dogs we are not, we Bitches of Art, so we will do it human-style: smiling, tentative, eager to please, polite; yet each standing our ground, apart.

We film in the front room, the music room. They bring lights, to penetrate the dark, and a different camera, larger, noisier. I think I hear them calling it Harry.

'Not Harry; *Arri*,' Mo tells me. 'The camera, it's an Arriflex. Sixteen mill, that's the film size, sixteen millimetres. The Hi8 was just video. This is the real deal.'

It is busier with three of them, with noisy Arri, with more complex lights and microphones. I sit in the kitchen, apart from them, and let them get on with it. I can hear them even from here. They are noisier than the two women together were; instructions fly across the room, no longer in lowered voices.

The filmmaker comes to find me. She wants me to play my theremin for them, wants to film that. Why not? They move me around – a light touch on the arm, a hand directing me to move just a little – stage-managing me. Caro uses a Polaroid, spitting out tongues glossy with image. She plucks them from the camera and waves them in the air, peering at them, wrinkling her nose, showing them to Mo before tweaking the position of the light, the camera, the theremin, the old lady.

I set up the machine, and then I play for them. I start with some scales, some trills, improvise a little to check the sound. Then – without meaning to, although I feel my body as it does so – I straighten my spine, hold my head high, relax my shoulders, and start playing. Bach. The first cello suite, in G major. So beautiful. I forget they are there, lose myself in the music like the cliché that I am.

They film me in my chair, in the kitchen, everywhere. She doesn't interview me, today. Mo (with Jonno, and Caro, tra-la) mills about me all day, has me make coffee, stand in my kitchen – just so, with the light like that – then stand by my front door. *Static shots*, she calls them. *Flavour. Atmosphere.*

'You're good at being still,' the filmmaker tells me, lifting her head from the viewfinder of the camera.

I am the stillness at the centre of things, the focus of their attention, their reason for being here, and yet separate from them. I am their subject, and yet somehow not here. Lena (understood).

They are busy at the end of the day, carefully coiling leads, packing equipment. At a sign from the filmmaker, the three of them huddle together briefly, speaking quietly, nodding, making plans. Caro and Jonno make their goodbyes, then disappear to heft their kit to the car.

The filmmaker gathers up the remaining gear-bag and her big shoulder bag, balancing them to hang one from each shoulder. I walk her to the door. We make a time for our next session, a week away. She wants to work a little on the footage she has, she says, think about what's still needed.

'Give you a bit of breathing space.'

'Time to work on my improvised life?'

'Yeah,' she laughs. 'See you!'

Coffee cups and water glasses are scattered around the house, the day's detritus. I ferry the dirty dishes to the kitchen sink. I wash them, dry them, put them away, thinking on the day and its busy-ness, its activity punctuated by stretches of quiet. The filmmaker looked wan, today. Pale, behind the lights. At one stage she disappeared to the bathroom. She took her voluminous bag. She was some time. She came back – refreshed – but she wouldn't meet my eyes.

I wonder; I wonder: does she use? Wouldn't that be the damnedest thing.

DUNEDIN
1932–1937

Grey stone, and damp

TOMAHAWK ROAD

Sydney never had a cold like Dunedin's. Trix's position teaching at the School of Art took us to the small, dark southern city, all grey stone and grey clouds when we arrived that winter. Trix loved the low light, the very southernness of it. Of course, it was coming home for her; she'd been born in Dunedin, then a thriving place of industry and gold and frozen sheep; nearly half a century since, her parents long-dead, Trix came back for its art and learning. But for me, there was nothing but damp chill, huddled in layers of woollens that first winter, in the big, damp house in Tomahawk Road, out past South Dunedin, that we moved into during our first week there.

The outgoing teacher who Trix would replace at the school had offered her the lease on the house he and his wife and their tribe of children had lived in for six years. We took it, eager to settle somewhere, anywhere. He told us the neighbours wouldn't complain about rowdy parties; the house turned out to have a view across Dunedin's cemetery, to the wild empty ocean. We didn't mind; we could live freely there, the two of us in that solitary house, out of sight of the conservative eyes and minds of the good grey Presbyterian people of Dunedin. We moved our belongings into the house on a Friday morning while the wind off the ocean blew across the cemetery and howled like the waking dead. Two men and a truck deposited our trunks, cases and tea-chests on the south-facing verandah, where they chilled in the bitter wind until we were ready to move them inside. We walked in through the front door, down a narrow hallway. Doors opened off to each side into old-fashioned rooms, generously sized but with mean little Victorian windows, heavily draped against the weather. The darkness of the rooms was immense, tangible, solid. I flicked on the electric light switch, then opened the curtains in the first room we entered, to let in light – but the dim overhead bulb and the pale winter light through the window failed to penetrate the dark. We stepped backwards from the room, and closed the door on it. The hallway zigzagged, and we opened another door into a big kitchen that spanned the back of the house. The pale sun eked into it through north-facing, pale-curtained windows that let in the wind, too.

The previous tenants had left a linoleum-covered table and three wooden chairs in the kitchen. I pulled one of the chairs out and collapsed onto it. Trix put her hand on my shoulder, and bent down to kiss the top of my head.

'All right, doll?' she asked.

I nodded, smiled at her, patted her hand with my hand, and wondered how I might survive this chill southern place.

*

Trix slotted into life at the art school easily enough. After the move from Sydney, she was re-energised, enthusiastic about everything – the students, the other teachers, the facilities, the generosity of the La Trobe Scheme that had brought her there, the whole idea of learning and teaching. There weren't a lot of students, but at least a few of them *had something*, she said, some spark. She relished the freedom the position gave her to paint, to work, even after being warned, within her first week at the school, that she would have to rein in her more modern ideas in front of the classes she taught. Dunedin was, she was reminded, an upright and deeply conservative city. Even that failed to dim her delight.

'Time for the quiet life after Sydney, eh, doll.'

She taught classical skills at the art school, perspective, figure drawing, landscape, portraiture; made contained sketches and demure water colours with the students. She saved her own art for home, working long into every evening in the room that soon came to smell like Trix, permeated with turpentine and cigarette smoke.

She'd leave for the school early each morning, wearing a voluminous separated skirt – *Trousers, Mrs Carmichael, are as entirely inappropriate for a female teacher as for our female students*, she had been warned on her first day teaching – clipped in at the ankles, safe from spokes and chain. Satchel over her shoulder, she cycled her big black bicycle into the Octagon then walked it up the steepness of Stuart Street to King Edward Technical College, where the art school was housed.

I'd still be in bed when she left, curled around a no-longer-hot water bottle. My first weeks were taken up with unpacking our things, making a home in the house on Tomahawk Road, but I soon completed this task. I found myself in the role of stay-at-home wife, a role to which I was unaccustomed.

But eventually, like Trix, I too settled into a routine. Mine revolved around the house, the landscape surrounding the house; a private routine, a private life, to balance Trix's public one. When the rain held off, I'd walk to the shops in South Dunedin. The air was cold, even on sunny days in the winter. People walked with heads down, eyes following the movement of their feet, staring at their toes. I bought meat from the butcher, vegetables from the greengrocer, and cooked great warming stews for us to eat by the fire. I bought beer from the pub in South Dunedin; on occasion they had wine, and sometimes it was drinkable.

I walked often through the cemetery, the wind whistling in my ears, walked between gravestones and plinths and obelisks and angels, and on to the beach. It was too wild for swimming, cold and wave-beaten. I walked, instead, listened to the water pounding on the beach, the ocean pounding at the margin of the land. I hauled great leathery seaweed, heavy as seal hides, up and into the garden, to form sculptures that would soften in the moist air, then stiffen on days when the air was dry.

And so we settled into quiet domesticity in Dunedin, a mild suburban couple after our heady, busy bohemian time in Sydney. On the rare occasions when anyone enquired as to our domestic situation, we felt it best to leave questions vaguely answered or, better still, unanswered, until it somehow came to be understood that we were relatives, the widow Mrs Carmichael, her niece Miss Gaunt, an orphan. The narrow grey city seemed able to tolerate this much.

My musical talents were not called upon to grace the stages of the theatres of Dunedin – my former fame seemed barely to have spread to this corner of the world. There seemed nowhere in this city's social life to match the modern music culture that Sydney had offered, although for Trix, the small art scene seemed to provide some stimulus, at least. Each of us felt a gap where our social circle had existed. We missed being able to be ourselves, together among friends. Trix had not been teaching for a month before she invited a small, carefully selected group of students and fellow teachers home to Tomahawk Road for the first of what became regular nights of eating, drinking, smoking and talking. It didn't take long before I managed to introduce a heavy dose of music to the evenings. Someone had a brainwave, and the group gained a name: the Brush and Blow Group – Brush for Trix and the others, and Blow for Tom, one of the students, who played the trumpet while I played piano. The Brush and Blow-ers – or Beebees, as we soon called ourselves – had as its core me, Trix, and another teacher from the school, Armin de Groot; and the students Armin and Trix gathered closest around them, Tom, Alastair, Mardi, Celia. Others came and went, but that core remained. We all thought of ourselves as bohemian, as modern, as artists apart from the workaday world around us, and free from its morals and strictures, its curtain-twitching and mouth-pursing.

We'd sit in the kitchen, the narrow room stretching across the back of the house. The wood-fired stove at one end cooked a stew, warmed the room, heated water. A piano stood against one wall. At night we'd pull heavy curtains across the windows. In winter I pinned old wool blankets up on top of the curtains for extra warmth. In the daytime, the blankets and curtains pulled aside, sunlight would steam the windows, cross the room, heat it to a pale yellow warmth. But at night, when the Beebees met there, we were wrapped in wool and warm and dark, fugged with beer and smoke, noisy enough to wake the dead across the road and invite them in for a beer.

I was wife, and I was lover. Trix and I huddled together in the draughty house, heavy blankets shielding the windows of our bedroom, eiderdowns piled upon us so that we could hardly move under their weight. But we moved – we moved! – our bodies slick and curving, slipping upon and into one another, until we erupted from the eiderdowns, pushed them to the floor, melting hot, gasping, musky with our cunning.

We survived in the curtain-twitching south only by being careful, so careful. As aunt and niece, we were almost respectable; as respectable, at least, as a woman artist and her household could ever be. And every night, as we held each other, curved into one another, we cared not what the world thought of us. We were entire, within ourselves. Perfect.

*

Trix's painting changed, in the low light of Dunedin. In Sydney, she had focussed outwards, on landscapes, on views through a window; or on still life studies: branches of lemons plucked from a tree, or oranges tumbled from a string bag arranged on a table, rendered strange by her kaleidoscope eye and its breaking of light and shape. Only rarely had she painted portraits – of Delphine Britten, of me. In Dunedin, although she said she loved the way the light fell on the land, she felt that she couldn't paint it, and she shifted her art from landscape to portrait. But the light and the landscape would sneak into the portraits, their backgrounds the St Clair waterfront, the harbour, the hills of the Otago Peninsula. She painted me, had me pose in the kitchen by the piano; I wore a blue shirt, but in the painting Trix made it green, a rich, deep, lustrous green, like satin. Instead of the kitchen and the blankets and curtains, she painted gravestones behind me, the cemetery across the road; a horizon line of gravestones in front of the seascape in the far distance.

Trix painted me a handful of times in those years at Tomahawk Road, but her self-portraits from that time are almost beyond number. In the end, they were piled against the walls in the room she used as her studio; as she finished one, she would stack it and move on, turn almost directly to the next, and the next. I can see her, the mirror she used propped by her side, her eyes staring into it, flickering back to the canvas – that constant motion, eyes moving from mirror to canvas, but her body retaining its position. Sometimes she painted the clothes she wore into the portraits; at other times, she invented costumes for herself, changed her hair, painted herself earrings she did not own, a flower behind her ear or in her hair. The landscapes that formed the background to these paintings became more fantastic as time passed. Her colour palette changed with each painting, expanded beyond what she saw in front of her in the house in Tomahawk Road, the cemetery and beach at our doorstep, or the painting studios at the school in Stuart Street; even the colourscapes we saw when Armin or Mardi drove us out to the plains to the south or to the hills of Otago couldn't provide her with all the colours she put into her paintings in those years. Trix came to live and paint from behind her eyes, from inside her mind.

ARPEGGIO

I don't know if Trix felt the lump before I noticed it. She must have: by that time it was the size and hardness of a pebble from the beach, rounded by the passage of time, by wearing against fluid; or of a small egg. It sat, her pebble, her egg, under the soft skin in her right armpit. Once I knew it was there, when I saw her lift her arm – or if she rested it behind her head, on the bed, against cold sheets – I could see it, hard under the surface as she held her arm aloft.

There was nothing that could be done, the doctor told her when I made her go to see him. She'd cycled in to town, her satchel over her shoulder. I waited in the kitchen for her, drinking tea. I heard her bicycle clank against the gate at the front of the house, heard her footfall on the steps, on the verandah; heard the door open, heard her walk down the hall; all these sounds came to me as if through liquid, under water, slowed down and other-worldly. Trix sat down at the kitchen table opposite me, her satchel draped over her shoulder. She sat very still. I went to the stove to fill the teapot, to make fresh tea. When I poured it for her, she put her hand over mine on the table.

She started a painting that day, when she returned from

town, tired, grey-faced, started it in a frenzy that day but came to finish it, that week, with a strange sort of calm. She faced out from the canvas at a quarter turn, so that you could see the outline of her right breast, clearly, against a background of pebbles, grey stone, damp, on a beachscape littered with grotesque sculpted seaweed, bull kelp blades like seal corpses, kelp stipes white like skeletons. She stared out of the painting with clear, blue eyes, her mouth a thin strip of lips pale as death, but smiling, turned up, just like that, at the corner. In her left hand, cupped gently between her breasts, there was an egg, mottled grey on ivory. Reflected, barely there on the top surface of the egg, you could see her eyes. She wore a pale blue smock, a simple shift, its texture quite clearly that of linen, the nubs of it silky, soapy on the surface of the canvas. The sky in the painting was a calm blue-grey and in it were two birds – one to the left, one to the right – with their wing tips almost touching in the middle of the painting, in the sky above Trix's head, almost forming a circle surrounding her. In the open palm of her right hand, extending into the foreground of the painting, defying perspective, she held a sea star.

I could not bear to look at the painting then, when she seemed well. Later, as she became sicker, and sicker, I could look within it and, seeing her calm, feel some comfort.

Trix was able to finish the teaching year, though her health slowly ebbed, leaving her thin, tired, and grey. In June we moved to a furnished flat in Tennyson Street, to be nearer to the school, to save Trix the bicycle ride each morning and evening. From Tennyson Street, she could walk up the hill to Stuart Street in the mornings, when her energy was at its peak for the day. In the afternoons, I would walk up and wait for her by the steps of the school; we'd walk home down the hill together, quiet, Trix leaning into me, her thin body against my side. She'd drink tea, eat a small meal I put in front of her, then she'd fall into bed and sleep a hot, restless, fitful sleep. We'd kept separate rooms as studios in the big house in Tomahawk Road, but – out on the coast, away from people – had shared a bedroom. In Tennyson Street, in town, we kept separate bedrooms once again, as we had years before in the house in Mosman. I cleaned the house, cooked for us, washed her sweat from bed sheets.

On occasion – to escape the sense of enclosure, of tightness I felt in town – I'd ride Trix's black bicycle down to the beach at St Clair and along the road skirting the coast, prop the bicycle by the gate of the house in Tomahawk Road, and walk down to the tide line, picking over the pebbles and seaweed strewn there. I'd walk back up from the beach, back between the salt grey stones of the cemetery and up through the gate, letting myself into the house, walking through its quiet rooms, filling them with the sounds of my footsteps, my breathing. I'd draw open the curtains in the kitchen; lift the lid of the piano and play an arpeggio, play scales, play anything that came to me. Often, I slammed my hands into the keyboard, up and down the length of it making noise, uncontrolled outbursts of noise, no musicality, no organisation to it, just pure, horrible, terrible noise; mimicking the thunder of the waves on the beach but without rhythm, without tone, just pure noise.

I raised my voice with the sound of the piano — hammers against wires — raised my voice to hammer against the air, in a wail, a scream, a cry; I screamed until my throat was raw. I'd sit then at the piano, dry-faced, empty.

Trix's studio in Tomahawk Road was filled with her paintings, her sketches and notebooks, an easel. Paintings were propped up, most of them facing the walls, covered with dustsheets; dotted around the room, Trix stared at me from other paintings left face-out. The smell of her was everywhere: turpentine, smoke. In my room was my theremin. There was no electricity to power it. I stood by it, stood in the position in which I would play it, held my hands as if to play, but it was dead, silent. My hands dropped to my side; I closed the doors to the rooms as I left, closed the front door behind me, locked it with the key I wore on a plait of red wool around my neck, and rode back to town.

FROCKS AND FURS

The graduate show was her last hurrah. We chose our outfits with care, dressed more extravagantly than we had in years, as if to acknowledge the significance of the night.

I drew a bath for Trix, warm, full, and knelt beside her while she washed. I sponged water down her back with a flannel; she shivered, although the water was warm. As she stepped from the bath I wrapped a towel around her shoulders, wrapped her in my arms, her back against my front. Her clothes were laid out on the bed, and I helped her into them, straightened her jacket, buttoned the silver buttons, buckled her shoes; although she could still do all of these things for herself, it was somehow a service I could perform for her, a gift, that night. I dressed quickly, gathered the train of my dress in my hands and, from the mantelpiece, took the ampoules of morphine the doctor had left that day. Trix sat at the kitchen table. I injected her as the doctor had shown me, watched relief suffuse her face.

When Armin arrived to pick us up, Trix and I sat, quiet, her hand on mine, at the kitchen table.

All our friends gathered around us that night, the whole group. But Trix tired early; I could see the labour behind her eyes as the night progressed, as the morphine wore off. Armin drove us back to the flat in Tennyson Street. We slept together – just slept, just held one another – that night for the last time, my arms around her thin body feeling her restlessness, her fitful sleep, and the deep, strong heat of the sickness all through her.

ART SHOW GALA
A LA MODE

Otago Daily Times, 13ᵗʰ November, 1936.

Teachers and students from the School of Art joined together for a sparkling ceremony in the Town Hall on Saturday last to mark the opening night of the graduate art show. Others more learned in the artistic world could comment knowledgeably on the art works on show, but your reporter was delighted by the array of jaunty outfits on display by our brightest Bohemians. The acclaimed artist and teacher at the school, formerly of Sydney, Mrs Beatrix Carmichael, wore a charcoal coloured skirt and matching jacket trimmed with silver buttons, a small black velvet toque and silver fox furs. Mrs Carmichael's niece, the musician Miss Lena Gaunt of South Dunedin, also formerly of Sydney, was elegant in a beautiful frock of pale blue ring-velvet, with fish tail train lined with silver. She carried a muff of rucked velvet to match her dress. Miss Mardi Devenish, a student at the school, wore a frock of flowered georgette in colours of white, geranium red and touches of black and pale blue, a necklet of red camellias, a hat of velvet, with shoes en suite. Miss Celia Beilby, also a student, wore a gown of midnight-blue, trimmed with white satin and large white buttons, and a small white hat with blue feather.

SELF-PORTRAIT, WAVING
GOODBYE

That summer, after the end of term, we moved back to the house in Tomahawk Road. Trix stopped painting me, stopped painting anything or anyone but herself. She painted many self-portraits during her illness, charting the course her body took, the effect of the disease on her body, her face. But she didn't paint what she saw in the mirror. Her image in the mirror was a reference, like gridlines on a page, like the converging lines of perspective drawn as guides to the eye. Trix didn't paint to the image; she painted away from it. She painted herself from the inside out.

She painted again with a frenzy and fervour, in the first weeks back at Tomahawk Road, needing little morphine and less food, surviving on tea and cigarettes and the smell of paint. I walked to the shops for food, even walked again on the beach, but never far away, and never for too long.

Armin visited most days; Mardi, Tom, the others came often. They came in the daytime, brought sandwiches and fruit, cigarettes and gossip, and we'd sit in the kitchen, talk, eat, drink tea. Trix would curl on the daybed pulled close to the stove, pillows behind her, red wool rug over her feet. Ash from her cigarettes would drop to the floor, gritting the rug in front of her. When she'd had morphine, her head would nod as we talked, her cigarette held aloft, held lightly between her fingers, dropping lower, burning lower; I'd watch it, carefully take it from her to stop it from burning the mattress, the rug, her clothes. Armin and the others didn't stay long, when they visited. They'd kiss Trix's cheek as they left, bend over her as she reclined on the daybed. I'd walk them to the door and it was me they embraced, tight, hard, as if I was dying; as if it was me they might not see again the next month, or week, or the next day.

She stopped painting, just stopped. She moved herself to the daybed, to the red rug, the pillows, the ashtray, although the cigarette in her hand remained unlit, there for comfort.

I went to the studio where she'd been sleeping, to strip the sheets from the bed, to wash them, wash away the sweet sick smell of her. There was a canvas on her easel. She'd told me it was finished, but there were great patches of white on it, the prepped canvas underneath showing through, lacking paint. Where there was paint, the colours were muted, grey. The usual fracturing of light that always fragmented her works was missing from this. Her face shone with pallor from the centre of the canvas, her brow wet with sweat. Her right hand was raised, the painting of it not complete, half of it in outline still.

BENEDICTION

People are quiet in the house of the dying. Armin and the others would let themselves in, walk softly, reverently to the kitchen, kiss me, take my place by the daybed, rest their hand on Trix's. We'd all speak in lowered voices, like the genteel murmur of a cocktail party. We didn't play the piano; no one sang. We ate sandwiches; no one cooked any more.

It was quick, in the end, although it didn't feel quick from within; time seemed to drip by, moment by moment, like honey, or treacle; like paint. The doctor came, and nurses. Morphine stayed the pain, for a while; then it could no longer. I would sit with her, sit by the stove, by the daybed. I would sit, hold her hand in mine.

When I slept, I slept in her studio, surrounded by her paintings. I made the bed with clean fresh sheets, thin wrinkled waves forming a front as I smoothed the white cotton across the surface of the bed with the palm of my hand. From the canvas on the easel Trix's hand was raised in greeting, or farewell.

*

On the last day, sun shone through the window in the kitchen. I prepared the morphine, as the doctor had, as the nurses had. I held my breath; I exhaled. As her breath eased, I slid beside her on the daybed, lay the length of her, our bodies still.

She was buried, of course, in the cemetery by the sea. We stood there in the wind, the salt on our lips, all of us – you could have seen us from the window of the kitchen of the house in Tomahawk Road if you'd leaned far enough out. We walked back from the graveside to the house, arms linked, eyes gleaming, ready to make noise again. We drank beer, then the wine in flagons that Armin had brought. There was bread and cheese, sausage rich with garlic, a plate of curried eggs; there were oranges, and grapes, and apples. A bowl of walnuts was in the centre of the table. Someone had made a fruit cake. Tom played the piano, and we sang. Someone brought more beer, perhaps sherry. I was sick in the flax bush by the verandah, in a great, hot, wine-dark wave.

A cool cloth bathed my forehead; a glass of water pressed against my lips. The bathroom was dark; no, the bedroom was dark. The sheets were white, smooth, cool against me. Trix, her hand raised in benediction, was by my side.

I slid my arms around the smooth, broad back above me, over me, felt prickling lips on my lips, my forehead, my breasts. I felt hard pain, where I had not felt pain before. It felt like the pain of loss. I cried out, sang out, loud, still alive.

BONFIRE

With Trix's death came a strange, in-between time, the house busy with solicitous visitors, but hushed, reverent. I missed the noise, from the time before sickness. But at least there were people. Mardi and Celia came often, would bring me food, stay for tea, then leave me, kissing me gently on each cheek, rubbing my back, smiling sadly. Armin and Tom came one day with boxes of Trix's papers and paints, cleared from her desk, her studio at the school. They brought two bottles of beer, and we drank them sitting at the kitchen table, as we always had. As they left, Tom hugged me, the empty bottles in his hands clinking together behind me. While Tom took the bottles to the car, Armin took my hand, the two of us framed in the doorway. He pressed my hand between his hands; I felt his beard brush first one cheek, then the other, felt his stubble then his lips on my forehead. He patted my hand, then dropped it, and walked to the car. I walked to the edge of the verandah, and waved to them both as they drove away.

I had nothing to do, no job to attend to, just myself to feed. I shopped for groceries, just enough for one, ever-thankful for the money in the bank that funded it. I walked on the beach each day. I tended the garden. I slept in Trix's studio, her paintings around me. I stopped expecting to hear her voice, smell her cigarettes, every time I walked through the front door. I realised that a week had passed, then a month, then two.

I lay on the bed in her studio, my hands on my belly, thinking of her hands, thinking of other hands. I had not bled since Trix was alive.

My uncle had sent me a telegram the week Trix died: *Darling Lena so so sorry for loss. Love always Val*. A letter had arrived a week or so later. *My darling girl*, he wrote, *you must know you always have a home here if you want it, in this house that is too big for me alone*. I had not known what to reply, had not been able to decide what to do, where to go.

I walked to the cemetery, stood by the mounded earth where Trix lay, no longer Trix. I crossed my arms, tucked my hands in hard. I bowed my head against the cold wind, closed my eyes against its stinging. This cold, conventional city was no place for the artist's unmarried, orphaned niece to have a baby.

That afternoon I walked to the post office and sent a telegram. *Dear Uncle. Yes please. Coming home. Will send details. Love Lena*.

In the weeks before I left Dunedin, although my belly had not yet started to swell, I could feel the subtle changes in my body, and knew that Trix would have felt them too.

I noticed changes in my mind too; an inner anaesthetic calmed me, soothed my days and nights, as a drug might. I hummed to the shape forming inside me, hummed too to Trix, sent vibrations into the air, the aether, to connect us. I spent less time in the house, with its furniture and quiet, and more on the beach, walking into the keening wind. On the beach I felt alive, felt Trix close, felt the three of us together.

One warm day, I watched from the kitchen window as sudden spring rain pelted in from across the ocean. I ran from the house, ran down to the beach, my dress soaking and dragging at my legs, the smell of me rising from the wet wool of my cardigan. There was no one but me on the beach. I stripped off my cardigan, my dress, threw my arms wide, my face to the sky, let the rain soak me, let myself cry to the sea and sky. This was how Trix stayed with me; I did not need corporeal reminders. And so, as I prepared to leave Dunedin, I determined to rid myself of our possessions.

Furniture Trix and I had accumulated, softened with the shapes of our bodies; tools we had used to dig and tend our cold, salted garden; these I left in the Tomahawk Road house for whoever would live there next. All of Trix's clothes, her notebooks, her paintings – I could not bear to keep these; I could not. I burned the clothes in a great bonfire in the back yard at Tomahawk Road, on the night before I handed over the keys to the land agent. Her notebooks, her paintings, I handed over to the care of Armin and Mardi and Tom. I took with me few things: one trunk of clothes, another of linen and sheet music, my fat scrapbook tucked inside; and other than these, my theremin, packed in its crate, with just two small paintings – one of me, one of Trix – nestled beside it, turned inwards, facing one another.

All of the stories of my life have begun and ended with the ocean. And so I left Dunedin, boarding yet another ship. While I considered myself an old hand at travel by sea, the voyage was my daughter's first. It was to be her only voyage by ship. She was doubly buoyed on that journey, by waters exterior and interior – my daughter travelled from Dunedin to Fremantle within me, *in utero*, not yet her and yet her, already kicking and rolling with the waters' movement.

COTTESLOE
1991

Weather turning

KIA ORA

The weather is turning; you can feel it in the mornings most, see the difference in the light, smell the cooler weather. It's still beautiful to swim; there's not yet the bite of winter, the cold touching your skin, getting under it. Even so, this morning the other bathers at the beach are fewer in number. As I hold the towel around me after my swim, absorbing the salty wet, I watch an old woman hobble to the water's edge, leaning on a stick. She pushes the stick down into the wet sand just up from the water, and gently sashays into the ocean. She bobs, her head in a rubber bathing cap studded with floppy rubber flowers; bobs on the waves, not swimming, just being there. She bobs back and forth on the water, bisected in my sightline by the upright of her walking stick in the sand. I turn away from her, stuff my towel into my bag, pull my cotton shirt over me, slip my feet into sandals and head up the sand, off the beach, to home.

Mo is coming again tomorrow. Not with Jonno and Caro. She just wants to *kaw-reh-raw*, she says. I beg your pardon, I say. Talk, she says, *kōrero*. She is using strange words, today, words I haven't heard her use before, as if she has just had a language lesson and wants to show off. They are like ripe fruit, round and heavy off her tongue. *Kia ora. Kōrero. Kai.* They are not familiar to me, these words; I have to ask her their meaning. She touches the bone pendant at her throat when she tells me. Hello or thank you or agreement. Talk. Food.

Kia ora, I tell her.

She brings only her audio recorder, as she did for our early sessions together. She sets it up on the kitchen table, fussing with the business of it, placing the machine and the microphone, adjusting their positions, carefully uncoiling leads, making connections. I busy myself with the coffeepot, my back turned to her as I face the stove. We both work in silence, saving our words for the machine.

I hear her exhale – a deep whoosh of breath – and mutter *fuck* under her breath.

'I've forgotten the power lead. Shit. I'm sorry. Look – I don't like to rely on battery to run it. *Shit.* Do you mind – shall we just forget it for today? I can't believe this.' She is flustered, not herself.

'No matter. I don't mind.'

'Thanks. I'm so sorry, I don't like to mess you around. I guess I'll pack up.'

'And we shall have coffee, at least.'

She starts unplugging and recoiling leads, packing the gear back into the plastic box she brought it in. I finish making the coffee, and turn to serve it. As I hand hers to her she – both hands busy – gestures with her eyes, her head, to the table, where I place both cups. She lifts the last lead, finishes coiling it, and bends over to put it in the gear bag on the floor by her feet. She straightens up, holding the lead, and staggers a little, then steadies herself by placing her hand on the table.

'Are you all right?' I reach out my hand towards her, but don't quite touch her. 'You look pale. Are you not well?'

'Sort of. I'm pregnant.'

'Oh.' I understand now the cause of her pallor, the bathroom hijinks. Not a user after all. 'Well, congratulations.'

Still standing, she puffs out breath – *pfou* – and her shoulders relax. 'Thanks.'

'But you should sit. You look dreadful. I'm sorry – tired, I should say.'

'I'm okay. It comes and goes. It's getting better.' She sits, the audio lead still coiled in her hands, resting in her lap. 'I'm past that first trimester thing.'

'Are you – I'm sorry, I don't mean to pry, but I'm a little surprised. Was it planned?'

'God, no! I mean, that sounds dreadful, or irresponsible. It was…' There's the puff of breath again, *pfou*, and she lifts both hands, palms upward, in a gesture of resignation, or acceptance. 'It was completely unplanned. The product of a reckless New Year's Eve fling, and – ah – contraceptive failure, if you must know.' She looks at me over her glasses, with something approaching a sly smile. 'Classic, really. An ecky at New Year's and I'm anyone's. I should know better, at my age.'

'Anarchy? At New Year's?'

'An ecky. Sorry, I thought you'd…' She shakes her head. 'Never mind. Ecky. Ecstasy. Kind of a love drug. A party drug. I hardly ever – ah well, that'll teach me, eh.'

She bends down – is it to avoid eye contact? I can't tell – and places the lead in her hands into the plastic box at her feet. She wraps both hands around the coffee cup and sips from it, holding the cup close to her mouth even when she has finished drinking. Her face is hard to read.

'What will you do?'

'Do you mean am I keeping it? Having it?'

'Yes, I suppose that's what I mean. Are you?'

'Well, yes. I didn't really think about not keeping it. Once I was pregnant, I realised I wanted it. You know, I'm forty. Now or never.' She shrugs her shoulders.

'But it's hard, you know. You should think carefully, if it's not too late to do something about it. A child; it slows a woman down. Anchors her. Perhaps artists shouldn't have children.' I lift my chin as I say it, as if to challenge her to disagree.

'But – do you really think that's true? Plenty of men who are filmmakers have children. I dunno. Francis Ford Coppola. It hasn't stopped him. Why should it be any different for a woman?'

'Well, put simply, because it *is* different. Any male artist who has a child also has a wife, or a woman playing that role. If you had a *wife* to look after it, *then* it wouldn't be different. You know that, if you think past the rhetoric. It is simply different. The biology of it. The sense of connection. I have – seen it happen. It can suck the creativity from a woman, if she's not careful. Suck her time and her energy, so that she has nothing left for art, for music.' I sip my coffee before uttering my final curse, only half-believing it. 'Your art will suffer if you do this.'

'I've heard the arguments before. I just – I've always been able to do whatever I've decided to do. I don't think having a child will fundamentally change that. There has to be a way to do it.'

I sigh, shake my head. 'Is there a father to have some say in the process?'

'Of course. I just – we're not – he's not in a position to be part of a couple.'

'Ah, so he's married.'

'No, no, not that. He's – he's not father material. It was just a thing, a fling, sex, not a relationship. He's a nice guy. Young. Too young.' She smiles, shrugs.

'He knows?'

'About this?' She touches her belly. 'Nah. I haven't told him. I don't think – I don't think I'm going to tell him. He'll notice soon enough. But I'm going to do it. On my own.'

I clap my hands, raise them together, clasped in a salute. 'Excellent! That's precisely the way. If you're set on doing this mad thing, do it by yourself. Make your own decisions. Don't rely on anyone staying in your life, being there to take things over. Pay someone to look after it for you. Pay a nanny, that's my advice. Then when they leave, you can find someone else to pay. It's the best way. People don't stay.' I look past her, out the window. Then I shrug, drain my coffee, stand up, pull myself up straight. 'When will I see you next?'

She gathers the last of her things, swipes them into her bag. 'Can we go again tomorrow? Caro and Jonno are keen. Would that be all right?'

'I have no other commitments. Tomorrow is fine. Let's start earlier. Eight o'clock. I like the mornings. It may not suit you and the others, of course. I know the young tend to rise later. And perhaps mornings are difficult for you, with this…'

I gesture with my hand towards her belly.

'No no, it's fine. This isn't going to change the film. Tomorrow. Eight o'clock. Thanks for today. I'm sorry about the lead. And everything.'

I see her to the door, wave her away as usual. Her confiding in me – my response to her – has not changed her view of me. I have responded to her news in the odd, embittered fashion of an old, childless woman. I have played my childless part.

THE HEART OF THE MATTER

And so she comes back, and she keeps asking me questions, endless bloody questions. Why did I agree to this? I cannot bear to think back on my life, now. Sometimes I make things up, when I don't want to answer her. Spin stories. And yet, somehow, she manages to hit to the heart of the matter, seeing things through the cool glass eye of her camera.

'What I'd really like to know is what's kept you coming back here, of all places. I mean, just before the war; why here, after you left Dunedin? After the war you left again; then, all those years later, you came back. You settled here – left and settled – time and again. What is it about this place; what's sent you away, but always brought you back?'

The grey-green eyes of the filmmaker look at me from behind the solar flare of the lights; I can't see them but I know they're there. Oh Mo, what can I tell you about the losses that have shaped the paths of my life, the forces that have pulled me from here so many times, and yet drawn me back? Is now the time to tell? Am I old enough not to care?

I sip my wine. A drop of condensation falls into my lap, spreads wetly; I feel it, cool against my leg.

'There is an extent to which it is just easier to return to one's homeland. If I can call on a musical analogy, maybe it's like the motif of an orchestral piece – you come back to it; it flows through the music, anchors it, no matter how far the music wanders from it. It comes back to that motif. It centres around it. Its heart is there. I guess this place is somehow at my centre. It's where I refer to – it's my reference point. My life has been lived relative to this place. And so, while I've flung myself far away from it many times, I return to it as if I'm on elastic. God, I'm mixing my metaphors, aren't I?' I sip again. I've responded to her questions – done my duty – but really, I've told her nothing.

The camera continues to roll, the light to shine, the condensation to form on the side of my wine glass and trickle down onto the coaster at the glass's base. I breathe in, breathe out, consciously, calming. I hear the house shift and creak as it heats in the warmth of the sun.

Perhaps I will get away with it, this time.

I see her to the door, nearly-empty glass in my hand. Closing the door behind her, I walk through to my bedroom, draining the last of the wine as I walk. I place the empty glass on the dressing table. Condensation wicks around under the base of the glass. A ring will form, will mark the wood. Well. So it shall.

I open the door to my wardrobe, and part the clothes that hang lowest, the long dresses, skirts, silky trousers, their wire and wooden hangers screeching on the rail as I push them aside. I kneel down – slowly, as I must, with age. At the bottom of the wardrobe, long left untouched, is my box of scrapbooks, of cuttings and clippings and keepings. I lean forward to lift it out. As I bring it close to my chest, I smell old books, papers, and dust. There is a faint, soft smell, too, like face powder, or flowers in another room. I stand – slowly, again – turn, and place the box on my bed. This is the story, in this box, the public story that Mo – or anyone – might find if she looks hard enough, through newspaper microfiche and musty library archives. Does it answer the questions she's asked me, though?

Behind where the box was, in the shadows at the back of the wardrobe, I see the dark curves of my old typewriter and, underneath it, another box, smaller than the one on the bed. I push the metal hooks of the hangers, and my clothes fall softly, densely back into place, curtaining the typewriter and the box. I close the wardrobe door on them, for the moment.

COTTESLOE
1937–1944

Grace note

A PLAIN GOLD RING

Uncle Valentine met me as we disembarked in Fremantle. The voyage had put in at Melbourne and Adelaide en route from Dunedin, but we had not had the opportunity to go ashore at any of these ports. I was tired of the roll of the ocean, ready for land.

Although we'd exchanged many letters and telegrams, I had not seen my uncle for a decade, since he'd delivered me to the port in Singapore. I watched him part the Fremantle crowd with his portly walk – he was, having kept his head above water during those financially depressed years, well-off and well-fed. He took me by the shoulders, locked his eyes with mine, then grasped me to him in a bearhug, patting his hands on my back until he released me from the embrace.

'My girl, so good to see you. You are all grown up.'

'As are you, Uncle.' My arms had not reached around him when we'd embraced.

'Wicked girl.' He linked his arm through mine, and started walking me back through the thronging crowd on the wharf in the direction from which he'd appeared. 'Come on, I have a car, let's get you home and wrapped around a drink. I've directed the shipping office to deliver your trunks, we need do nothing else about them. You're home now. Uncle Val will look after you, my love.'

Uncle Valentine drove like a demon, both hands clutched tight around the steering wheel. We opened the windows of the heavy black car and the warm wind blew through our hair (or mine, anyway – Uncle's had thinned to nothing, a shiny globe exposed when he removed his hat and placed it on the back seat of the car). We drove along the coast from Fremantle, north along the railway line. I stuck my head out of the open window, like a dog in a farm truck. The wind blew my hair across my face. I could smell the ocean, even as I only glimpsed it behind the sand dunes and buildings that now spread up the coast. I felt light for the first time in an age, for the first time since Trix had gone. I pressed a hand to my belly, my Grace, whispered, *We're home.*

Uncle Valentine – *Call me Val, darling, no need for the uncle*, he said as he handed me a glass of whisky no more than a moment after we walked through his front door – still lived in his big, comfortable house in the street that ran down straight as a die to the sea. We stood facing each other, glasses in hand, in his dark, curtained, familiar front room.

'To your return, my dear.'

'To being back.'

We clinked our glasses together.

'And to your dear Beatrix.'

He put his big arms around me, then released me, and

tossed the contents of his glass down his throat. I sipped mine – I had not had a taste for alcohol since Grace had been with me – and raised the glass towards him.

'To Trix.'

'Sit my dear, sit! You must be fagged. Sit and tell me something lovely about your journey. Or was it all tedious?'

He waved his hand at the soft chairs and lounges arranged in the room. I sank into cushions, grateful that they didn't sway and rock with the sea under them. Uncle Valentine pushed a velvet-covered ottoman towards me with his foot.

'Feet up old thing. Another drink?'

I shook my head, holding my glass of barely touched whisky up towards him. He poured himself another glass at the sideboard, then sank into the cushions opposite me, and we fell back into relaxed conversation, melted the years away. I'd always been comfortable with Uncle Valentine. Being with him did feel like being home. I felt justified in my compulsion to return to this place of my youth – not quite home, and yet more home than any other I could claim.

He waved his whisky glass in the direction of the gramophone dominating the room.

'Got all your recordings, my girl. Very proud, you know. Tell everyone I'm solely responsible for your musical education. And your various talents.' He winked at me, swirled the whisky in his glass and downed it in a big swallow. 'But you stopped playing, eh? Done with it?'

'For the moment,' I told him. I took a tiny sip of whisky, smiled at my uncle, looked around the room for a topic of conversation, anything to change focus. There was a small brass vessel on the mantelpiece, an odd little pot, almost like a teapot. I stood, walked to the mantel, lifted the pot. The lid was on a hinge. Within it was another, smaller container, a shallow bowl that fitted within the outer vessel neatly, snugly. A faint smell, smoky, sweet, arose from the open pot. When I closed the lid, there was a pleasing *ting*, a clear, bell-like note.

'Ah, memories of days in Malacca, the eastern sojourn, misspent youth, eh?' He wiggled his eyebrows, as he used to when I was a child. I laughed, shook my head. 'It's for smoking opium, darling. Lovely filigree work on the lid and the base. They're collectors' pieces now. Got it on my last trip up there. When your father...' He paused, waved his hand in the air. 'When I went to sort out his things, tidy up the loose ends. Sad business.' He smacked his lips together, sighed, drained his already empty whisky glass.

'But life, my dear Helena, is for the living. Here, more whisky!' He poured from the decanter into his glass, and my own. I stood, and we faced one another, clinked our glasses. 'To those gone, much loved, and to those of us who remain!' His voice was loud in the room. My right hand clinked my whisky glass, raised the glass to my lips to drink. My left hand slid to rest on my belly, rubbing lightly, slowly, hardly at all.

Uncle Valentine installed me in a comfortable bedroom facing north onto the wide verandah that shaded the room from the sun, and insisted I make myself thoroughly at home. My trunks arrived and were carried up to my room late in the afternoon of the day I arrived. I went upstairs to unpack, shaking each garment as I took it from the sea trunk before folding it into drawers dry and scented with sprigs of lavender tied with kitchen string.

The next day I woke early, in the relative cool of morning, Grace churning within my just-bulging belly. I left quietly through the back door, leaving the house before it had started its day. The back door led to a path through the garden, past the old outhouses at the back and down, through a low gate in the back fence, to the laneway that ran parallel with the street, down to the ocean. The unpaved laneway had dirty sand in wheel ruts on either side of a central mound, topped at that time of the year by browned grass, the odd green weed. Weeds fringed the laneway on either side, frilled up against the back fences of the houses. Bougainvillea hung over back fences, thunderboxes backed onto them and through them. Back gates were sized to high-step through, cut so that they began a foot above ground level and reached only chest high at most.

On that first day, and on most days that followed, I would wake early and walk the laneways and streets that ran to the ocean. In the cool dark, the nightcart men clattered; later in the day children played; but I had the laneways to myself in that in-between time, my pathway to the beach, to swim each morning as Grace swam inside me. Then I'd return to the front of the house as the streets were commencing their days, people starting to appear from front doors, milkos to deliver, motor cars and bicycles to veer from their parking places. The streets were for the daytime. The laneways were mine, in that liminal time.

*

Grace grew and took me over, as the months passed. Uncle Valentine and I failed to talk about this, even as it became obvious, even as my belly grew to match and then exceed the size of his. Finally he acknowledged my by then obvious state by leaving a slip of paper folded on my breakfast plate one morning, his neat writing spelling the name and address of his physician; *Pop along and see Davidson*, he told me, *he'll look after you, and look after the little one when it comes*.

He gave me one other gift, that day. He took both my hands in his plump hands, and pressed them together around something cold, hard. I parted my hands; they cupped a plain gold ring, barely remembered.

'Your mother's, my love. And our mother's, before that. I was saving this for when you married, but I think that you have need of it now. Wear it proudly. Stare them in the eye, my darling girl.' He kissed me on the forehead, and sat down to read his newspaper. I slipped the ring onto my finger, perfectly in place.

THE NORTH TOWER

A woman with blue eyes in a plain face, and dark black hair roped into a thick plait, took money at the public bathing pavilion that stood guard over the beach. Two turnstiles funnelled people through on a strict separation, men to the right, women to the left, to wade through a shallow foot pool reeking of bleach – for hygiene – and on through to the changing rooms. The blue-eyed woman sat between the turnstiles, eternally smoking cigarettes while overseeing pennies dropped onto a tray for inspection before she fingered them down a smooth wooden ramp and into a metal box. When I reached the beach each morning it was too early for the turnstiles to operate, but by the time I had swum and was ready to climb back into my clothes, the door would be open, the wooden sign would be out, and I would nod to the woman as I dropped my penny into the tray. She'd nod back at me, blow smoke from her nose, and smile, smiling more – as the months passed – at my belly than my face.

There came a day when, as I waddled up to the turnstile, the blue-eyed woman stepped off her high chair and, waving her cigarette at me, indicated that I should walk through at the side, where she unlooped the heavy rope that hung across from the edge of the turnstile to the far wall.

'Through here, love, don't want you jamming halfway.'

I thanked her, handed her my penny, and she looped the rope across behind me.

The next day, she smiled over her cigarette as I approached and, as she unlooped the rope, told me, 'I'm Cath.'

'Lena,' I nodded at her, smiling back, dropping my penny into her palm.

A week later, on an overcast morning, there was no one behind me at the turnstile as I went through under the unlooped rope. Cath waved me through, screwing her nose up at my penny, 'Through you go, love.' I saved my pennies from that day on.

Cath was a brick-shaped woman who, though she looked much older, was close to me in age, thirty to my twenty-eight. We progressed quickly, after that week when the rope first unlooped, from learning first names to taking a cup of tea together in the sunshine while her husband, Eric, limped in from his maintenance work and spelled her at the turnstile midmorning. After my early swim, dried and dressed in the pavilion changing rooms, I'd come out past Cath, blinking into the sunshine.

'Cuppa?' she'd ask as I came through past the rope.

'Lovely.'

I'd install myself on the limestone retaining wall in the shade, bring out the novel or magazine I carried in my bag, knowing that by the time the sunlight moved enough to heat me, Cath would appear from the entrance to the pavilion carrying two thick china cups and saucers in her hands, with the cigarette clamped into the corner of her mouth somehow balancing her as she walked.

We sat and smoked and talked and drank our tea in the shade. Cath soon knew that I was due to give birth in early May; that I'd been living in New Zealand; that I was comfortable but unsettled living at my uncle's house; and that, while I didn't want to talk about it, I was a recent widow. I found out that Cath and Eric had been married for ten years; that they'd come up to the city from the bush three years ago; that Eric's leg had been mangled in an accident on the farm and Cath didn't want to talk about it; and that she grew sadder and sadder with every month and year that passed without her falling pregnant. These things were enough for each of us to know. They were the basis on which our friendship grew. Cath and I would sit in the sunshine on the limestone wall, my hair drying into salt curls on my cheeks, me dobbing smokes from Cath, my belly growing bigger by the day.

It caused disapproving looks on the beach, that big belly, more disapproving the bigger it became. It seemed it wasn't proper to be seen in a swimsuit, stretched alarmingly, no matter how carefully, how demurely, I covered myself with a loose, long cotton shirt until the very moment I plunged out of sight, into the water. Complaints were made. But they were made to Cath.

'Bugger 'em,' she said to me. 'Silly straightlaced buggers. What, do they think babies are found under a bush? Bloody bugger 'em.'

I began to spend more and more of each day at the pavilion – Cath and Eric called it the Pav, so I did too. They lived frugally at the Pav, rent-free in exchange for working the turnstiles and some light maintenance, their small wage from the council supplemented by the proceeds of an insurance payment after Eric's accident. When March came, summer – despite the searing heat – was deemed officially over and the Pav was open only at weekends and so, on weekdays, I would knock on the door and walk through to the kitchen, and Cath and I would sit and put our feet up on the low windowsill that looked over the ocean and we too would look over the ocean, smoking and drinking tea. Often, we found that we didn't speak. Cath and I were comfortable just sitting. We did a lot of that, that autumn and winter. Just sitting.

Cath started calling me Princess. She told me I spoke like one. I talked about Uncle's house as if it was a castle, she said, or a palace or a museum or something posh where I couldn't make myself at home. She'd ask me why I spent so much time at the Pav with her and her crip hubbie. I'd just smile, shake my head at her, *oh, Cath*, and we'd sit and smile and talk when we needed to.

We were there in the kitchen one such afternoon. I'd brought horseshoe rolls fresh from the bakery, a pound of butter. The three of us, Cath, Eric and I, had demolished the rolls, Vegemite smeared on thick butter, lettuce wetly crunching, washed down with cups of tea. Eric had disappeared again after lunch. He never stayed with us unless he was eating.

Cath asked me again what it was like living where I

was – whether I was happy there, whether I'd stay.

'Oh, I don't know, Cath. My uncle's lovely, but – well, it's hard to say. It's not that he's said anything to me, but I think a baby in his house is the last thing he's ever imagined.'

'What, he doesn't want you there?'

'No, he's happy for me to be there. He's – bemused, I suppose. I think he just can't imagine what he'll do with a baby.' I realised as I spoke that nor could I imagine what I would do with a baby. I rubbed my hands over my belly.

Cath butted out her cigarette without lighting another from its glowing tip. She stood, rubbed her hands together as if she were trying to make fire, or warm them.

'Well, Madame Princess, what about coming and having a look upstairs.'

I remember being surprised – Cath had never talked about an upstairs. She led me down a hallway and through a door at the end. Four wide steps led straight up, then turned a right angle to the left, then turned back again on themselves – just a half-storey up from the level of Cath and Eric's flat. At the top, the steps opened out into a square room soft with sunlight trying to get in through windows whitewashed to block it. Through the whitewash though, through the big, arched, paned windows stretching across two walls of the room I could see the Indian Ocean, so close, so blue, spreading forever. Furniture was piled against one wall of the room, and boxes; I poked at the corner of a bookcase, a chair with a broken leg, a narrow iron bedhead, a tea-chest. Dust rose, further softening the light. The smell was of dust, and dried salt.

'Oh Cath, it's beautiful.' I felt surrounded by the ocean; not in the way it surrounds you on a ship, but with the height and groundedness that being on land provided.

Cath stood in the doorway, unmoved by the ocean view she'd seen every day for the past three years and was afraid she'd be compelled to see for many years more.

'What would you reckon'— Cath leaned forward to me, pivoting herself free of the doorframe —'to paying us a bit of rent, just on the q.t., and moving yourself and your bub in here? Share the kitchen with us, of course. There's the little bathroom at the bottom of the stairs you could use. We're at the other end of the building, so Bub can scream his head off and we won't mind. And I could give you a hand with things, with Bub. What d'you reckon about that, Princess?'

I stood with my face pressed against a gap in the whitewash on the window, where I could look through and see all the way to Rottnest Island, a flat streak of ribbon floating hot above the water on the horizon. Heads bobbed on the surface of the water below. The white sand stretched forever up the coast, towards the north, past where the houses ran out, the city ended. I unlatched one of the windows; it stuck at first, but opened with some persuasion. Now I could taste the salt in this room — the north tower of the Pav — hear the gulls, the waves.

'I reckon that'd be perfect.'

I walked across the room and put my arms out towards her. We hugged, tentatively at first, then tighter.

'Move when you want, love,' she said. 'I'll get Eric to sort a key out for you.'

ALL THE PAIN IN THE WORLD

Rather than, as I feared, having to be convinced of the sense of my move, Uncle Valentine – bless him – was so transparently relieved to see us go that he showered us with money and made us promise to come to tea every Sunday. I happily agreed.

Eric handed me a key the following morning when I went for my swim. I turned the key over in my pocket, until it felt warm from my touch. We moved the next day. Uncle Valentine organised his man, and the gardener and his cousin, to tote my trunks, my theremin, and some furniture that Uncle Valentine insisted we choose for the room, *to be comfortable, don't want you camping.* His housekeeper reluctantly handed over a rattan basket piled with linen, sheets and pillowcases, towels. A tea-chest filled rapidly, as Uncle Valentine cycloned through the house pointing at random.

'She'll need one of those, and one of those – fix it, will you, Mrs Anderson, you're a dear.'

Uncle Valentine's small army trooped to the Pav carrying scraping tools, a ladder, and dropsheets. They took away the dusty pile of unloved, broken furniture, then draped the room with dropsheets, and spent the afternoon removing the whitewash from the windows while I sat and drank tea with Cath in the kitchen downstairs. Some hours later, we watched them carry my belongings, brought in procession from Uncle Valentine's house, up the narrow stairs of the Pav, huffing and shifting and arranging themselves cleverly to fit. Mr Anderson saluted as they left, *All done, Miss*, ladder under his arm.

Cath and I climbed the stairs to the north tower. The windows and floor shone. My belongings were clustered neatly against the wall where before a pile of broken furniture had been. Across the floor of the clean new room we unfurled an oriental rug in deep burgundy silk picked out in cerulean. 'I'm sure it was your mother's, darling; you must take it,' Uncle Valentine had told me. I drew my hands over its surface, wondering if I remembered its colours from long ago.

Cath helped me arrange the furniture in the room. We placed the wide bed against the wall opposite the windows, so that I could lie and look out on two sides, have two ways of looking at the world.

I grew larger and larger in that bed. I would lie there until I heard Eric leave each morning, then waddle down the stairs to slump myself in the warm kitchen with Cath. She'd knit, fragments of wool left over from a hundred different garments forming a rainbow rug for my Grace. She tried to teach me – I had never learned to knit, although I could sew, the Misses Murray had seen to that long ago – but I never got the knack. The metal needles slipped in my hands so that I held them, somehow, in a cello bow grip that could make no sense of the strings of yarn, forming a tight tangle I couldn't be bothered loosening. So while Cath knitted, I'd sit and read, or talk with her, or just look through the windows at the darkening, wintering ocean, rubbing my taut belly with restless hands.

Cath and I were warm, enclosed, in the kitchen. Eric drifted in and out, always quiet, sometimes smelling of beer a little earlier in the day than he ought. A little rain came as the months progressed. I stopped my morning walks when I moved into the north tower – I was bigger, the rain stopped me – all these were excuses, but really I felt the restlessness slip away from me once I came to the tower. I inhabited it; the tower room around me, me around Grace.

Every Sunday, I waddled up the street for tea at Uncle Valentine's, as promised. Sometimes I persuaded Cath to join us, but Eric wouldn't come. Mrs Anderson would make us cakes and sandwiches, too much to eat in a sitting, and send us home to the Pav with a not quite approving look and a basket of food.

It was on one such Sunday that Gracie decided to arrive. I felt a pain start from somewhere far away, saw it approach out of the corner of my eye as Uncle Valentine offered me a plate of lamingtons. I stood up as the pain got closer. It reached my core, and started to radiate out from my centre to all the parts of my body all at once, like a sonic radiation, or like starlight. I remember Uncle Valentine calling for the car, still holding the lamingtons. My uncle drove us away from the ocean, across the railway track, and over towards the river, and in no time at all I was installed in a high-ceilinged room in the little maternity hospital called Devonleigh. Uncle was waved away by the busy women who bustled around me, hushing me, stripping me, shaving me, shushing me. But I would not be shushed, I who had always made sound. And when our time finally came, it came with a roar, and I – making sounds like keening and lowing all at once, like the cattle on the boat so long ago up the coast – pushed Gracie out of me, all slick and new.

Holding her to me, I felt as if all the pain in the world had been funnelled through my body and made good, turned into light.

FIRST WINTER

Grace lay in Mrs Anderson's old rattan washing basket, sunlight through the windows warming the white sheet covering her. The blanket that Cath had knitted was folded down to the bottom of the basket; the late autumn sun was warm, most days, after cool nights. I sat by her side, my hand on the basket, near but not touching my little dark-haired daughter, and watched her sleep and breathe while my body healed and flowed back to its former shape, but softer, fuller.

We kept ourselves in the tower for most of that first winter, once Grace was in the world. Rain threw itself against the windows. The ocean swelled up close to the footings of the pavilion building, big wintry waves thrown up high and hard by storms far out at sea. When the rain stopped, I would open the window and lean out over the high thrashing waves eating at the limestone that formed the base of the building, the limestone made of long-dead sea creatures, the waves taking them back to the deep. Salt saturated the air; a light crust would form on my face. Running my tongue around my lips, I could taste it.

*

Grace was three months old before I swam in the ocean again. It was a beautiful calm late winter day – not spring, that wouldn't come for a month. But a taste of it. Midmorning, milk-full, Grace slept in the washing basket, pushing out to its edges, only just fitting within it. She was a big bonny baby, pale skin under dark hair, eyes like dark steel; or like coal, sharp and shining. In the kitchen, I could hear Cath clattering cups, humming.

I wasn't sure then what made me want to swim, that day. I ran down to Cath in the kitchen before I could change my mind; of course, Cath was happy to watch Grace. I ran back to the tower, then carried the basket back down to the kitchen. Grace seemed to settle deeper into sleep with the jigging of the basket down the stairs, along the passage, into the kitchen and onto the table in the sun. Sun was good for babies, they said.

From the drawer of my dresser I took my black swimsuit, laid it on the bed. Grace and I had pushed it out of shape, stretched it, as we swam into the late summer, bigger and bigger. I removed all my clothes and stood naked by the bed. My emptied breasts drooped, dark blue veins running through pale flesh to long dark nipples. My stomach bulged, soft. I missed the taut containment of pregnancy.

I stepped into the swimsuit, pulled its straps over my shoulders. It sagged on my soft, changed body, pouched at the belly and over the crotch. I shivered, grabbed my towelling gown from the hook behind the door, eased my feet into moccasins, and stepped towards the stairs and down, out onto the beach.

The tide was high. I dropped the dressing gown off my

shoulders and draped it on a limestone wall where the water wouldn't reach it, slipped my shoes off and placed them on the wall. Before I could think about it, I ran into the water.

The cold took my breath away. A pain shot through my crotch as the water hit. I dived under the water, and my head felt as if it would burst. My teeth screamed in my skull. Salt water filled my nose, ballooned my swimsuit; I felt my breasts float free from the slack wool, as if they were trying to escape from me. I felt the wool of the swimsuit pull up between my legs, still Grace-sore. Salt water eased into every corner of my body, every empty crevice and cranny. As water flowed in, so sound came from my mouth, a deep guttural sound that changed to something high and yet from the back of the nose, from the sinus cavity. I shouted, something that sounded like *yes!*, but that wasn't quite a word. I thought of Trix. Finally, now, I let myself think of Trix, a year to the day in the cold, damp ground overlooking the beach by Tomahawk Road.

SEA STAR

Spring gave in to summer, and the pavilion uncurled itself in the warmth. Cath and I would take turns at the turnstile, Grace gurgling in her basket, sitting up smiling at everyone as they filed through. Eric prowled the grounds, leaning on his broom more than he swept with it, dragging his gammy leg, propping himself against the wall to roll a smoke and watch the women, the winterwhite bodies that started to appear on the beach and baste themselves in sunshine. The weather grew warm, then hot, then – after Christmas – too hot. By then we were dark brown from mornings on the beach, slimmed down from the appetite-sapping heat. Grace was brown all over, golden brown apart from the white depths of all her folds and creases. She was quick to smile, to laugh. She dribbled as her teeth appeared, and the sand collected and dried in the streaks and runnels of spit around her mouth and down her chin, and in the fat white creases under her fat little face. I'd dip her in the sea – *one, two, threeeeeee!* – and she'd burble like the waves, matching their pitch and the shape of their sound. Then I'd bundle her up in a sun-warmed towel, cuddle her to me and we'd roll on the sand, giggling, tickling.

Afternoons were for sleeping, still and quiet, staying away from the sun. Thick velvet, blood red curtains hung from the windows of my room, a gift from Uncle Valentine. I'd close them each morning when we woke, as the sun rose and the early morning cool remained in the room. When Grace and I returned to our room after lunch, we walked into a deep violet darkness, trapped cool behind the curtains and the thick limestone walls of the building.

I'd lay Grace on the bed and lie beside her. She spread her arms like a little fat sea star, always gravitating to the middle of the bed. I arced my body around her, crescent moon to her star. We hummed to each other, call and response light with fatigue in the dark of the room, until we fell asleep. We'd sleep the afternoons into evening, drawing back the curtains only once the sun had dropped behind the ocean, orange piercing blue.

Nights were not for sleeping. Nights were for walking, while others slept.

From an early age, Grace would wake at night, unable to be fed or otherwise persuaded back to sleep. One hot night, my head nodding with sweat and tiredness, I scooped her up in my silk robe, tied the sleeves to fasten at my back and, Grace cocooned as I remembered Balinese babies in batik cocooned, we stepped out of our room in the tower and onto the squeaking white sand to walk ourselves towards sleep. I hummed as we walked, my voice in my throat low under the roll and phizzle of the waves and foam. I walked on the edge of the ocean, on the cool sand angling down to water that sucked at my toes, kissed my ankles. Lulled by the jogging action my walking made, Grace's head would loll, her humming fade to a gentle snore. I'd walk under the jetty's wooden uprights, feel it cooler, smell wooden must. While Grace slept I'd sit on the jetty's edge, rocking her gently against me, my whole torso moving with her. No lights showed from the pavilion, and few from the houses beyond. Looking to the north, up the curve of the coast, only occasional pinpoints of light pitted the dark. I felt alone, yet no longer alone: I had Grace.

I started writing my story, that summer – this story; writing it for Grace. The story of us. I'd been alone, then I'd had Trix; Trix had left me, but I was no longer alone. I had Grace. I wanted to tell her my story, the story of before her, of how she'd come to be. There was no one to tell her but me. I bought a typewriter – a big black Underwood – and set it up on a table in the corner of the north tower of the Pav. I'd never used one before. I was slow, my fingers not used to the heavy hand they needed to make the keys shift the levers, the hammers with their little metal letters, like the hammers of a piano, nothing like a theremin.

I started with my first memories. Would Grace's first memories be of sounds, of water? My fingers stabbed the story out, made hard imprints on the thin paper, sometimes ripped it in my enthusiasm. I tapped out the story of Uncle Valentine before he got too fat to swim at the beach, of the Misses Murray, of ships and sound and light; I tapped monkeys and snakes; butterflies, dolls and bees. I tapped the story of the Professor. I tapped out Trix, how she came and went. I typed it for Grace, a few pages each day, while she slept. As the pile of paper grew, I kept it in a box, kept it safe with a lid. I was no longer alone; we had each other. And I would write our story for Grace, so she'd have it when I was gone.

BLOODY BUGGERY

Grace didn't walk until she was sixteen months old. A fat healthy baby, she was passed from me to Cath, from Cath to whoever happened to be with us – and there were many people with us in Grace's first summer as we worked and lazed by turns at the beach. Grace would go to anyone, her arms outstretched, sticky spitty face ready to press into any shirt front or chest. She was everybody's baby, beloved. She rolled and crawled where she needed to on the sand, and had only to put her fat arms out to be picked up, whizzed from here to there with a kiss on her fat brown cheek. And so, summer turned to autumn and Grace turned one; and autumn turned to winter, and still Grace crawled and slithered and demanded, raised her arms to be lifted, relied on others to move her. She had no need to walk.

If Grace didn't walk, I too had my lacks; I hadn't played my theremin since before Grace's birth – indeed, not since some time before her conception. The theremin – dragged with me across the oceans – now rested in the corner of the room in the north tower, covered with one of Uncle's old sheets; not neglected, not abandoned – just not played.

There was some sense in which I needed to make music with my body – just my body – without the electronics intervening.

So, I hummed.

It had started when I was pregnant with Grace, when I would send vibrations down from my mouth and my tongue and my throat to her, the growing Grace inside me. I closed my lips, felt them relax against each other, felt my soft palate relax and engorge, the drone swell from my throat, inside my head, through my sinuses and down into the depth of my belly to my darling girl.

I hummed for Grace tunes I didn't remember remembering until she was there to prompt them, lullabies my mother had hummed and sung to me. French words, remembered phonetically, half understood from lessons with the Misses Murray, bubbled out of me; Malay words from my earliest memories, the sound of bees, of paper on comb; and sounds I pulled from the air, assonant, feather-soft.

I hummed to Grace, the vibrations in my lips and my throat. As I hummed to her, I moved my hands, close to her body but not touching her. She began to sigh, *aaah ah aaah*, in time with me, in response to me. Later her response would gain a consonant, *maah maa maaaah*. Her sounds echoed mine, responded to my voice climbing up and down the register, my rhythms quickening and slowing. We developed it into a game, Grace and I. Our humming game.

And perhaps I tested her, at times – higher, lower, faster, slower. Three-four time, an arpeggio, a scale.

Grace responded differently each time, sometimes in close harmony, sometimes shouting across and above me. Always though, I would see her eyes on mine, as if she could interpret the music through my eyes. Or perhaps she just saw the reflection of her own face, recognised herself through the mirror of my eyes.

Perhaps there was electricity, machinery in the air, on the day that I drew the dust sheet from the theremin. I connected the wires from the machine to the wall, from the machine to its speaker. I heard the hum of valves warming. Grace said *maaaah maaaaah* behind me, from the rug in the middle of the room where she sat like a buddha, watching. I raised my arms into the old accustomed pose – ready to dance, right arm high, left arm at waist height. My old partner's humming turned to harmonic keening. I twitched my finger and the keening sang *vibrato*. I played a scale, up then down, the timbre brittle, malformed. I adjusted the dials at the front of the machine to change the wave shape. I played again, the same scale, up then down – yes, that was better; sweeter. I played the scale again, faster. I remembered this; my arms and body fell into remembered patterns, my muscles settled. I felt the electricity surge in me, through my fingers and down through my belly.

I felt wetness on the backs of my knees, a tight clasping.

Fat dimpled hands were hanging on for dear life. Grace had walked to me.

'Maaaaaaaaah. Ma-maaaaaaah!'

I turned, bent and swept her into my arms, 'Clever girl, Gracie! Walking girl!' I showered kisses on her fat face.

I twirled her around the room, both of us giggling and wheeeee-ing. Holding her up, kissing her face, I ran us downstairs to tell Cath.

The kitchen was empty. I filled the kettle, put it onto the stove to boil for a cup of tea, to celebrate. While it heated, I knelt on the ground with Grace, urging her to walk to me again, across the room. She keened at me, a sound like the theremin, then walked, clapping her hands, before collapsing onto me, both of us giggling.

The kitchen door jiggled then opened wide. Cath stood framed in the doorway, a string bag fat with groceries in her left hand, a bunch of boronia, green-brown and yellow, fragrant, an upside-down V in her right. I scooped Grace up in my arms and we stood, the table between Cath and me, the kettle steaming up to the boil on the stove behind me.

'Cath! You'll never guess! Grace walked! She walked to me!'

Cath hefted the bag of groceries onto the table. The bag collapsed, limp, the contents shifting to their new arrangement.

'Oh Princess. We've declared war on Germany. We've declared bloody war. Bloody buggery bloody war.'

Her face was shiny with tears. I stepped around the table, moved towards her and put my arms around her; we both supported Grace between us, held her there and cried on her until she cried too – like us, not understanding, but knowing the need to cry. The boronia had dropped from Cath's hand and its scent rose as it crushed under our feet: dusty lemon, sharp with spice, a smell like bruised purple.

THE STRONG ARM BOYS

Lives are lived at a different speed in times of war. Grace's childhood, like mine, was spent in the shadow of a distant war, her life inked in by the actions of men.

But there are some things that war doesn't stop. People will always make music. And people will always dance. There were dances everywhere in the city, but the dances at our beach were the best. Bands played in the rotunda, and people would dance up and down the pier. But the best dances were at the Pav.

Don Armstrong and his Strong Arm Boys held dances at the Pav every Wednesday and Saturday night, from spring through to autumn, when the weather was forecast fine, which was most of the time. The dance floor had no roof, was open to the stars. It had as its ceiling a violet sky, picked out with starlight and a slice of moon. On rare nights when a rainstorm arced across the sky and dumped sudden big, hard, hot rain on the dancers, they'd run to huddle at the edges of the dance floor, under cover of the porticoes that lined it. Tables and chairs were set up there, for supper. The raised stage where the band played was under cover, so the band would keep on playing through the rain, playing louder to drown it out.

The Strong Arm Boys played the songs of the moment, jazz and swing, anything the dancers wanted. They were good enough, rough enough, fast enough for dancing. Two guitars, drums at the back, Don on piano with a microphone to sing into; a horn section of trumpet and saxophone; and Danny, a farm boy from Dandaragan, on bass. They dressed in matching black suits. All of them but Danny were over fifty; Danny was younger, and no one quite knew what kept him out of the forces – and of course they called him Dannyboy. They played with gusto, the Strong Arm Boys.

The dance floor was next to our flat in the Pav. A door led through to the hallway that led in one direction to the kitchen and Cath and Eric's room, in the other to the north tower. When you walked through from the dance floor to our flat and closed the door behind you, the music would hum through the wood of the door, vibrate your spine and arse if you leaned against it. Up the stairs, in our room, Grace would rock herself to sleep, to the sound thumping and thrumming through the walls and the floor and the limestone of the building, up through the still night air and in through the open windows of the room in the north tower of the Pav. I'd come to check her in the night and find her asleep, legs splayed, on her belly in the warm night, one hand down her pants and the other in her mouth, jammed in to the knuckles, fingers wet with spit.

Eric, of course, with his gammy leg, hated to go to the dances, and he hated Cath to go. But she went. We'd go together. After I'd put Grace to bed, tucked her in tight, rocked her to sleep, sung her a song, I'd dress for the dance, put my make-up on, curl my hair. My old clothes came out, the old clothes from Sydney, formal clothes that had lain long unused in the bottom of the trunk. They were years out of fashion, but because the fabrics were so fine, so rich, the cut so beautiful, I didn't change them. I looked out of time; but that was how I felt anyway, so I didn't mind. Silk and satin skimmed my body, hugging it tight – I could fit into the dresses again, since my body had lost the softness from Grace's first year. It felt delicious to dress this way again. I enjoyed the outline of my body in the mirror, under the cloth. I liked myself hard, after the Grace-softness.

Some nights saw just a score of us at the dance. We learned to dance the man, or the woman, as required; to play the part, take the position. Other nights there were hundreds, especially when our boys were in town, and anything female was in high demand.

Our boys, that's what they called them, and most of them were just boys: farm boys, city boys, skinny and uninteresting, either hardened from war, or yet to go and scared. And they were scared of a woman like me; I terrified them with my old-fashioned clothes and my haughty way of speaking.

God, I loved to dance! It took my mind and my body back to the days in Sydney, took me away from the war. At the Pav, we couldn't have stayed away if we'd tried, the music would have come to us. I loved to walk through that door – both ways. Men would say to me, to Cath, 'Can I walk you home?' and we'd say yes, link arms with them, and get them to walk us to the unmarked door at the edge of the dance floor. Then we'd turn around, wave at them and close the door tight behind us. We'd lean against it, on the safe side, breathing hard, laughing hard, hearing the music distorted and muffled on the other side, hear them knocking, confused.

And on the nights when the dances weren't on, Cath and Eric and Gracie and I'd troop across the road to the Lido, to the pictures. Even Eric loved the pictures. From the beginning of summer, the deck chairs and screen were set up, and the projector started its clickety whirring once it became dark enough to see the pictures moving on the screen. Gracie – like all the children – ran wild between the deck chairs, or she'd sleep on a rug by my feet, curled into herself, her fingers in her mouth. The air smelled of hot chips in newspaper, cigarette smoke, and beer from sly bottles stashed under the deck chairs.

To tell the truth, our lives didn't change much because of the war, not in those first years. The boys, the men, went away – but they came back in uniform, and ready to dance with the girls with a new urgency. That was what changed – there was an urgency to people's lives in wartime. People were reluctant to waste time. They grabbed at things they might previously have held back from. Grabbed not without thinking, but with a different way of thinking, a different way of seeing the world. This only increased when, instead of the men coming home, their names started to appear in lists within a sombre, black-bordered box on the front page of the newspaper, in rank order, alphabetical, all lined up in columns, uniform.

DINKY-DI

Our beach streets had always had their share of hostels and boarding houses. With the war, more families took in boarders; everyone crammed in together. Those who could afford it kept their households as they always had. Uncle Valentine remained in solitary splendour in his big old house up the road from the Pav, with the Andersons in attendance. One of the big houses was rumoured to be a brothel, and the doctor's house, conveniently next door, was said to be where the young women went when their precautions failed or the clap caught them out.

The hotel on the corner was commandeered by the US Navy, used as a billet for submariners. They'd parade down the beach in their uniforms or their civvies. You could tell them, even when out of uniform, even before they spoke. There was something about the way they held themselves, a kind of poise; not the arrogance of youth, of soldiers, but somehow a sense of righteousness, an old-fashioned courtesy holding in place the instincts that war teased men to display.

There were black men among them, an exotic chocolate-black, bringing me memories of musicians I'd met in Sydney, in the partying musical days and nights in the Cross and at the docks. They'd strip down to white, short-sleeved, tight cotton undershirts through which you could see the hair or smoothness of their chests. It was the first time we saw what we learnt to call t-shirts. They'd sit on the verandah, arms bulging from those undershirts, all limbs and shoulders, arranged like warriors in the classical paintings I saw in books in Uncle Valentine's library, like *The Rape of the Sabine Women*. No, they were more like *The Raft of the Medusa*, as if they were survivors, safe for a brief moment in time from the ocean, the war; but it was just that, a brief moment in time. Snapped. Adrift. Homeless. Stateless. A bit lawless too – there was a sense of danger, of not being sure what was going to happen next.

When I walked Grace in her pram along in front of the hostel, their eyes would overlook me instead of looking me over; they'd turn to look for the next unencumbered woman. But when I walked without Grace – sometimes detouring especially to pass in front of the men as they lounged and lazed and sprawled and threw balls and kicked and stretched on the lawn and the verandahs, top and bottom, of the hostel – *then* they'd look at me, then they'd call out, and whistle. It was Ma'am when I had Grace with me. Single, alone – *sans enfant* – I became darlin', or doll, or baby; would be called with a whistle, a shout.

I was lucky enough not to have to work to keep myself and my daughter fed and sheltered and clothed. Our rent was cheap at the Pav, and often I put in a little extra for Cath. We still went each Sunday to Uncle Valentine for tea and as we left, each week, he would press a crisp note into my palm, clasping the money into my hand and wrapping it between his big, soft hands. I had my inheritance, my small nest egg in the bank, left by my parents. We were comfortable, Grace and I, better off than most. And our days and nights were our own, not chained to the need to work. I could wallow in Grace's babyhood, her childhood, watch her learn and grow and discover. I enjoyed being a child with her in a way I had never quite been allowed to be a child myself.

We spent days on the beach, Gracie and I. Grace's third summer, the second of the war, was busy for the two of us, busy with playing. We made peg dollies play in the sand, built sand cities for them, sand houses, sand castles. We looked for shells and seaweed, mermaid's-purses and cuttlefish washed up from the ocean, and we brought them back to the tower above the sea where Grace would sit and arrange them and rearrange them for hours at a time, building houses and stories and muttering them under her breath as she went.

I taught her how to make a comb buzz and hum, to make the sound of bees. She laughed at that, even though I'm not sure she'd ever seen a bee. Flies she knew, but not bees. I think she thought that *bees* was the word for the sound.

It's not entirely true that the trooper boys would ignore me when I was with Grace. Sometimes, as we played on the beach, the older ones, the bolder ones, the ones with children of their own would come up to us on pretence of my Grace. *What a cute little doll she is, just like my little sister / daughter / cousin*, they'd say. *Does she look like her daddy? Do you look like your daddy, honey?* they'd ask her, and Grace would beam her smile at them, beam back at them and introduce me, her mummy-and-daddy, all rolled into one. *Is your daddy a Yankee or a dinky-di Aussie, honey?* they'd ask her, and she'd echo them back in a singsong, *dinky-di, dinky-di*, not for the meaning but for the sound of it.

They'd want to give Grace pennies. And I let them. Why not? I taught her to curtsey – almost before she could walk – and she'd curtsey, her head down, eyes cast up to catch the response. She had a good sense of audience, my little one. She'd take the proffered penny with another quick bob from the knees, and tuck it into her fist. Then she'd hand it to me, sticky and hot and specked with sand. And then they'd sit down next to Grace and me in the sand, stretching their brown arms back behind them, spidering them out to splay across the sand but they'd sink into the fineness of it; their hands would work themselves up to the wrist in the sand, silvery, hot, making its way into cracks and crevices.

The Yanks were bolder than the Australian boys. And the Australian boys mostly went home for their leave. It was the Americans who colonised the beach during the years of the war, transformed it. The beach, the streets, the air, the dances were filled with their twanging voices, their t-shirts, their strangeness, the smell of their cigarettes.

CUSP

There was a night on the cusp of autumn when humidity added to unseasonal heat, and the crowd at the dance was huge, bigger than I'd ever seen. The press of bodies, the sweat, the smell of cigarettes and perfume and rum and beer and powder were overwhelming. Even Eric was keen to go to the dance that night – it had the feel of a last hurrah before winter, the weather perilous, edgy, full. I'd put on one of my favourite old Sydney dresses for the dance. As I'd dressed, looking at myself in the mirror in the north tower had felt like looking back into time. I'd even set my hair in a style from then – the dress seemed to require it.

The Strong Arm Boys were already playing when I stepped through the door from the flat, swinging it, the dance floor full and teeming, swarming with bodies. Limbs were bare, brown from summer. Arms and legs moved loosely, flung out and all about with abandon. The band sounded tight, different, the bass up-front. Dannyboy was gone – maybe he'd finally been called up. The lights were low on the crowd; we could see the boys in the band, but they wouldn't have been able to recognise faces in the crowd, not easily.

But I recognised the face replacing Danny's behind the bass. I knew Gus immediately, placed him, felt a jolt in my gut, a rush. Gus was from long before, from Sydney. Trix and I knew him in the Buzz Room days – well, the nights really, long smoky dreaming nights, dancing and music and minds escaping bodies. Gus had been quiet in the Buzz Room days, not much of a player, in the background. But even so I'd noticed him; and he was good-looking still. Long, feminine fingers, a slightly effete way of holding his hands with a droop of the wrist, a relaxedness that likely came from playing bass, but that was balanced by the breadth of his shoulders, and his rich, low voice. His curling dark hair, almost black over olive skin, made him look Italian, or Greek, even Aboriginal.

I turned away, breathed in deeply, settled my shoulders, and didn't have to wait long to be grabbed to dance. An airman pressed himself against me, then swung me away. I felt him pull me in to him, and our fronts pressed and brushed, the buttons of his uniform hard against me. I smelled his sweat, felt it slick on his hand. It had a chemical effect on me, lightning to my brain, to my body. I observed it, then lost myself in it, in the dance, in the darkness, in the music.

I danced two more dances with the airman, then begged off. He swung me over to the chairs lined up around the edges of the dance floor, winked as he let me loose and sashayed to the next girl. I found Cath in the crowd as the band announced a break between sets. Cath linked her arm through mine, winked at me.

'Nice dance, Princess?'

As we walked to the supper table, laughing, I felt a hand on my shoulder, a voice say my name.

'Lena? It's you, isn't it?'

I turned to face him. I could read the years that had passed since the Buzz Room in the depth and shadows of the lines by his eyes, and from his nose to his mouth.

'Hello, Gus.' I leaned in to kiss first one cheek, then the next, as we all always used to back in Sydney. He smelled smoky, and of sweat. I closed my eyes and breathed in hard.

'I'm Cath, pleased to meet you.' Cath nudged me with her shoulder, held her hand out towards Gus.

'Gus.'

They shook hands, but Gus kept his eyes on me.

'Haven't seen you with the Boys before, have we? You new in town?' Cath asked.

'Just over from Sydney. Been travelling.'

Cath dug her elbow into my side. 'You two old friends?'

'Ages ago. I've told you I used to live in Sydney, haven't I, Cath?' She shrugged at me. 'Gus was in bands there, too.'

'Well.' Cath looked at me, looked at Gus, screwed her mouth into a shape designating reluctant acceptance. 'I'm going to go and find a drink, and then I'm going to find someone to dance with. Nice to meet you.' She turned away from Gus, and winked at me as she left us.

Gus and I hung off to the side of the dance floor and talked, tentatively. He told me he'd not been in Perth long, was sniffing around in the hope of continued work with the Boys. He didn't say why he wasn't fighting, and I didn't ask.

'Where are you playing these days?' he asked me. 'Still playing that crazy machine? You haven't got yourself a real instrument yet?' He smiled as he said it.

'Not playing anything much lately.'

'Where'd you and Trix get to? You were there one minute, then – not.'

'New Zealand.'

'Ha! End of the earth after all! That's what I heard, that you'd dropped off the end of the earth.' He laughed. 'You been here long?' he asked, lighting a cigarette. He offered the pack to me. I took one. He flicked his lighter and I leaned in to it, steadying his hand with mine as I did so. Such little routine actions, so familiar, so clichéd. I exhaled.

'Since 'thirty-seven.'

'Why here? It's a fair way from New Zealand. Fair way from anywhere.'

'I have family here,' I told him, figuring that could cover Uncle Valentine and Grace. 'You?'

He screwed his mouth up, looked away. 'Not sure. Just ended up here. Travelled with one mob, then another. Found myself here before I knew it.'

Then he asked me. It had to come.

'And Trix?' He blew smoke out of the corner of his mouth, but towards me, so that his breath mingled with mine.

I sighed, put my hand to my mouth, a little as if the fingers could stop the words coming out. 'Trix died. In New Zealand. We were there for – a while. We were happy. I came here, I didn't want to stay.'

He fumbled, then managed to put his hands around mine, held our hands in between us in a pose of prayer. Cigarettes stuck out, mine on one side, his on the other, like flags, like little incense sticks, the smoke wringing up from them and joining, entwining, in the air above them.

'Oh, Lena. I'm so sorry.'

And that was it. I fell into him, and he wrapped himself around me, and I felt enclosed and warm and lost and found all at once. I missed Trix. But somehow, somehow, there was something of Trix in this man, even if it was nothing more than a shared memory. Something to hold onto, for a time, at least.

When the music and dancing had finished, when the Boys had packed their instruments and made their noisy exits, when Eric had locked up after all the punters had gone, and we'd declined Cath's offer of a cuppa, Gus and I tiptoed to the door of my room in the north tower. I turned to him at the top of the stairs, my finger to my lips.

'Shh.'

'Cath won't care. She's got smiling eyes, that one.' He leaned in, kissed me lightly, then harder, pressing me back into the door.

'Not Cath. Shhh.'

I pushed him gently away, turned to open the door, my hand on his chest, holding him back. The room was lit by the bedside lamp I always left on for her when I was out. Grace was asleep on her low bed under the window, fingers in her mouth, the pillow wet with spit.

'Grace. She's Grace. My girl.'

He brushed one hand back over his hair, put the other hand on his hip. He looked at me, looked at Grace.

'She looks like you. Little Lena.'

I crossed the room, turned off the light. Grace moved in her sleep, pulled her hand away from her mouth, murmured, rolled over to face the wall. I looked over at Gus, backlit in the doorway. I couldn't see his features, just his shape. I walked towards him.

I leaned back against the doorframe. Gus, opposite me, leaned against its other side, our legs angled towards each other, our feet touching at the toes. He reached both his hands towards me, and I reached out to him.

Gus was living close, a room in one of the boarding houses clustered near the beach. He travelled often with the band, but when he was around, he'd come and spend time with us in the kitchen, on the beach, in the room in the north tower. Cath liked him; Grace loved him; Eric tolerated him.

And me? I wasn't sure.

I knew one thing, though, and I loved him for it: I didn't need to explain anything. Gus didn't ask, he just accepted. I was there, Trix was gone; Grace was there, Grace was mine.

I also knew that with Gus around I had someone to talk to about music. We'd dissect the Strong Arm Boys' performances over cigarettes and whisky after the dance, Don and the other boys filing off home one by one, leaving Gus and me sitting on the edge of the stage, our backs against the piano, talking rhythm and set lists and harmonic structure and jazz. Gus could play anything; he'd jump up, pick out a melody or a line on the piano to illustrate what he was talking about, or step his fingers up and down the neck of the bass, keeping his touch light, soft, muffled in the still, late night.

It was Gus who talked Don and the Strong Arm Boys into it. I didn't take much talking around, by the time he suggested it.

'Lennie,' he said, 'how about playing that machine of yours with the Strong Arm Boys? Just a couple of songs?'

I smiled. 'I thought you'd never ask.'

We worked up a short but punchy set, where I'd start by playing a couple of bars of my signature *Aetherwave Suite* – even if no one remembered it any more – then crash into the songs the crowd wanted to dance to, the songs the Boys always played. Gus and Eric hauled my theremin down from the tower to the stage of the dance floor, and Gus and I practised there in the daytime, every day for weeks, with Gracie running and dancing and clapping her way around us. At night, when the dances were on, we'd drape the theremin with a heavy sheet of canvas Eric found down in the store room. We practised twice, three times, with the Strong Arm Boys. And then, the next Saturday, we played.

After the Boys' first set, after the break, I walked on stage alone while the lights were down. I wore the dress I'd worn on my eighteenth birthday, still slinky, still fitting. I stood behind my theremin, took the stance: ready. The lights came up on us, spotting us there at centre stage, and

I played the first bars of *Aetherwave Suite*, piercing the night. Everything was silent but me, my machine. Then the lights crashed on, the Boys crashed in, and the crowd screamed and stamped as we hit a danceable beat. You could almost forget I was playing, but the sound of the music had changed; the sound bounced into parts of bodies and parts of the room that it had never bounced into before. People's dancing changed too, subtly.

And as I looked into the crowd swirling below, I saw Gracie. Cath was holding her, holding her up above the crowd to watch her mama. Gracie was clapping, and the look on her face was entranced, ecstatic, her eyes wide. I looked across the stage at Gus, slapping the bass, holding it hard. Gus was watching me too, with the same look: wide-eyed, ecstatic.

WITH ME ALWAYS

We fell into a loosely linked life, Gus and I. We lived in the moment, but then everyone did; it was wartime. I never quite knew when he'd be there, when he'd be gone. I learned not to rely on his presence, just to enjoy it when I could. Uncle Valentine, too, was away more and more, doing I knew not what. Eric, though he rarely strayed far from the Pav, kept himself to himself to such an extent that he too often felt absent. Though our men were not away fighting a war, we were as often without them as if they had been. When they were there, when their presence demanded it, we lived the complex lives that men and women do, together. When they were not, we settled back into a simpler routine, we women, we girls. Each had its benefits, each its lacks. If I thought about it, I felt lucky to have both.

Grace, though; Grace was ever-present, my constant one. I kept her with me always, as my parents had not kept me with them always. We were close, intimate, connected. Grace looked at me with unblinking, unquestioning love.

We leaned upon one another, my Grace and I. Increasingly, as she passed from toddlerhood to childhood, it was I who leaned on Grace, trusting her constancy, her dependability. She seemed older than her little handful of years, perhaps because I failed to treat her as a child, as all those who had cared for me when I was younger had done in their turn, for better or worse. I treated Grace as my equal, as Uncle Valentine had treated me; indulged, beloved, but equal.

And as Uncle Valentine had done for me, so many years before, so now I was quick to show Grace the delights of the ocean from an early age. Living so close to the sea – sleeping with the rhythm of it in our ears, the rime of it in our mouths and nostrils – how could I not? I said to her, as my uncle had to me, 'Taste the salt, Old Briny; that's what keeps you up, keeps you floating.' We cupped our hands into the ocean and splashed the crisp, mineral water on our faces and into our mouths. We dipped our bodies in the water, gently at first, easing in. I taught her to respect, but not to fear, the ocean's pull and power. Her quick confidence in the waves was a delight to me. We spent our days on the beach, in and out of the water, under the watchful gaze of the lifesaving club stalwarts.

But we were not the only ones on the beach. The crowds at summer would start arriving with the first train, milling down the streets from the station to the ocean until the beach throbbed with people. They were everywhere, on the sand and up and down the grass terraces. Flesh was exposed to the sun, skin browning to dark perfection until it was just too hot; then they'd retreat to the shade of hats and umbrellas and the dark pine trees overhead. People came to make a day of it, brought a picnic lunch in a billy or a basket, or treated themselves to hot chips, ice-cream and ginger beer from the kiosk. Grace and I would avoid the crowds that mulled and pushed, whenever we could; and we were lucky, we could escape to the cool retreat of the Pav whenever the crowded crush on the beach became too much.

Grace loved to lie on the cool wet sand under the jetty, tucking herself up in the highest cranny, the tiny space there, where she'd draw pictures in the damp packed sand, or make up games. Although there were hundreds, even thousands of children on the beach, Grace wasn't interested in spending time with them. I was her playmate; and when I wasn't available, she had her dolls. She'd line them up in the cool shade of the jetty, make them castles of sand, serve tea and cakes in shells, laid out on a table of finest cuttlebone. Her favourite doll she called Sallyrags, oblivious to the incongruity of the name for the delicate china face that topped a floppy body, hand-stitched in exquisite pearl-white silk. Sallyrags was a gift from Uncle Valentine. She travelled everywhere with Grace, in sickness and in health, slept with her every night from the moment she arrived. The doll had become frail and fragile from spit and sick and sweat and cuddling. Sallyrags' wardrobe was all that kept the doll's fraying, mended limbs together, sewn and knitted over the years by Cath from remnants and scraps of fabric and wool. Best of all, in Grace's eyes, were the dresses that Cath made for Sallyrags from the scraps left over from Grace's own dresses.

She'd carry out self-important conversations with the doll, providing both voices.

'Sallyrags is my twin sister. I'm the oldest though, by seventy thirteen hours.'

'She's the oldest, but I'm the cleverest. And we're both the prettiest, because we're twins.'

Grace liked to take Sallyrags to the beach, even though I warned her of the doll's fragility.

'Don't put her in the sea, love. She's not made to swim, not like you.'

Sallyrags, though, like Grace, was drawn to the water, so there inevitably was a day when Grace came to me shamefaced, holding a bedraggled, sandy, salty and very sad-looking Sallyrags in her arms.

'I didn't mean her to go in the water.' She wiped a tear from her eye, then wiped the same tear from Sallyrags' eye. 'She slipped in while I wasn't looking.'

Grace helped me bath Sallyrags in warm fresh water. She cooed to her as we washed her, like a mother to a baby, bent down to her, supported her heavy head. We washed her gently with Sunlight soap, then pegged her up carefully on the line. Grace sat by the line, quietly reading, waiting for Sallyrags to dry. She'd get up and touch her, gently pat her hand, her foot, then she'd shake her head at the doll, tell her *Just a little longer, be a good girl* and settle back to her watchful reading.

When Sallyrags was finally deemed dry, Grace dressed her carefully – cooing, talking to her, making soothing noises – in a dress that matched her own.

Be careful with her, I almost told her, but how could she take more care? It was like having an invalid in the house.

Grace tiptoed everywhere with her doll, cradling her, shushing me and Cath and Eric, asking for the milky treats a sick child might want – custard sprinkled with dessicated coconut; an egg flip, flavoured with honey and nutmeg; creamy bread and butter pudding.

Within a week, though, it became apparent that her vigilant nursing had failed. Sallyrags' stuffing started to rot and crumble – worse, to smell. Her arms and legs fell apart at the seams, the delicate fabric decaying. Even Cath couldn't mend her. Only her chinadoll face remained intact, smooth, beautiful.

'I'm sorry, little one,' Cath said as she turned the foetid, fraying doll over in her hands, picked at her unravelling seams. 'She's beyond me, love.' Cath offered to make Grace another doll, a replacement for Sallyrags.

'No, thank you,' Grace solemnly told her. 'It wouldn't be the same.'

I watched her put the stinking remains of the doll in an old shoebox and, that evening, she asked us all – Cath, Eric, Gus and me – to come to the beach to say goodbye. I watched her place offerings in the tattered box, treasures she'd picked up from the beach: a seagull feather, a piece of cuttlebone, a shell; a sand dollar, half a mermaid's-purse. I saw her mouth move, although I could not hear words, as she pushed the box out on a wave, and threw a handful of sand after it. We all stood there, watching until the box bobbed out of sight. Gus picked Grace up, swung her onto his shoulders, and we walked, the five of us, back to the Pav, to have our tea.

*

When it was not being used for the twice-weekly dances, the dance floor – the roof of the Pav building – was women's space, a place for Cath and Grace and me. Cath and I strung washing lines from firm hooks in the wall, to stretch right across from the road side to the beach side of the building, and we'd peg out our laundry every Monday, with plenty of time to dry by the next dance on Wednesday. Wide wooden edging framed the dance floor. On the road side of the building the edging dipped low, conveniently at belly height, at leaning-on height. We'd smoke, drink a cup of tea, watch the world go by in the street below us.

Grace loved to crawl into the rattan washing basket, even when she was far too big to fit. When she was a tiny baby, Grace had slept in the basket, and I'd pushed it across the floor with my feet to keep her in the healthy sun, in the warmth. It had stood up well to use. She'd sit in it and read a book, or sing a song, but Grace loved nothing more than to be in that washing basket, pretending it was her boat. Often, she was Ratty, poling purposefully down the river.

'Push me, Moley!' she demanded of me, one afternoon as I hung out the bed linen.

'Oh Gracie, I'm busy,' I told her, peg sticking from the side of my mouth, hands full of washing.

'But Mama, there is nothing half so much worth doing as simply messing about in boats! You know that! Push me! Please, Mama Moley.'

I pegged out the pillowcase I was holding, then I bent down, grabbed the basket, and pushed her across the floor, my hands on the scratchy rattan of the basket's top edge. She squealed with delight, with movement.

'God, Gracie, I can hardly shift you, you big fat Ratty!' I pushed harder.

The basket stuck and scratched, and itself gave out a squeal. I looked behind us. A crisp jagged line followed accusingly from where we'd started next to the clothesline, carved into the polished jarrah of the dance floor. I looked back at Grace, and saw her mouth widen in an O to match her eyes, to match mine.

It was Eric's job to polish the jarrah floorboards. He was furious with us – well, not with Gracie, who could do no wrong in Eric's eyes, but with me. He muttered and cursed while he sanded and buffed and shined and buffed some more. He swore you could still see the scratch, although it looked fine to me. But he liked to mutter and curse, and Eric must have forgiven us, as – after he finished his buffing and cursing – he fixed a thick old scrap of carpet securely to the bottom of the basket, before shoving it into my arms.

'Won't scratch next time, bloody thing.'

When Uncle Valentine was in town, we went for afternoon tea on Sunday, as always. Grace would rush to him, and he'd sweep her up in his arms, rest her on his big rich belly.

'My graceful Grace! As delightful as ever.'

He'd kiss me on both cheeks, squeezing Grace between us, then let her down. Cath came with us, sometimes; Gus did not, although Uncle would have welcomed him.

We'd feast on freshly baked treats, neat sandwiches with fish paste or egg or tongue, all washed down with tea in fine china, and milk for Grace. There was no indication, at Uncle's big house on a Sunday afternoon, of the austerity that was becoming apparent elsewhere in the shops and houses around us. We laughed and ate until we could eat no more, then we retired to the front room to settle in the big soft chairs there. Uncle would play his musical recordings for us, music old and new, and his first command after tea on a Sunday would be to Grace.

'Graceful girl, give me a twirl!' He'd take her hand, bow to her (as low as his ample figure would allow), and they'd swirl and whirl around the room, my dear uncle lifting my darling girl up onto his paunch, clutching her to him, then letting her down as he collapsed into a chair and telling her to *Give us a solo, darling*. She'd step and turn and point her toes, then shimmy her shoulders, her whole body, as she saw the submariners dance at the Pav. Then, finally tired, she'd climb onto Uncle Valentine's knee and settle to listen to the music, my cue to change to something quieter, calmer.

'Play your music, Mama! Play the wave music,' she'd command, but only sometimes could I be persuaded to place the needle onto one of my own recordings, and only when it was the three of us, me, my uncle and Grace, never when Cath was there. It was difficult to listen to myself. I could only really listen by pretending it was someone else playing.

Grace would lay her head upon her great-uncle's

shoulder, and his arm would support her, his hand gently stroke her hair. Indeed, he loved her almost as much as I did. But never did I regret my decision to move to the Pav. We lived our own lives there, in the mist of salt spray rising from the beach, and Uncle was free to live his.

A NOTE PINNED TO HER DRESS

We were tired of the war by 1944. Even the dances had lost their shine, their ability to pull us out of ourselves for the night, for even the duration of one dance. There was now a feeling of time dragging, of killing time – in all its meanings – that was too hard to shake off.

I was still playing my sets with the Strong Arm Boys; we'd developed them into quite a central part of the act. But I only played with them at the Pav. They toured around the city during the week, and sometimes toured away, playing a circuit of country towns, for weeks or months at a time. Dannyboy hadn't come back so Gus stayed with the band, with us. We almost felt like a family, an extended family, temporally complicated: me, Grace, Cath and Eric all of the time; Uncle Valentine on Sundays; and Gus, who came and went, without comment, without discussion.

Grace started school in February. I'd walk her up the hill and down to the railway line, across and up to the school each morning, and pick her up in the afternoon. We'd take a different route each day, looking at houses, trying to see through windows and curtains and blinds to catch glimpses into other people's lives; lives lived in houses, not on the beach. Grace was quiet at school, her teacher told me. Her teacher, I gathered, did not quite approve of me, even less so when, on occasion, Gus would walk with us to school, Grace swinging between the two of us, lifted high, laughing. At the school gate she'd kiss us both, two cheeks each in the European way, then bounce off to the classroom.

We were tired of the war. But life went on.

In the second week of Grace's first school holidays, not long after her sixth birthday, I woke up bleeding – just my usual monthly interruption, a morning of pain, a few days bloated, then the cycle would begin again. I hobbled to the kitchen, slightly bent to ease my cramping belly, and boiled water for tea. I ferreted in the bathroom, in the kitchen, in our room, for a bottle of Bex, to ease the cramp and ache. I found the bottle, but apart from its cotton wool plug it was empty.

Grace skipped into the kitchen. I don't recall where Cath was, nor Eric – why can I not recall this? Why was Cath not there, as she was nearly every other day?

'Grace, love, I need you to pop up to the shop and buy me some medicine. You're a big girl now; I can trust you to do that for me.'

She looked at me with wide eyes. 'The shop on John Street?'

I nodded. 'I can pin a note to your dress, so Mrs Watson'll know it's all right. You can pop the money in your pocket. Come on, big girl.'

Grace looked at her feet, scuffed one against the other with a sliding, scratching sound.

'Do I have to?'

My belly lurched then, a cramp that made my eyes water, light dance behind my eyes. I swallowed hard, screwed up my eyes against it.

'Oh for goodness' sake, Grace.' I rustled in my pocket for money, counted coins and pressed them into her reluctant hand, scribbled a note and pinned it – taking a pin from the cracked teacup on the windowsill by Cath's sewing basket – to Grace's dress. The dress was winter-weight cotton, patterned with blue and white vertical stripes. She wore a navy blue cardigan over it, with only the top button done up. Her short hair was bunched at the back in a patch, where she had slept on it, grinding her head on the pillow. 'I was put on the ship on my own from Singapore when I was four years old; I think you can go to the jolly shop for me.'

She turned to me at the door. I waved her away.

'Go on! And come straight back, love.' She looked unsure. 'Go on, darling, straight there and straight back. Careful on the road. I'll make us toast and honey when you get back and we'll take it back to bed.'

Another wave of cramping passed over me, and I grimaced as she closed the heavy door behind her.

It should have taken Grace no more than fifteen minutes to walk to the shop and back, even if she dawdled – it was only around the corner. When Cath arrived home half an hour later, shopping spilling from her bag, Grace had not yet returned. Cath yelled for Eric, who raced off as fast as his gammy leg could carry him. He quickly reported back that Grace had at least reached the shop; Mrs Watson had exchanged the bottle of pills for the coins in Grace's pocket, sent her on her way back home. Eric had checked at Uncle Valentine's house; my uncle was at work, but Mr Anderson in the garden, Mrs Anderson in the kitchen, neither of them had seen Grace.

I ran to the boarding house where Gus was staying, hauled him out of bed. The three of them – Gus and Cath and Eric – prowled the streets, circling out, while I stayed in the kitchen at the Pav, waiting for her to come home. Someone must have called the police; uniforms appeared on the street, men from the submariners' hostel – my friends, men I'd danced with, had played music for – spread through the streets of our little community by the sea.

I sat at the kitchen table at the Pav, drinking cups of tea. A cold, hard pain knotted in my belly.

It was late in the afternoon when they brought her home. Cath pushed open the door and ran to me, held me, *oh Princess*, she said, *our little darling*.

Gus carried her. He walked through the doorway into the kitchen and he held her, her little dark head lolled against his shoulder. Tears streamed down his face. Her hair was darker where his tears dripped down, matting it together. I stood and moved towards them. I touched her bed-matted hair, the back of her head. There were leaves in her hair, stuck to her cardigan, tiny leaves from a ti-tree; I picked one from her hair, crushed it, smelled the sharp medicinal smell of it. I reached out my arms and Gus folded me into them, into him and Grace who was no longer Grace. I could not believe the terrible lifelessness I felt in her body.

A man in a dark uniform and a woman in a nurse's frock came. They stood by the kitchen door, his head bowed, hers upright, waiting. I held Grace, Gus held us both; Cath cried at the table. I brushed the hair from her eyes with my hand, kissed her on both cheeks, in the European way, then kissed her cold lips. Then – too soon – they took her away, my darling. I did not understand what had happened. As they carried her away, I turned to Gus and fell into his arms; we gathered Cath in, and the three of us stood, shaking, trembling, as the sun dropped lower in the sky through the window behind us.

Then I broke away – burst through the kitchen door to the street, watched as the ambulance and the police car pulled away slowly. A sound came from me, a sound I had never heard and have never heard since; a low keening, not of this life.

I turned away from the ocean and faced the land, the dying light of the day at my back. I saw the lines of the streets marked by the rising tips of the tall dark pine trees, black-green triangles above the houses, their branches reaching down in curves towards the ground. I walked away from the ocean, towards the land, the trees. The arms of the pines stretched out to me.

COTTESLOE
1991

Ghost notes

SWEET SMOKE STILL

I remember ti-tree leaves in her hair, on her dress, remember the smell of them. I cannot stand that smell, still; it makes my guts roil. I remember the note, remember pinning it to her dress, remember the pain in my belly. I recall her now, as I have tried all these years not to. Dark hair, dark eyes, humming on the beach, the tiny star around which I revolved.

She was my grace note, my *appoggiatura*: she added to me, accented me, augmented me. Linked to me with the most delicate of curves, she was not quite there; then she was gone, leaving me bare, unadorned, raw, all alone again. The Italian *appoggiare* means *to lean upon*. We leaned upon one another, and when she was gone, for a long time I didn't want to hold myself up without her.

It is May, now, this month. Her birthday was in May. She was born in weather like this, heavy, thick weather. It was May when she left me, too. What an awful, awful month, all leaves turning, weather with cold on its tongue, thunder in its bowels.

*

She is filming me, again. She asks about then, about that time. Her questions come to me as if through glass, or through water.

'You came back here, as an adult, just as war was announced, in 1939, is that right?'

'Before then. Before the war.'

'And you lived right down on the beach. Could you talk about that?'

'At the pavilion, yes. I wasn't there at first though. I stayed with my uncle. He was close by. I moved to the Pav quite soon though, and I was there by the time the war broke out.'

'Why there? Did you work there?'

'Mmm? Work? No, I paid a little rent to the people who did though. It was – oh, I suppose an escape. A place to be away. To have my own space, you might say.'

'You were there for some time, until after the war, is that right?'

I close my eyes, block out the light. How can I tell her why? I can't, I can't tell her. How can I, now, when her body and mind are growing a child? And *why* should I? Everyone who knows is gone; there's no one left but me.

I imagine a woman, dark-haired, not thin – with meat on her bones. Fifty years old; older than Mo. Perhaps with children – God, even grandchildren! – of her own. I imagine her humming, under her breath, as she works.

'Lena?'

I open my eyes. 'Mmn?'

'You left here soon after the war, is that right?'

'I don't remember.' I shake my head, try to muster my thoughts. 'I suppose – let me see – I left in 'forty-seven. Yes. Went to Paris, at first.'

'What prompted you to leave? I imagine Europe was so much more damaged than Australia, from the war.'

She sits with her notebook balanced on her knee. It is not just her. The three of them are there. I can't see the boy, Jonno. Caro is behind the light. In the silence I imagine I can hear them breathing. All I can see is Mo, and all I can see of her is the notebook balanced on her knees, the pen resting lightly in her hand, her feet in their heavy black boots, close together, pointing towards me, in the backwards spill from the bright light.

'Lena? Are you all right?'

'No.' I start to rise out of my seat, then sit back down. 'Can we – I don't really want to talk about it. I'm happy to discuss my work, my music, but I really don't want to talk about – can you please turn it off?' I hold my hand up towards the camera, shielding my face. She is standing now, reaching out. 'Please.' The sound from the camera changes as she switches it off. I drop my hands to my lap, bow my head. 'Thank you.'

I make an excuse, tell her I am feeling unwell. She bustles out, hustles her little team away with her; I hear her tell them to pack up, to finish up. She comes back to me, brings me a glass of water. I take it, drink from it. My hand is shaking. She takes the glass from me, places it on the table. She is solicitous, asks what she can bring me, if I need anything. *Poor old woman, no one to look after her.* I'll be fine, I tell her, I just need to rest. The strange humidity this past week, I say to her, it's harder on me than the strict heat of summer. I find it harder.

I stand in the doorway, she on the verandah. She asks me again if I am all right.

'Yes. Yes. I'm fine.'

She holds out her hand, takes mine, wraps her other hand around it.

'You know...' she starts, then stops, then starts again, as if with a prepared speech. 'It's the untold stories I'm interested in, the stories that hold secrets. That's my challenge as a filmmaker – to find ways of showing those secret stories, especially the dark parts, while still respecting the subject. Respecting you.'

I shake my head. 'It's difficult.'

'I know. I know. But – you know, I've always felt that, when I'm making a documentary, I have moral obligations that I don't have when I'm making a dramatic film. When I'm making a documentary – telling your story – my responsibility for you goes beyond the finished film. I'm responsible for the emotional aftermath of the film. I feel very strongly about it. If I didn't, I'd make it all up – it's as simple as that. I wouldn't be interviewing you. I wouldn't be making documentaries. I'd make movies, make it all up.' She is still holding my hand in hers. She pats my hand, squeezes it, then releases it. 'I want to tell your story. If you'll let me.'

I nod my head, but I don't speak.

'May I come again?'

I nod.

'Give you a few days, though, eh? Perhaps after the weekend?'

'Yes. After the weekend. Yes.'

'Okay. I'll call you, we'll set a time.'

She turns, steps off the verandah, then turns back to me.

'It's good, you know? This story, your story, this film – it's good. You're remarkable. People want to know about you.'

There's no answer I can give her. I smile, grimly; I nod.

I watch her walk up the path, under the jacaranda tree, through the garden, and away out of sight.

My scrapbook contains press cuttings, charting my musical career over the years. It bulges with newspaper articles – in English, French, German, Russian – photographs, clippings from magazines, programmes from shows I have played. In truth it is not so much a scrapbook as a scrap box, spilling out and only barely contained.

I open the lid of the box. The smell of old paper meets me, and under that, the ghost note of light perfume, of stage make-up, faded to must. At the bottom of the box is my oldest scrapbook, from the beginning, from Sydney. The paper is old, thick, and dark brown, coffee-brown, more stiff card or board than paper. Memories are tucked within the pages, spilled as I leaf through them: a programme from the State Theatre, wild with the colour and shapes of Trix's design; a letter from the Professor; a sketch Trix made of me, draped in a kimono, my hair loose, my body formed by her in quick, loose lines on the page. From the very back of the book – tucked there, out of time – I take a photograph. It is small, square, its black, white and grey bordered by a frame of white. I kneel on the sand on the beach. I am wearing my bathing costume, dark in the photograph, and a large-brimmed sunhat. I am holding my arm upright, reaching out in front of me, my finger pointing directly towards the camera. I am smiling a deep, wide smile. Enclosed by my other arm is Grace, naked and brown, dark hair wet and rimed with salt, eyes screwed up against the sun, fat little hand up to shade her eyes, nose screwed up, laughing as she looks toward the camera.

I touch my fingertip lightly to her face, the glossy surface of the image sticky, almost liquid. From a drawer in the kitchen I take an envelope. In it I place the photograph, a newspaper cutting, and a flattened sprig of ti-tree, pressed deep in the spine of the book, grey with age. I lick the sweet mint gum and seal the envelope, place stamps on it, write the filmmaker's address.

I walk to the postbox by the shop on the corner, and drop the envelope through the slot. I do not have the energy to walk further, to go to the beach, to swim. It feels hot. *It's gunna be a hot one.* No, it can't be hot, winter is coming. It is May. The rain will come soon, the winter rain. I walk home, slowly, through air that feels heavy. Perhaps there will be thunder.

I go to my bedroom. I lie upon my bed. I prepare a smoke. I feel the hit. I feel its numbing, welcome it. My hands clench, fingering the air, tapping time on the surface of the bed. I curl into myself, climb in.

Stay with me. Nearly there.

The filmmaker is here again. I open the door to her. She says my name, then she stands, immobile. She puts her hand on my shoulder, on the top of my arm, and rubs the thin skin there, like rubbing a sore muscle, or patting a dog. How long it is since anyone has held me. How very long.

'I'm so sorry,' she says. 'I didn't know.'

I turn, and she follows me. We go into the front room, the music room. I stand near the theremin. I can feel the droop and stoop of my shoulders. I can feel the sweet smoke still. I can feel the filmmaker's sadness.

'Thank you for telling me,' she says. She tries to meet my eyes with hers. I look down, look at my feet, the rug beneath my feet. 'I can't begin to know how you must feel, must have felt then, but – well, at least I know, now. About Grace.'

I flick my eyes up when she says *Grace*. My head nods lower, sadder; it feels heavy on my neck, too heavy to bear. She steps towards me; I step back, as if following her lead in a dance.

'And they never found out what happened? Who did it; if anyone—'

'No,' I interrupt her. 'No.'

'Lena,' she says.

I can't look at her.

'Do you want me to stay?'

I shake my head: no.

'Do you want me to go?'

I lift my head, drop it, lift it, drop it, a slow motion nod: *yes*.

She reaches out, touches my arm again. I nod, just slightly. And then she leaves me.

COTTESLOE, EUROPE, COTTESLOE
1944–1991

Singing my daughter down

JUST WALK AWAY

Sometimes, you just have to walk away. As it turned out, it took me a couple of years to walk away, after Gracie died.

In the meantime, I walked; at first, all I did was walk. Up and down those streets, and through the back lanes, under the Norfolk pines, along the beach, my head down, alone. I don't remember much of that time. Gus was there, and Cath and Eric. Uncle Valentine gently suggested, I seem to recall, that I move back into the big house with him. But I stayed at the Pav, in the tower, sometimes looking out at the sea, but mostly folding myself in on myself, curled in a ball on the rug on the floor, just holding on for dear life; just.

I couldn't bear to think of her under the ground, so she turned to ash and smoke, my Grace. Ash like chalk, like limestone, ground. I stood with her in my hands, cradled the box that held her, the wind behind me in rhythmic gusts and soughing troughs blowing out over the wintry ocean. I let Grace fly from my fingers on the wind, whispered her over the water, humming low in my throat. She whorled, a perfect chalky spiral on an eddy of water, before turbulence dispersed her. Soon she would be everywhere, in every ocean; but the grit of her stayed deep in the cracks in my hands.

There was a sheet of paper still in the typewriter, in the room in the north tower, words filling half the page. It stayed there for days, then weeks, then months. Then one day, I ripped it from the machine. I packed the papers – all of them, the unfinished story, my story, our story – tied them neatly with blue manuscript ribbon, put them in a box, put the box in a drawer. The typewriter stayed where it was, another cold machine in the corner of the room. I didn't need it; I didn't need to finish the story, now. But I couldn't throw it away. I just put it in a box. Put it away.

I became very thin, I know that. Eating didn't seem appropriate. I became so thin that my flow stopped, my breath stank. My body started to eat itself from the inside out. They would all have worried about me; I understood that later. And they were grieving too, of course. But I was her mother. I grieved hardest.

I don't know when I first used opiates to dull the pain, to take its sharp edge away. Gus knew a man, who knew someone else, who knew one of the Americans. Smoke soothed smoothly, ate the pain, uncurled me, at least while it unfurled through my body. Gus and I sat in the tower, sat and smoked. It was dark, often; perhaps I slept during the day. The war ended, I remember that. I remember it not meaning anything – so, the war was over, so what?

And the dances continued, sound drifting through the walls and under the door and in through the glass of the window on the night air, hoots and hollers and horns and loud stamping glory, all happiness and peace. What did they know? Gus and I sat in the tower. I've said that. We sat in the tower, and we smoked, and sometimes the pain edged away enough so that I let him hold me to him, my face against his dark hair, the smell of it, the smoke, the sweat.

And in the daytime, people came there too. They came to the beach, paid their coins at the pavilion and put their swimsuits on and padded out on the sand and lay there in the sunlight. I saw them. I saw them swim in the water, swim out to the pylon, around it and back to the beach, saw them haul themselves onto the beach and lie on the sand, brown and dripping, as if nothing had happened, not the war, not anything. I saw them climb onto the pylon and leap off; I saw joy on their faces, damn them. Sometimes I would stand with my face pressed against the glass of the window overlooking the beach and imagine myself outside my body and in that water, inside it and underneath it and letting it rush through me; imagined cool beads of water effervescing up my arms, on my thighs, on my eyes.

I stayed in the tower. Gus and I sat in the tower. Stay with me. I'm getting there.

I came back to the world, slowly, and so did Gus. He came and went with the band; sometimes he was away for months. He would stay with me in the tower when he was in town. With time, I could function in the world again; I ate, moderately; I could smile at someone in a shop who did me a small kindness. Still smoke smudged the edges, kept me afloat.

In time, I started going to watch Gus play. I could listen to the music, sometimes, listen without it hurting. Gus wrapped himself around the bass, swayed it, closed his eyes and moved into it. I closed my eyes and moved, alone, sometimes with the music, sometimes against it, felt the boom of the bass move the bones in my chest, felt it in my teeth.

You could almost forget there'd been a war, a few years after its end. No more uniforms; the Americans had all gone, our boys came home and packed their uniforms away never to be seen again, burned them, buried them. It was on the inside that people carried their wars, like I carried Grace.

I got my chance to walk away, finally, in 1947. Gus had decided to chance his luck in Europe, convinced by one of the Americans he'd met during the war and kept in touch with, a jazz pianist of some skill and renown.

'Come with me,' Gus said; it was as simple as that.

I packed my things into crates and tea-chests, and we shifted them back to Uncle Valentine's, to the old cottage at the back of his house. He gave us money in an envelope, *something to fall back on*, and made me promise to telegraph for more if ever I needed it. He drove us to the ship – once again, to voyage by sea – and Uncle Valentine and Cath stood on the wharf and waved us off, on our way north, to Europe.

BLUE SMOKE

Paris was dark blue, night time, moonlight, deep blue smoke and noise. So soon after the war; so scarred, when we arrived there – and I mean Paris, as well as me. We arrived in the middle of winter, to a cold different from any cold I'd known, a cold with the weight of the whole continent behind it, wind blowing harsh from the east. I bought a coat, scarlet red wool, boiled and thickly felted, and wrapped myself tightly in its warmth.

I dredged schoolgirl French from the depths of my memory. My prim accent soon had the edges knocked off it though, and I added to my limited vocabulary as I copied the sounds I heard in the bars and streets, learned by listening for the music of the language, listening for its tones and timbre, repeating it, copying it, improvising.

Gus played most nights, somewhere or other in the city. I'd go with him, sit at the bar, or at a table, at the side of the stage if there was one, and listen, drinking wine, smoking the Gitanes that Trix used to smoke when first we met; smelling of her. Paris reminded me of Trix. I saw everything through her eyes, remembered her descriptions of it, paintings she'd made of it. Light became fragmented in my eyes, dark blue, moonlight. Noise became fragmented too; I heard sounds in the streets that rang in different ways in this northern light, at this distance from the ocean. The sounds I heard changed as I learned more of the language, as I came to understand what was said around me in the streets, in the markets.

Over time I fell into conversations with other musicians in the bars, students of music, professionals as well as amateurs. Music was a serious business in Paris. Theories were discussed, new music was played. There was talk of *musique concrète*, found sounds, of the recording and manipulation of sound. But the new magnetic tape technology lacked the immediacy of music performed in the moment. Gus and his band kept on playing their music in real time, on real instruments, making the music new through the bending of sound, the manipulation of wind through metal, or wire forming nodes and antinodes, of wood against skin or metal; they chopped the sound and looped it as they played, tweaking each loop to argue back on itself, emphasising motif and repetition, resorting to melody when they felt the music warranted it.

I stood to the side while all of this happened, talked and listened but did not play. I could have begged or borrowed an instrument – mine was packed away in a tea-chest in the little cottage behind Uncle Valentine's house – and played with Gus, or found an ensemble to play with, could even have played on my own. I could've found an audience if I'd wanted one; the name Lena Gaunt, after all those years, was still known. But I wasn't ready to play. I could listen to the concretists, the jazz musicians, the classicists, the Fado singer in the bar on our street, but I didn't have it in me to play, not then, not yet. There was a lassitude in me – not just from the smoke, although that gave me a blessed liquid heaviness, slowed my heart, coloured everything around me in shades of dark blue, smoke blue, deep water blue, stopped the brightness outside from overwhelming me. My limbs moved as if through honey; no, something more bitter, blackstrap molasses. There was a bitter taste in my mouth, constantly, that nothing could nullify – a soul bitterness – and a big gap in my heart. Gus couldn't fill it. We lived as sister and brother in our dark Parisian apartment, sharing a bed just to sleep, or to smoke, each turning to the outside of the bed, turning away from one another, backs hunched, as smoke or fatigue or alcohol pushed us out of consciousness. My red coat hung on a hook on the back of the door. Gus's black coat hung next to it, shoulders stooped away from mine.

Gus and I spent years in Paris, watched the decade click over, left the war years firmly behind. It's a hazy, smoky time, difficult to remember. We were there. Then we were not. In the end, we drifted apart; that's one way to describe it, a modern way, a way from a time that hadn't happened yet. He stayed in Paris. I took the train, then the ferry, then the train, and moved to London; there was a man I knew there, had met in Paris, it's not important who. But London was a broken place, as it turned out, holes still in the landscape of the city, and in its people. You could turn a corner and encounter a whole block of rubble, an entire street flattened. Almost worse were the streets where a single house was missing, picked out, gouged out, blank. The whole place still felt raw from war.

If Paris had been blue, London was grey. My red coat felt too red, stood out against the ugly, damaged landscape. The people I knew there were damaged, too. The sounds on the streets, the voices, were ugly, harsh, lacked music. And so I walked, one day, with my clothes in a suitcase, to Paddington station. I stared at the board listing departing trains, and found myself seeking the seaside. I caught the 1:20 to St Ives.

SUMMERTIME

St Ives was blue, but a different blue to Paris, a pale blue, watery, salted, marine. The whole sky was brighter. It felt as if the war hadn't happened. I spent a week in a hotel by the harbour, during which time I found a house to let, a small stone cottage with whitewashed walls, a blue door fronting straight onto the street, a piano in the front room, and a single tiny bedroom at the top of narrow stairs, with a small, paned window through which I could see, framed by narrow houses, a glimpse of the sea.

This was a nursery rhyme place – *as I was going to St Ives, I met a man with seven wives* – removed from the world. I spent most of my time walking, at first; on the beach, and up and down streets that tipped down to old stone walls containing the harbour. I had money still, from Father, my little nest egg that sat quietly in the bank and provided for me. I was not unusual in St Ives, living on my own, no visible means of support. Artists clustered in the town to paint, to sculpt; they came for the weather, the light, the blue; and where there are artists, there are musicians. I kept well outside the complexities of allegiances forming and unforming, of groups and schools and styles. I had had enough of artists and musicians in my life, by then. I was content to camouflage myself near them.

But after some time in St Ives, something changed in me, and it felt right once again to sit at the piano in my front room and play. I played the music of my childhood, simple pieces, picked melodies from the air – found sounds – played what pleased my ear. As I played, so I found a rhythm to my life. Everything in moderation: music, food, light, morphine. For the latter, I had registered with a sympathetic doctor in Penzance, where the chemist's shop in Market Jew Street legitimately supplied what I needed, not that it was much. Just a taste. Just a sweet taste. My hands on the keys moved slowly, picked their way up and down the keyboard, through its range. My head dropped low over the keys, eyelids dropped, my eyes closed. I heard not just the music from each key as it was depressed; I heard too the click of my fingernails on the keys; the pop as the pad of each finger pressed against the key surface; the percussion of hammer on wire; the resonance of the wood of the piano, connecting it to the slate floor of my cottage and up through my shoes, my feet, to me. I hunched my elbows in tight against my sides, nodding my head with the sounds I made.

I reached middle age in St Ives, slipped past bearing the summer I turned forty-five. I'd slipped away from people, too; celibacy suited me. I could connect – but with myself, in a closed circuit. The air compressed against me, formed a bubble, cushioned me, preserved me, somehow, like eggs preserved in lampblack.

I lived each day from start to finish, never planning too much in advance. I was a woman who lived in a small town on the edge of an island. I lived by the sea. I played my piano. I kept to myself, although I was on nodding and good morning terms with people I encountered in my day. I settled into life in the town. My shoulders relaxed. Sometimes, I reached the end of the day and realised I had not thought, all the day, about those I'd lost.

But those days were few, even then, even though – by then, before I knew it – ten years had passed since I'd lost Grace. I tried to think of her there, ash in the sea, smoke in the aether, but she felt far away. I didn't feel as if she was still with me, no matter what I did. I felt as if I'd abandoned her, left her on the other side of the world. But being away was how I could live, then. I didn't imagine her grown near to adulthood, as tall as me, didn't wonder what she would have done, who she might have become. I felt only an emptiness, a lack, a failing; a falling apart, when I thought of her. There was a dark black hole in my gut, or my heart, or my soul.

I started swimming again that summer. The water in the bay was cold, always took my breath away. Waves formed, rose and fell, gentle in the cove – no more than a cranny in the rocks, really – where I swam. The rocks reached out from the shore, enclosed me, calmed the water around me. I would leave the salt in my hair each day, let it stiffen; then wash it away, a small weekly ritual, washing my hair in the cold stone basin in the kitchen in my cottage. It was that summer in St Ives that I first cut my hair man-short, nun-short; I kept it so ever after. I could run my hands over it, feel its thick felt, no longer hair-like, but animal, or like the pile of a silk rug. At first I missed the pressure of long hair pinned at the nape of my neck, balled there. It felt strange to roll my head on my neck muscles, right around, without hitting the smooth, tight bun of hair that I'd worn for so long. Those muscles and tendons and vertebrae had started to creak in complaint; I heard and felt the crunch within my neck, felt it in the back of my teeth, contained within me; not old age – not yet – just middle age.

I would wrap myself in my red coat – even in summer, it was cold when the wind came through – and walk up to the cliff-top, walk into the wind and the sky and the salt air. The wind would push my coat against me, press it into me. I wrapped my short hair in a woollen beret, tucked a scarf around my neck. Salt lined my nostrils, my eyelashes, burned my throat raw.

From the cliff-top, up above the town, I would sing to the wind, scream and howl songs with no words. Sounds I found on the wind I echoed back to it, from deep in my guts, from my throat. I pulled sounds from the air; I made the sounds without thinking, without knowing what they meant, without touching the heart of them. The sounds were blue, pale blue, salt blue, the blue of the sea around me, and the sky reflected, refracted. Those sounds had depth behind them and raw salt rubbed through them.

FAME (REPRISE)

I thought of my fame as a thing of the past – or, more to the point, I did not think of it at all. I was concerned with smaller things, things closer to me: rising each morning, eating, walking on the cliff-tops, swimming, playing my piano, my weekly trip to Penzance. I received little mail, just short letters, irregularly, from Uncle Valentine, usually with money tucked into the fold of the blue onionskin paper, his love formally declared at the bottom of the page over the flying *V* of his signature. There was no telephone in my cottage. I was contained, local, unconnected to the outside world.

It came, then, as something of a surprise when I received a letter one day, the unfamiliar return address – Rose Watford Summer School of Music, Cripplesease, near St Ives, Cornwall – typed on the back of the envelope.

Dear Madame Gaunt,

I should like to invite you to present a masterclass at our Summer School of Music here at Cripplesease. The Summer School has been run each July for the last three years, and its success relies on the involvement and commitment of a cross-section of the avant-garde within St Ives, and from the wider community. We expect students from Britain and the Continent to attend, as has been the case in previous years. We also have some interest from American musicians this year. We would be honoured if you would consent to appear at Rose Watford this summer.

If you are interested in participating, please contact me and we can meet and discuss details. May I take this opportunity belatedly to welcome you to St Ives. We are delighted to have a musician of your innovative talent within our small community.

Sincerely yours,
Jeremy Landsdowne
Director
Rose Watford Summer School of Music

*

On my first meeting with Jeremy, the following week, he walked me around the grounds of the school – a once-grand, crumbling house on the hill near the tiny, unfortunately named village of Cripplesease – and showed me the wing where the school would run, the Folly where small groups could retreat, the Glen where a marquee would be erected and recitals take place, the Salon where students and tutors would meet to share meals each day. I learned that there was no Rose Watford – hers was a name he'd pulled from the air when he started the school, reasoning that the Cripplesease School was hardly a name inspiring success. He made a jug of gin and lemon, with elderflowers and lemon slices floating prettily on the surface, and we sat on old faded armchairs dragged into the sun, and drank and talked.

Jeremy was a fey man of indeterminate age with a little bit of money, a passion for what had come to be known as avant-garde music, and a talent for bringing the two – musicians and money – together. He had started the summer school after a great-aunt had left him the crumbling pile in Cripplesease. He had, he said, heard that I was living in St Ives. I couldn't imagine from whom, nor who would be interested. He tapped the side of his nose with his index finger, sipped his flowery gin.

'You can't hide fame like yours under a bushel like St Ives, if you'll pardon the mashed metaphor.'

Always susceptible to flattery and recognition, I raised my glass to Jeremy. We drank gin, we talked of music. We connected, just a little. And so it seemed right to agree; yes, I would play.

I held a masterclass that July at the school. Jeremy appeared at the door of my cottage a week after we first met with a brand new theremin for me to play, to practise on. I kept the theremin – *Got it from America last year. If you'd store it at your house for me, you'd be doing me such a favour*, he said – all that year, and ran a masterclass and a performance class at Cripplesease the following summer, and again the next. Jeremy, I'm sure, was behind the visits of journalists who came to write about me, the odd musician making music that wasn't music. It was Jeremy who put the BBC onto me, when we made the first of many broadcasts and recordings after that first summer at Cripplesease. And I suspect it was he who can be thanked for the invitation I received to record and film the performance of a piece to show at the Philips Pavilion at the World's Fair in Brussels in '58.

Indeed, before I knew it – and through no fault nor action of my own – I was famous again.

It was strange to find myself riding on the wave of electronic music as it – the modernity of it – again found its time, its place. Articles and photographs in newspapers and magazines followed the Brussels Fair, then a recording that sold well enough to lead to an offer to spend summer and *fall*, as they termed it, in America; that was how I spent the years of my fifties, the '60s. After the summer school at Cripplesease each year, I would close the door on my little cottage in St Ives, catch the train to Southampton, and board the ship to New York. I played Newport first in '60, then again in '62 when they recorded my performance. That record, *Lena Live at Newport*, sold best of all my records, better even than in what was usually, in magazine articles, called my *heyday*, more than thirty years before. I was, I could face it, an old woman by then – I was sixty-one when I played my last Newport Festival in 1971, the year the crowds stormed the fences. They called me *crossover*, then; I had crossed some mythical divide from what was called classical music to what was called jazz. Later they called me experimental. I didn't care. I just played the music I wanted to hear, played with people whose music excited me: Cage, Glass, Reed, monosyllabic names that sound almost musical as I recall them.

Again, again, I'm getting ahead of myself. Time is all over the place, *like a madwoman's breakfast*, as Uncle Valentine would have said.

So, through the 1960s I spent half my year in one place and half in the other, crossing the Atlantic each way, each year, on one or other of the Cunard *Queens*. I kept a small apartment in New York – I could afford to, as I paid next to nothing for my cottage in St Ives, and the inheritance I had from my father still sat in the wise investments my uncle had made for me, gave me money for nothing. I was comfortably off. I split my time between the city and the sea, lived separate lives in each. In New York I bought a theremin from an old woman my own age who also had known the Professor; the dear Professor, long-dead by then. I bought fine clothes, dressed myself beautifully again, chic. I bought a sleek chair, all modern lines and leather, from the Herman Miller store. It was all I had in my apartment there: my lounge chair, its ottoman, a bed, the theremin, and a closet for my clothes. I lived a musician's life, a busy life, there; I lived among people. I enjoyed the fame. I can't deny that. It was flattering for an old woman – oh, I looked all right then, they even still called me *striking* in those days. But I was becoming old, or at least older.

I appeared on television, once, after Newport. You still sometimes see the footage, fuzzy with age (as I was not yet, not then, not quite). I do look striking. I have seen myself, my flickering self: in a silk sheath, high-necked, pale, the black pattern appliquéd to curve down the front of the dress, black on oyster white, curving up over my shoulder.

My shoulders are straight, strong. My lipstick is dark. My hair is short, nun-like, mannish. I do not smile. I play the theremin, my arms and hands orchestrating music from the machine, a short piece to camera, then applause. My mouth smiles, briefly. I bow. The camera pans back across the set. I remember; I remember the light on me fading, so that I was again in darkness, the crowd's focus pulled from me.

Over the years though, finally, I did start to run low: on money, and on energy. Keeping up with the younger ones became a drain, and there came a time when I just – lost interest. Then, I stayed in my apartment every day, every night, with myself for company. I emerged only to play my music. I had no time for the energetic excesses of the young. I rejected their preference for the needle, which I'd always found too clinical, masculine. I retained my fondness for the primordial hit of the smoke. I lost my tolerance for them, the clever boys and girls who I had, in the past, been content to let milk my finances, funding their bands and their films, their drugs, their paintings and their parties.

I played; I kept to myself. Myself and the smoke, always smoke, my money up in smoke (just a little, just enough). Things slipped away from me – pawned, lost or stolen, I was never sure which – my mother's wedding ring, her jade beads. The silver cigarette case Uncle Valentine had given me. It was a strange time, hazy.

It was after the 1971 Newport Festival – I didn't know it was the final one, not then – that I received a letter in a buff-yellow lawyer's envelope. My uncle had died. I was his sole heir. He had left me his house, some money, some shares. Another death; but he was an old man, by then, his death timely, his life well-lived. And yet, with that letter in my hand, something was released. I wept and wept, wept for my beloved uncle, in a way I had not been able to, not for Trix, nor Grace, nor my mother or father. Such uncomplicated love he'd shown me. I wept and moaned until I was empty, wept all the weeping I should have done years before.

Uncle Valentine had come to the rescue in death as he had so often in life. Instead of returning to the salt blue, pale blue of St Ives, I would go to the place I had long ago called home, that southern place, that hot place, my uncle's house near the tower by the sea.

LEAVING ON A JET PLANE

I was tired of crossing the Atlantic Ocean. I had only some clothes and books in the cottage in St Ives – Jeremy could send someone to pack them for me, send them on. I would leave from New York, leave before winter set in. This time – the only time in my life – I made the journey by aeroplane.

From New York, we flew across the vast wide land to Los Angeles; from there to Sydney. The bridge arced across the water, flattened by the angle I viewed it from, smaller than I remembered, beautiful still. The new opera house, brilliant white stacked on the foreshore, reflected light in all directions. The light was high and the sky went on forever. I had been away from Australia for twenty-five years, from Sydney for nearly a lifetime.

I took a room in a hotel in the Cross, not far from where the Buzz Room had been, where now a sign advertised *Sex aids & XXX*. I walked where I had walked forty years before. I swam at the baths, named now for Boy Charlton. I walked to Mrs Macquaries Chair and sat watching the bridge, the boats on the water, the light, listening to the harbour and the city all around me. I caught the ferry to Manly, and saw the bridge again from the water, streaming now with cars as it had not forty years before.

I walked through the Domain to the Art Gallery. In the new wing, I stopped before three paintings on the wall. One showed the bridge under construction, its two halves reaching towards each other over aquamarine sea, green hills mounded soft against rooftops angled for the light to glance off. Next to it was the portrait of Delphine Britten; I remembered watching her standing in front of it, remembered Trix standing with her, touching the painting, tracing Delphine's face. Delphine perched on the edge of her armchair, pushing herself up into the foreground of the painting, as if about to burst through the surface of the canvas and reach out and kiss my cheek, take me by the hand, and show off the latest painting or musician she'd acquired.

The third painting was of a bowl of oranges. I had put those oranges in that bowl. There was an orange in front of the bowl, on the table, next to a glass. There was a knife next to the orange. I had cut the orange with the knife. I had placed the cloth under the bowl. I had stood behind Trix as she had painted the oranges. I had brought her tea, laid my hand on her shoulder as she painted. I couldn't remember what I'd done then. It had been so long ago. I couldn't remember. The painting no longer smelled like a painting, just had its look, its shape. I read the label on the wall next to the painting:

Untitled [Still life, knife and oranges], 1930
Beatrix Carmichael (1890–1937)

I reached my hand forward and stroked the frame surrounding it with the tip of my finger. I touched my finger onto the surface of the paint, traced the raised ridge of orange, edged with blue, that formed the arc of skin of the wedge of cut fruit. I closed my eyes, moved my fingertips lightly across the surface of the painting. Touching my fingertips to my lips, memory sensing smoke and tea, turpentine and sweet oranges, I turned away from the paintings.

After two days in Sydney I flew west across the continent, my forehead pressed against the fractured-looking perspex of the aeroplane's window, looking down at red earth split by lines of road, curlicues of dry riverbed, and southern coastline brilliant blue against white beach against red dirt, the contrast almost hurting my eyes. The aeroplane's engines cycled up and down in pitch, juddered through me to the bone. In the late afternoon, with the sun glowing low over the ocean to the west, we floated down over the Hills where the Misses Murray had schooled me, over red tiled roofs and swimming pools like evil eyes. The aeroplane coasted in slowly on the hot wind. I walked into a furnace of shimmering air, down the metal stairs onto tarmac so hot it took my breath away.

A fat man in a white taxi chain-smoked as he drove me towards the beach. He spoke in a flat nasal voice of money and mining, of the easy wealth that was being dug from the ground, of things I didn't care about. We drove around past the lights of the city – tall now, but not tall like New York – and the curve of the river directed us towards the ocean.

Uncle Valentine's house had stood empty for months, since before his death. I unlocked the front door and stepped through into the darkness of the hallway. It was clean, still furnished, but airless. Running my hand down the wall, I flicked the switch, but it remained dark, the electricity not connected. The house was quiet; there was no refrigerator hum, not a breath other than my own. I left my case in the hallway, climbed the stairs, and opened the door to my old bedroom at the front of the house. I opened the window, let the smell of the ocean in. I found sheets in a cupboard, made the bare bed with them, and slept as soon as my head touched the crisp cotton.

I woke early the next morning, when the sun only barely coloured the sky. From the bottom of my case I retrieved my swimsuit, put it on, covered it with a long loose shirt, slipped my feet into sandals. From my uncle's house – my house – I walked down the road, slowly, one hand clutched low across my belly. Magpies called from the branches of pine trees. I crossed the road and stood above the beach, looking down at it from the path, catching the smell of it, the sound of it washing over me. I turned to my left, to the building, the pavilion, much of its structure cement-covered now, rendered workaday. There was a large wooden sign on the side of the building, paint bright and garish, advertising ice-creams. I walked under the arched limestone, touched my hand to its grain; dragged my fingertip down it, felt its cool abrasion. I looked up, just briefly, to the windows of the north tower; they were whitewashed again, blanked out. I walked on down the steps, kicked off my sandals and sank my feet into sand, closed my eyes at the wet-dry squeak. I dropped my towel and sandals, slipped off my shirt and dropped it too on the small pile by my feet. I walked to the water's edge. I sank into the sea.

MY BACK PAGES

Uncle's lawyer had left me a cluster of keys on a brass key ring. There were small keys that opened cabinets, tiny keys that unlocked drawers; keys to back doors and side doors and front doors, to the gramophone and the liquor cabinet and my uncle's bedside table. I moved through the house, clanking and tinkling, trying every key in every keyhole, discovering, uncovering.

From the house's back door, I walked through filtered light down the neat path under the jacaranda tree, the carpet of blossoms underfoot, purple turning brown. The long, looped-head brass key turned easily in the lock of the front door of the cottage at the back of the garden. The door opened onto a dark hallway with a dry, stale smell. I opened the door to the room that led off the hallway to the right. Square shapes, uneven shapes, were piled against two walls of the room, draped with cloth, theatrical. I lifted the cloth; dust flittered in the dim light through the whitewashed window. There were tea-chests underneath, HELENA scrawled across them in black, or MISS GAUNT lettered in a different hand. On one was marked SCRAPBOOKS, on another, MUSIC.

I turned to the window, scratched a tiny patch of whitewash from its surface. I looked out to the dark shading protection of the long, low verandah. Across the room, behind the boxes and tea-chests, was a fireplace with a heavy jarrah mantelpiece. I imagined Uncle Valentine's brass opium pot shining upon the shelf, perhaps a vase next to it, with strong-scented roses, or orange blossom. Trix's sad self-portrait; the silver-blue painting she had made of me; I could imagine them there, too. This would be a fine bedroom in which to grow old.

I sold Uncle Valentine's house and all its contents for a good sum of money, employing a lawyer to rejig the land title so that I could retain the cottage at the back for myself. I engaged a builder to install French doors to the back of the cottage, turning the dark lean-to into a bright, light kitchen, with a small laundry and bathroom leading off it. I planted a lemon tree by the new back doors. Then I moved in. I unpacked the few things I needed. Mother's silk rug, my theremin, and Trix's two paintings, long in storage in the front room of the cottage, were uncovered now, mine again. Jeremy sent my books, my things from St Ives, packed into a trunk. My leather chair and ottoman were shipped from New York. I had left my New York theremin there, in the apartment, when I left. I imagined the next tenant moving in and finding it, there in the middle of the room, imagined arms outstretched in wonder, to touch, to play. The idea made me smile. I could afford such expensive indulgences again.

While no work came my way, interest remained in

what I'd done in my years overseas; a serious man from the radio telephoned to interview me about avant-garde music and, out of interest, or boredom, I agreed. You can find that in their archives, I'm sure; I staggered from vague to lucid, I can just recall it, but he edited me kindly and I sounded interesting, and sensible, my voice low and smoky. I sounded old on the radio; I sounded like the old woman I had become. Listening to myself, my voice, made me realise this in a way that looking in a mirror did not.

And then, of course, there was the dame-ing. It didn't take much to be made a dame in the '70s. I didn't go to the ceremony. I stayed at home and – I don't remember what I did, but I know I stayed at home. They delivered the thing, the medal, to me later. *In recognition of services to music*, apparently that was what I received it for. They like a bit of fame, here; they particularly like it when you're famous somewhere else. As long as you come home.

They replayed the interview after that, replayed the part where I said 'I am electrical by nature' – that mad quote! – where I talked of fame, and electricity. I sat in my bedroom, the day I received it, looking up at the twin portraits on the wall above the mantelpiece – of Trix, of me – and held the velvet case that contained the medal on its thick ribbon. It meant nothing, a medal for surviving. I put it in the bottom drawer in the kitchen, under the clean tea towels, and I called myself Dame when it suited me, if I needed to.

I went to the School of Music at the university one day a week, taught students, said wise things to them, nodded sagely. *Thank you, Dame Lena.* When you grow old, everything you say is wise. I swam in the ocean. I grew older. I drifted away on sweet smoke plumes – just a little, just enough – and drank my coffee and played my Aetherwave machine in the dark front room of my cottage. Just me, just quietly, comfortably, slowly eating into the pile of money that Uncle Valentine's house had provided.

There was another machine, too, that I found in storage when I came back to this house: this typewriter, the old black Underwood. I couldn't bear to read the papers I'd typed for Grace, and I couldn't bear not to. In the end, I left them tied with their blue manuscript ribbon, and I packed the typewriter and the box of papers into the bottom of the wardrobe, behind my box of scrapbooks. It's stayed there ever since, another twenty years in storage, my story – part memoir, part autobiography, part meditation – all tied up. But I knew the story needed finishing. I couldn't tell Grace – I couldn't even tell you, with your film and your lights and your cameras and your baby – so I've typed it for you, tapped it out on the machine. I bought a ream of thick bond paper, after you told me about the baby. I hauled the typewriter out of the wardrobe, put it with the fresh paper on the table in my bedroom. I straightened the pile of paper, fed a piece under the platen of the typewriter and – without thinking about where to start, or what to write – I let the story flow again.

COTTESLOE
1991

The lowest note in the universe

AETHERWAVE

She sat in her front room; she made coffee. These are the ways to measure my life: music, coffee cups, coffee spoons. *She stood there and played that damned machine.*

I have played my machine, played my music. I have swum. I have stood on the worn silk in the front room, feet bare on the pile, flat to it, grounded, and raised my arms and held them there and felt the music through my bones, in my back teeth, my jaw bone aching, the electric smell, ozone cracking the air in the room, lifting the dust, an aching arc of sound.

I have lived in this house, this cottage, for twenty years. I will die here. I have lived here and played my machine, pulled sound from the aether. I am electrical by nature; music invents me.

I suppose Mo will want to come back, perhaps next week. She will come back with Jonno and Caro, with the camera and microphone, the solar flare of light, and set them all up in my front room, again. Mo and Caro and Jonno, tra-la. The three of them will come and make their film. They will finish their film of the little old lady in the chair.

How tired of it all I have become.

I have not seen the film, what there is of it so far, and I do not want to. Mo will finish the film. She will make what she will of it – of me – tell a story, another story of me, her story of me. Add to the mythology.

If I were to write my own story again – to start from the beginning – I wouldn't write a great long manuscript, this time. I'd fit it all on a page of blue onionskin paper; perhaps just a list of names, or of places and dates, on that single page. Or I might write a list of objects, instead: a well, a comb, a doll transformed by water; a snake, a cigarette, and a paintbrush; a strange musical cabinet, a wooden box filled with wires and transformers; a bowl of oranges. Or perhaps I'd write a piece of music on the page, a musical phrase, or just a note; or a pair of notes linked by a curving tie – grace notes, ghost notes.

I have not swum for days now; weeks. The weather has turned; that has never stopped me before. But now, I do not have the energy to drop myself into the calming, anaesthetic waves, feel their soothing good.

The room is getting light now; pale grey seeps in under the shading verandah. I have sat in this chair all night. My lips are dry, stuck together like cigarette papers. I force my tongue between my lips. Even my tongue feels dry.

I press my hands into the arms of the chair, lift my body out of it. I am light; I can feel the slightness of my bones, fine, flexing as I stand. My feet bear such little weight. I feel transparent.

*

Perhaps Mo has filmed enough. Perhaps she already has what she needs to finish the film. Last week she asked me what she should call it.

'Aetherwave,' I told her. 'Call it *Aetherwave*.'

I presumed she meant the film, not the baby.

She is getting quite a belly; her pregnancy is obvious, now. She looks well on it, not sickly and pale like she did. I wonder about the father. She doesn't talk about the father. I understand why. Perhaps I should have told her that. Never mind.

She will grow, Mo will, grow big with her baby. She will make her film, make her baby. She will feel all the pain in the world, as I did; that particular pain of birth, like no other.

I hope…

I hope…

I wish her well.

I should have told her that, too.

I sit in my chair. Pale grey early morning light filters into the room. My feet are flat on the floor below me, on the silk rug that long ago was my mother's, that is now mine. Father bought the rug from the *pasar*. I can smell the *pasar*, durian, satay, clove cigarettes and dung, hear the sounds of the market, cacophonous.

The lacquered wooden cabinet opposite me is quiet, cold. I could flick a switch on the wall and it would warm, come to life, electrical, humming. It is not quite as old as me, this box of wires and capacitors, ceramic and metal. I recall when I first saw it, recall the wonder I felt. It will be here long after I've gone. I extend my arm, meaning to touch its surface, but it's just beyond my reach. My hands return to my lap, rest on my knees, fingers tapping in pattern to match my heart.

Next to the typewriter on the desk in my bedroom is the small box from the back of my wardrobe, dun cardboard, the size of a manuscript. I lift the lid, smell the dust smell. Blue ribbon forms a cross that binds the papers within. The pages are tightly typed, near-black with words packed line upon line, margins out close to the edge. Each page is crinkled with the imprint of the typewriter keys.

I untie the ribbon, lift the papers, and upend them onto the desk. The undersides of the pages are grey with the shadows of words bleeding through from the face. From the shelf behind the typewriter I take another sheaf of papers – new, thicker, fresh – and place them on top of the older pages. I retie the blue ribbon around and across the bundle, wrap it loosely with thick brown paper kept from long ago. On it I write her name – *MAUREEN PATTERSON* – in large capital letters.

She will make a better story of it than I could, than I have. She will make the connections, pull it all together, make it sing. Make sense of it. It's her job. It's what she does. I just make music. Pull music out of thin air. I am electrical by nature, musical by nature. The old lady in the chair, who once was striking, and is still there.

Across the room, the two paintings – one of Trix, so sad, so final; the other of me, silver-blue, electric – hang on the wall above the low, heavy jarrah mantelpiece. At full stretch, I can reach to lift them from their hooks. I place them on the bed: first Trix, face up; then me, face down, facing her, our frames matching, touching.

There is no more paper rolled onto the typewriter platen. The empty manuscript box is next to it, its lid askew. My scrap box is on the dresser, its contents spilled across the surface, onto the floor, in disarray. From the desk I pick up the bundled papers, take them to the kitchen, and place them on the table, neatly, in the centre. There is paper in a drawer. I sit at the table and write, concentrating to form the letters clearly, unambiguously.

> *Dear Maureen,*
>   *Keep this.*
>   *It's yours now.*
>   *Yours,*
>   *Lena Gaunt.*

I mean *use it if you want to. Tell the story*. I hope she understands that.

In my bedroom, I wrap brown paper around the paintings on the bed, wrapping them thickly, using all of the paper. The last layer of paper curls away, loosens, unwraps itself. I take a scarf, charcoal silk, from my wardrobe and tie it around the parcel, criss-cross it snug and secure. With a thick marker pen I write her name, large, and underline it. I carry the parcel to the kitchen, place it on the table next to the bundled papers. To the note on the table I add: *These two paintings, also, are now yours.*

I pick up a tea towel from the back of the kitchen chair,

fold it in half lengthwise, hang it on the hook by the sink, where it will dry. I take a glass from the draining board and fill it with water from the tap. I drink slowly from the glass, tasting the water, feeling it wet my lips, my mouth, my throat. I look out the window. The sun is low in the sky. The sky is grey, pale grey, watery grey. The light in the sky is liquid, limpid, cold.

I prepare my sweet smoke – just enough, and then some more. There is comfort – in the end, as always – in repetition, in ritual. My hands make movements that my conscious mind does not have to control, automatic, nerves firing electrical impulses, skin and bone and flesh responding. My gear is on the table by my side. I do not have to be careful any more. I am patient. Aetherised. I am acutely conscious of the sounds I am making. Even the smoke has sound.

I cannot move my body from this chair. But the smoke can take me anywhere. Blue smoke, ti-tree, the scent of oranges, turpentine and tea; sweet boronia, rosin, rosewood, on a wave of salt ocean air.

I hold the smoke in my lungs, in my body, sweet and bitter connected. My feet are flat on the floor, rest bare on the silk-warm pile of the rug. My hands rest on my knees. My fingertips tap a rhythm, pattern the blood and drug flowing through my body. Why do they call this *wasted*? This beauty. This stillness. This escape.

It's a long, slow dawn at this time of the year. The air is cold, as I walk down the road to the beach, cold but thick, like walking through cold honey. The streets are quiet. It is still early. I am facing west, facing the vast ocean, my back to the land. The sun will rise behind me.

The beach is empty. This beach is never empty; but today, now, the beach is empty. I am alone; just me. I stand by the limestone wall above the beach and look down on the sand, the water, look out to the horizon curved against the still-dark sky. I can hear the water move the seabed, if I listen hard enough – liquid on solid – and I breathe air, my breath shallow, shallow like the edge of the ocean, its margin, where I swim.

I walk down the stairs, kick off my sandals, feel concrete cold and hard before I step onto sand. My trousers drag, collecting grains at their hem, collecting damp from the night. I watch the moisture wick up the fabric of my trousers, a rising tide; I imagine molecules, their movement, their tiny orbits, their positive and negative, repelling and attracting. I cannot tell if the universe is in the molecules, or the molecules in the universe, or how they all connect. But I know that all is electrical by nature.

I slip my trousers down. I pull my shirt over my head, drop it at my feet. The air is cold on my skin. My skin is warm against the sky. I run my hands over my head, feel every short, silken hair alive.

My feet step into the foaming shallows. I stand at the edge of the ocean, the edge of the land. The water is cold, effervescent. I can taste salt – from the smell of it – raw in the back of my throat. I lick my lips, and taste salt there, too. I step through the shallows, my feet raising sand storms in the sea. I cannot see my feet. As I walk further, deeper, I feel the touch of seaweed against my legs, brushing lightly, delicate, frightening. I walk out until it is deep enough to swim. I lift my feet from the sand, pull my arms through the water from in front of me to the side. I hear the water bubble, hear it increase in pitch as I push it away from me, like a waterfall flowing uphill. I feel the *phush* of smaller, finer bubbles, their small bead on my arms, trapped in the pale hairs.

I dip my head below the surface of the water, lift my feet again from the seabed, my arms outstretched and circling to keep me afloat. I sing, under the sea, my human voice waking in the salt water, singing words I could not say in the air, singing, each to each. The sea sings back to me, humming syllables that make no sense, *maaaah maaaaah*. I push my head up, surface into the air, into quiet.

Nearly there.

Under the surface of the water I drop my arms into position to play – right hand raised to shoulder height; left hand dropped as low as my waist. My hands fall into place – left hand palm down, flattened, to draw volume; right hand with fingers pinched lightly together to form an eye. I move my fingers in the water, effect tiny changes in the waves that effect bigger movements. I play, with minute movements of each hand, long ago learned. Muscle memory takes over from my conscious brain as my fingers and hands move under the water's cover. I know the movements, from a lifetime of playing.

As I pluck the final note, I let myself sink under the water. Expelling air from my mouth and nose, as the bubbles rise to the surface above my head I hear waveforms, harmonic intervals; I can hear the sound waves mixing in the air and water, undulating, soothing. I will myself to be as heavy as I feel; I feel myself within the water, feel myself displace it, feel my body move through the water and make it eddy and roil, feel bubbles rise in my wake and turbulence all around. Trix is there; Grace is there. Grace is there, above me, her dark hair around her head like a halo, like a dinner plate, like a sea anemone's tentacles, like a star. Grace holds her arms out towards me, then rolls in the water above me and faces away, her hair tentacling around her, blocking out the sun, the sky, the world, the air above. I wave my hand at Grace, wave at her to turn back, not to go away, but she does not respond. I stop waving. The water is warm. It makes a pressure against my ears, a pressure I can hear inside my head as a single note, humming, musical, low. It is B-flat, like the black strip near the bottom of the piano. But it isn't played on the piano, it's a different sound, not a hammer on a wire, nor a bow across a string, nor an electrical field interrupted; it is a humming, inside my head, but low; lower than any note I have heard before. It is the lowest note in the universe; a grace note, a ghost note, the low hum of everything, connecting.

ACKNOWLEDGEMENTS

Half of the first draft of this novel was written while I was 2008 Emerging Writer-in-Residence at Katharine Susannah Pritchard Writers' Centre. Grateful thanks to the Katharine Susannah Pritchard Foundation and ArtsWA for funding the residency, and to all at KSPWC – particularly Mardi May – for support and encouragement.

I owe much to this novel's first readers, Barbara Polly, Robin Fleming, and Michelle Edgerley, for their honesty, their helpful comments, and their enthusiasm for the book's early draft.

To Jane Fraser, Wendy Jenkins and Georgia Richter, at Fremantle Press, I owe huge thanks, particularly for taking a punt on me in the first place. Thanks are due to my editor Nicola O'Shea, for her enormously helpful and thoughtful input. The clear-eyed wisdom and patient professionalism of these women were vital in helping me craft the novel into its final form. I cannot thank them enough.

I'd like to thank Jane Aitken, Emily Boyce and especially Scott Pack at Aardvark Bureau, for leading Lena into the bigger, wider world; and a great big *kia ora* to everyone who's championed this book, with particular thanks to Lisa Northcote.

This book was inspired and informed in part by the

documentary film *Theremin: An Electronic Odyssey* (written and directed by Steven M. Martin, 1994). I also found inspiration in the films of Gaylene Preston (particularly *Lovely Rita – A Painter's Life* [2007]) and rich reference material in the articles and interviews available on Preston's website (gaylenepreston.co.nz).

My great-grandfather, Charles Beilby, wrote a detailed account (as well as a sheaf of intriguing, incomplete notes) of travelling north from Perth to Singapore, and of his subsequent life in Malaya from 1907 to 1928. The transcription by my father, David Farr, of Charles's writing was an invaluable source. Thanks, Dad, for this and other family history material.

From anecdotes and family stories told by my grandmothers, Joan Farr and Betty McKenzie, and my mother, Dee Squires, I have drawn inspiration, detail, and a very long bow. Their stories provided points of connection and reference for Lena's fictional life – points for me to improvise from – and I am deeply grateful for them.

This book and I would also like to thank: all at Michael King Writers' Centre where I was visiting writer in 2009, particularly Ian Wedde (who then held the University of Auckland Residency) for helpful discussion and encouragement; Joe Hubmann and Michele Morris for providing somewhere to write when I needed it; Jan Rogers for additional family stories; Spencer Stevens for considered comment and lively discussion; and friends, colleagues and family – most especially Spencer – for tolerating and understanding my frequent absences and distraction.

While I have the chance, thanks for their support and encouragement, particularly early in my writing career, is due to Fiona Kidman, Elizabeth Smither and Bill Manhire: all gracious teachers, generous mentors, beautiful writers.

My biggest, most grateful thanks, for this book and much more, go to Craig Stevens, my first first reader, who introduced me to the odd world of electronic music. I doubt Lena Gaunt would ever have moved on from cello to theremin without the influence of his strange interests and curious mind.

READING GROUP QUESTIONS

• *I was a solitary child, lacking companions my own age, but I was not lonely. I was happy in my own company, dancing to my own drum.*
What kind of a character is Lena Gaunt? Do her childhood experiences shape the woman she is to become, or is there something innate in her character that helps to shape her life story?

• What is the impact of different relationships on Lena's life, beginning with her relationship with Little Clive and ending with her relationship with Mo?

• How would you characterise Lena's relationship to the concept of 'home'?

• It might be said that Lena's oldest and longest relationships are with Uncle Valentine, and with music. What difference do these make to her life?

• What is Lena Gaunt's relationship to grief? And what is her relationship to music?

• *In those magazines of my uncle's, and in the slim literary volumes on his shelves, I found pages alive with the buzz of the next new thing. Like me, they were of this century, not the last; they looked forward, not to the past. If these are possible, I* thought — *this machine, or this poem — if these are possible, then anything, anything might be possible.*

In what ways are aspects of the unfolding twentieth century revealed through the character of Lena Gaunt? In what ways are they metaphors for her life?

• Does it matter that we do not ever really find out what happened to Grace?

• What is Lena's reason for beginning — and then finishing — the writing of this story? Why does she choose to withhold and then deliver her long-kept secret to Mo?

• Why does the novel end in the way that it does? Does this book have a 'happy ending'?